THE CASE FILES OF MISTRESS MORRIGAN

SIX INTENSE SAPPHIC SHORT STORIES

THE EROTES CIRCLE

CHLOE SLATE

Cover art by [COVER ARTIST]

Created with Vellum

INTRODUCTION

This book was not supposed to be this long, I swear.

I started writing these stories about Brenda's devious domme persona while I was writing and editing *The Startup*, as a way to distract myself from it because I always need at least three projects to work on at once, I guess.

But as I got more and more into exploring this side of her, the more I loved it, and I sort of couldn't stop. Things sort of snowballed from there, and now you have in your hands the product of me getting way too carried away.

But, I think a word of warning is in order.

Compared to the other books in The Erotes Circle, these stories are more extreme and lean much more heavily into BDSM than those stories. These stories are going to put you through the wringer, and I genuinely implore you to check the trigger warnings listed after this introduction before you dive into these wicked tales.

If you do think these stories are to your liking, there's so much here for you to enjoy. These are glimpses into the darker side of Brenda and Wendy, the more wild times they enjoyed before (slightly) settling down as you see them now in *The Mansion* and *The Startup*.

If anyone's keeping track of canon for my books*, all of this takes place after the events of *Shopping*, but before the events of *The Mansion*.

---

* And if you really are serious about tracking canon and making sense of my very erratic and probably inconsistent story world, you might want to send me a message, because I could use someone to help me manage the timeline of the Chloe Slate Smut Universe (CSSU)

TRIGGER AND CONTENT WARNINGS

A full listing of trigger and content warnings can be found On My Website under the page for this book.

As a general warning, this book contains extensive scenes of BDSM, including verbal degradation, impact play, toys, binding and gagging, and other very intense activities.

All parties involved in these stories consent enthusiastically in the text, and consent is repeatedly established, along with healthy check-ins and cooldown.

While the author has made an effort to depict the BDSM activities within this book in a realistic and safe way, many of the activities are exaggerated for entertainment value. As such, this book should not be seen as instructions or recommendations on BDSM practices.

If you are interested in practicing BDSM, which the author believes can be an exciting and fulfilling part of any healthy relationship, please consult instructional texts or experts in the field.

PET

ONE

"BUT, babe, you look really fucking hot in it." Wendy said from the other side of the room.

I was staring at myself in the mirror, the brand-new dominatrix suit on my body for the first time. I'd opted for a dark purple bodice that covered my entire torso besides my arms with matching thigh-high boots, and of course, a full-face mask to cap it all off.

"It still feels strange, Wen." I said, admiring my form, but it still seemed so uncanny and odd.

"Well, my love..." Wendy stood up from the bench on the other side of the play room and embraced me from behind, "These little submissives don't have any idea you think it looks strange for you to be in an outfit like this... and I'm sure Mistress Morrigan definitely has a hell of a lot of confidence when she wears something like this."

Wendy slipped her hands down the front of the suit, her hands gliding along the latex. She hooked her thumb into the ring for the zipper at my crotch and pulled it down, the change in pressure and temperature as the suit opened up making me realize I'd been really missing out by not trying latex sooner.

"And I think you look utterly delicious in it. I can't wait to watch you work this woman over in front of me." She said in my ear as her fingers pressed between the folds of the bodysuit to stroke me, teasing around my clit. I could see Wendy's reflection grinning wickedly behind me.

The scene in front of me was incredibly hot, Wendy holding me and massaging my pussy, a huge smile on her face. "Mmm...that's perfect, baby...get me warmed up before I have to be so mean."

"Like you aren't going to enjoy every single second of it..." Wendy laughed.

"I guess we'll find out."

She laughed again. "Go get 'em, love." Wendy pulled the zipper of my crotch closed and smacked my ass lightly as she headed over to the chair to watch the session unfold. I initially thought that women at Club Crescent would have a problem with a domme bringing her wife along to watch the scene unfold, but I was quickly made to realize that something like that would not only be acceptable to a good number of women who were into BDSM, but some of them even saw it as a bonus.

So here we were, in Club Crescent, my wife in a sheer babydoll dress that didn't hide her nipples at all, me in a latex domme suit, ready to take on our first submissive. The first official one, I guess.

The music that played throughout the tamer parts of the club thrummed under everything, distracting me from my heart beat. The play rooms were pretty well soundproofed, as I couldn't hear a single shriek of glee or yelp of pained pleasure as we waited for our unlucky subject to arrive.

Wendy smiled and mouthed a word at me, "beautiful", and I blushed in response...even if she couldn't see it due to the mask. She always knew what I needed to hear and how I needed to hear it. Mistress Morrigan didn't have a problem being a ruthless monster, but Brenda sometimes needed a little bit of reassurance.

I was about to begin expressing my anxiety again to Wendy when the black door in the corner of the room shook with a knock.

"Showtime." Wendy raised her eyebrows.

I gave my wife a smirk and padded over to the door, my boots clacking on the slate tile.

TWO

"COME IN." I said, my voice not wavering a bit. With her entry, I felt the latent energy of Mistress Morrigan course through me, giving me a newfound energy.

The woman entered timidly and stood there with her head down for a few seconds before closing the door behind her and locking it, not a second of eye contact being made in that time.

"Your kink list and prohibited acts list, now. If you don't have it, get the fuck out of my dungeon." I snarled. I wanted this sub to get what she paid for, after all. "Don't even think about making eye contact with my wife."

Wendy shifted a bit in her chair on the far side of the room and crossed her legs, giving a show of the sheer, black lace panties that adorned her under that short dress of hers. It was hard for me to not look at her, resplendent in her curvy beauty, so it must have been nearly impossible for this woman.

The sub handed the paper to me with a shaky hand. "Thank you. You can follow orders, that's good."

"Thank you, Mistress." She replied softly.

I stood behind the woman, my height difference making her smaller body seem tiny next to mine. She was cute as hell, in that sort of sickly goth way that seemed to gravitate to places like this. She was wearing a black dress with lace straps and a red bra, a splay of silver necklaces on her chest. I noticed she didn't seem to have any tattoos, which maybe meant the goth look was a put-on, but if it was, it was a good one. Her big, watery eyes were rimmed with coal-black liner and her hair was braided into a tight single strand running halfway down her shoulders. I looked in the kink pamphlet she handed me and saw that 'Hair Pulling' was marked with an enthusiastic green dot, which gave me almost too much of a thrill.

"On your knees while I read this." I put my hand on the sub's shoulder as I held the pamphlet in my other hand.

She dropped to her knees without any resistance at all and sat back on her calves. I smirked a little. She seemed pretty malleable so far, which I wasn't expecting. Of course, she had signed up for this.

The list of hard and soft limits were a little daring, and I didn't know if I had the capacity for all of them, but I'd give it a try. Maybe Lilith, who ran Club Crescent, had made sure to serve me up with a somewhat easy one for my first session.

"What's your name?" I said to the trembling woman in front of me.

"Cassidy, Mistress."

I looked at her and tapped my foot on the slate, giving a quick, hard stare down, a glare that said that wasn't going to be an answer in the future. "Should we call Cassidy by the name she gave us, Aosoth, or should we not give her the honor?" I said, looking over at Wendy.

The two of us had way too fun of a time picking out our demon-themed names for our characters that we would play here at Club Crescent. Yes, BDSM was about pleasure and pain, but it was also about being a huge fucking nerd.

"She doesn't deserve her real name, Mistress Morrigan. We'll just call her Pet." Wendy replied, smiling as she said the name, as if she enjoyed how much that must have turned the submissive on.

"Is that alright with you, Pet?" I said, laying a trap. Imagine if she disobeyed her domme.

The sub nodded vigorously, a blush already coloring her cheeks.

"When I ask for an answer, I want you to say it, Pet. Don't just nod at me." I cradled her face in my hand, ensuring she was paying attention to me.

"Yes, Mistress, I like the name." She replied, her eyes cast to the ground.

"Good...very good, Pet. I was going to use it whether you liked it or not, but at least this will make things a little easier."

I stood in front of the kneeling woman, the latex hugging my body, looking at the pamphlet she gave me to find some good things to tease her about.

"I guess since you're being compliant, I'll look at your favorite things first." I scanned the list and then looked up at Pet. At this point, I'd forgotten her real name. "You marked nipple play as one of your favorites.

Is that true? Do you like having your nipples played with, Pet?"

The sub blushed and her voice trembled, "Yes, Mistress, I love having my nipples played with."

I walked around the back of her and knelt down a little, then reached around to squeeze at one of her tits, giving it a firm pinch to the nipple through the fabric.

"They're a little small, aren't they?" I said with a haughty tone. In reality, they were just as big as my own, I'm sure.

"Y...Yes, Mistress. I know I'm a little small."

I smiled at her response. She really was quite the compliant one.

"More than small, Pet, don't you think?" I grabbed at the woman's braid, forcing her to tilt her head upward. I placed my lips right against the outside of Pet's ear and whispered, "But, as insignificant and lackluster they are, my lovely wife is looking at them, Pet. She can see your little nipples getting hard already." I squeezed Pet's breast again, loving the feeling of the lacy bodice against my hand and the heat from her body coming through it. "You're getting so turned on, lovely little Pet, I bet you're going to come before we do much of anything, and we can just end this whole session in the next few minutes, right?"

"N—no, please, Mistress Morrigan. I'll be a good girl, I won't come until you say I can."

I slapped Pet lightly on the cheek. "Slapping (Face)" was marked in yellow on her sheet, so even though Pet seemed to have the capacity to take a hit on every other part of her body, I knew I had to play nice when it came to her face.

"I don't believe you, Pet. I think you're going to get so overwhelmed at the thought of me sliding my tongue between your little pussy lips that you're not going to be able to hold back." I slid my hand down Pet's stomach and pressed my middle and ring fingers just below the waistband of her panties, enough for a tease but certainly not what she wanted. "And we'll leave, Pet. We'll leave while you're coming, we'll find someone else to fuck tonight, someone who can endure us, who can respect us, little Pet. It's going to happen..." I pressed harder and lowered my fingers, feeling just the beginning of the underside of her panties. I knew I wanted to get her going, to get her primed and begging.

"Just give up, Pet. Come. You need to do it. End this night before it gets worse. You won't be the same woman on the other side of what we're going to do to you tonight." I licked Pet's ear and dragged my bottom teeth along the sensitive arc at the top. "You can come, little Pet. You can prove you're not capable of handling us. There's no shame in coming when a hot fucking domme has her fingers against your begging cunt. It feels good, doesn't it, Pet? I can practically feel your body begging for you to do the smart thing here."

Pet held firm, showing no emotion or tells. I imagined she was an experienced sub, because if someone had done this to me, even if I wanted to keep the night going on forever, I think I would have at least moaned in ecstasy. But not Pet, she suffered through it deliciously.

I pulled my hand away from Pet and grabbed her

shoulders. "Bad choice, Pet. Very fucking bad. Remember that I gave you this opportunity when you're strapped down and having your frail body ravaged by me. This could have been easy."

"I am yours, Mistress Morrigan. My body is your subject." Pet said, nodding. There was also a little flicker of smile there, a bit of Cassidy showing up for a second. I knew she liked it scary and villainous, and I was ready to serve that up for her all night.

"Enough kneeling." I stood up and grabbed Pet's braid, using it as an improvised leash. "I know you probably find it natural to be your knees like this, Pet, but now, you're going to stand up and show me your little tits, and you're going to show them to Aosoth as well."

Her eyes were wide and she swallowed hard.

I could feel her shake in my grasp. "Now, Pet!" I said.

THREE

YES, MISTRESS." She whispered as she stood and brought her hands to the thin straps of her black dress.

"God, I don't need to see you naked right now, you fucking idiot, just push them up over your bra, so I can see how pitiful they are. You're not allowed to be topless in front of us yet."

The woman looked so dejected, and I loved every fucking second of it. Wendy shifted in the chair as she watched, her eyes fixed on Pet.

The sub pushed her tits up over the cups of her red bra, exposing a pale expanse of skin in the valley between her breasts, her thin frame looking a little more bony than I liked, but she would do.

"Pinch your nipples. Get them hard for me. Show me how hard they can get, Pet."

Pet was breathing heavily as her small hands gripped her nipples and squeezed at the nubs, twisting them as they hardened at the stimulation. Her chest heaved with the sensations and the blush on her face spread down to her neck as she did her best to make her tits ready for her domme.

"She looks like she might be enjoying that a little too much, Mistress Morrigan." Wendy said, watching the scene. My wife's nipples were beyond hard and begging for attention, and it burned me up that I wouldn't be able to give it to her...not yet, at least.

"That's not for your enjoyment, Pet, you're only supposed to do that because I want you to. But tell me truthfully, sweet little Pet, are you enjoying the feeling of fondling your little tits in front of me?"

"Yes, Mistress. I like the feeling."

Wendy's eyes lit up in an unbridled glee, "God, that was the wrong answer. I am so, so sorry for what is about to happen to you."

Pet looked at me and her eyes widened, both in shock and arousal. I was dying to put her through her paces, so I was so happy that Wendy moved us along.

"She's right, Pet...you see, Aosoth is smart, and she does what she's supposed to do. You, on the other hand..." I reached behind Pet and grabbed her ass roughly, eliciting a yelp of pleasure, "you are in so, so much goddamn trouble."

"M--Mistress Morrigan, I'm so sorry...god...I'm sorry." Pet begged. She was getting into it too, and a decent actor at that.

"Since you've been good before this...unforgivable slip-up, I'm going to let you pick your punishment, Pet. But, I will warn you that if the punishment you pick isn't the severity I was imagining...well," I walked away from Pet, making sure she saw my ass, because it looked phenomenal in this bodysuit, "I don't think you even want to think about how severely I'll punish you for getting it wrong."

I saw the fear in Pet's eyes and I knew she wasn't just acting. There was a moment of truth here.

"I...I choose..." Pet started, a few beads of sweat forming on her brow.

"Answer, now." I pushed, trying to fluster her.

"Now." Wendy echoed. How on earth did I land the best domme assistant in the world?

"I choose to be spanked, Mistress Morrigan."

I smiled, "And how many?"

She swallowed hard. "I'd like to be spanked 30 times, Mistress Morrigan."

"30...do you think I was imagining giving you more than 30 or less than 30, dear Pet?" I grinned, turning back toward her.

"I...I was hoping not less than 30, Mistress Morrigan...I didn't want to underperform for you." Pet's voice trembled as she said this, which just made me more and more aroused.

"Mmm...I was thinking about giving you 29 and making you sit there and close those big doe eyes in anticipation of the last one that would never come, but I guess I've ruined the surprise a little, haven't I?" I leaned in and kissed Pet on the mouth, my body craving intimacy after denying it for so long. I was more than glad to see a green check next to Kissing on the sheet, because most people in BDSM really shied away from it. They didn't know how fucking satisfying good kissing could be, though.

And Pet's kissing was satisfying. Her body was

pliable in my grip and I pressed her small body into mine, making her feel how big and dominant I was over her.

I pushed her against the wall as I kissed her and bit at her lower lip, her moans reverberating inside her mouth and onto my lips. "You're quite the good kisser, Pet. Did you learn these skills for being a wanton slut that will kiss any woman she sees?"

I pulled at her lip as I spoke, her moans of pleasure filling the space.

"Y...Yes, Mistress..." Pet's face was flush.

I broke away and licked my lips, her taste still on them. "I'll need to punish you for that as well, I suppose." I looked over at a small wooden bench, its seat wide enough to allow someone to lean over it. "Pet, present your ass for spanking, if you don't do it in the next five seconds I will pick you up and put you on that goddamn stool." I threatened. While I was strong, I don't think I really could have picked her up, so I was glad when Pet gleefully bent over it, her lily-white thighs looking delicious against the black tile floor.

"Do you want her bare, Mistress?" Wendy said from the corner, her eyes sparkling as she looked at Pet's ass.

"I'm a little disappointed she hasn't already pulled her panties down for us, if I'm being honest, dear Aosoth."

"S--sorry...Mistress Morrigan." Pet reached up and pulled her black panties down, exposing her ass to myself and Wendy. From this position, I saw a peek of black pubic hair between her thighs, a delicious preview for later.

"You sure do say sorry a lot, don't you, Pet?" I

scratched my nails along the woman's ass cheeks, loving the sound of my fingers scraping her skin.

"Y...Yes, I do, Mistress, and I'm sorr--uhh...sorry."

Wendy smirked in response and I continued my path on Pet's ass, making red scratches down her legs. "She's pale, Mistress...a girl that pale, can you imagine the red marks it's going to leave?"

"Well, my lovely assistant, we don't have to imagine..." I reeled back and slapped Pet's ass, the contact making a satisfying cracking sound that reverberated through the mirrored room.

"Mmph...god..." Pet bit back the cry of pain, not wanting to sound weak to her Mistresses, but it was already evident.

"Did you say something, Pet?" Wendy said, the joy evident on her face. "Mistress, Pet sounds like she's enjoying this..."

"No--no...it's so painful...no..." Pet said. It was really fucking adorable because I could very clearly tell that one spank had gotten her so turned on, but I was glad she was playing along.

I brought my hand down on her ass again, another snap. "Two."

"Guhhh...oh...no, no...so bad." Pet's moans and pleas continued to ring out as I struck her, making the count reach 14 in no time. Her ass was now a rosy pink, and it made me smile.

I got behind Pet and grabbed her ass, kneading it under my hands. It felt so warm and raw, and I was only half done. "Oh, dear Pet, are you blushing...for me?"

"Y--Yes, Mistress..." Her ass clenched in my hands as I felt her shiver under me.

"Do you want a rest? Do you need it?" I teased.

"Yes..."

"God, Morrigan, Pet just does not know what to say, does she?" Wendy laughed as she watched intently for my next move.

"She truly doesn't, Aosoth. You'd think by this point she'd learn her lesson, but..." I smacked her for number fifteen, making sure this one hit hard, "Some pets can't be made obedient, no matter how *fucking* hard you try."

I didn't give her any time to breathe after the hit and quickly rained down hits on her, the speed picking up. I reached 23, 24, 25...

"God...I'm fucking dripping..." Pet snarled.

"What? What the fuck did you just say, Pet?" I said, grabbing her ass roughly.

"Oh no..." Pet said, and I could see tears in her eyes as she looked at Wendy, the realization of what she just said dawning on her. "Oh my god, Mistress, I'm so sorry..."

"No time for sorry, Pet. Pull your panties up right now. You're enjoying this too much, it's not even punishment."

She pulled the black fabric up over her ass, her hands shaking. "I'm so, so sorry...please don't...punish me too badly..."

"You're in no place to demand not being punished, Pet. Aosoth, fetch me a strap-on, I need to teach Pet yet another lesson."

FOUR

WENDY SECURED the strap-on harness around my hips, the green dildo feeling wonderful against my body. The latex bodysuit already squeezed me so much, but the addition of the tightly pulled straps of the harness made me feel even more deliciously confined.

I stepped forward, rubbing the head of the strap-on against Pet's red asscheek. "Do you know what this is, Pet?" I said.

"It...it's a dildo, Mistress Morrigan."

I slapped the dildo against her ass in admonishment. "Wrong, Pet. It's called a strap-on, and I am very particular about terminology. So, what is it?"

"A strap-on, Mistress."

"Good..." I rubbed the silicone dildo along her ass, up the back of her thigh, teasing her with it. "Now do you know what someone does when they are wearing a strap-on like this, little Pet?"

"They fuck greedy little sluts who can't learn their

lesson, Mistress." Pet's body was shuddering in anticipation. I wanted so badly to just give her the fuck she wanted, but teasing was the most wonderful part of all of this.

"Pet, your language. My god, where did you even learn to speak like that?" I said, now rubbing the head of the dildo against the small strip of fabric covering her pussy.

"S...Sorry, Mistress..." Her body tensed as the toy moved against her most sensitive spots, making the fabric shift as it passed by. I knew it felt good for her, and I wanted to tease her in that way.

"Aosoth, I have some bad news." I said, pressing the dildo harder against Pet. "Little Pet here is probably so used to being ravaged from behind that me doing this isn't even going to be punishment for her. I doubt she'll even feel it." I took my hand and slid the small strip of fabric to the side a little, teasing the head of the dildo into Pet's wetness. "Do you feel that, Pet? Is that registering at all?"

"God...no...please stop...please don't fuck me with your strap-on, Mistress, I won't be able to take it!" Pet was pushing against the bench as she begged.

I could have easily pushed myself in at that moment, but instead I just pulled the strap-on away, returning her thong to its position. "She's lying, Aosoth. This shameful little slut is such a liar." I slapped Pet's ass again. "Do you know the position they call 'cowgirl', dear Pet? And please don't lie."

"Y--Yes, Mistress. I know the position." She sounded almost apologetic to know such things.

"Then let's have you straddle me, little Pet, I think I

need to see you show a little devotion to your fair mistress."

I stepped away and walked over to the small bed on the other side of the room. This being a BDSM room, I was pretty sure the lowly, boring bed probably didn't get much attention, but it was perfect for my purposes. I sat down, feeling some relief from standing on the sturdy but uncomfortable boots for the better part of an hour. I stayed sitting up, the strap-on jutting out at a weird angle, but I didn't want to miss seeing Pet's approach.

"Pet, take off your panties, then stand up and come over here. Keep your dress on, I don't need to see your disgusting body while you do this."

"Y--yes, Mistress..." Pet slowly stood up, her red ass on display as she peeled the panties away, letting them drop to her ankles. "M--My ass is so sensitive now, Mistress, can you..."

"Can I fucking what, Pet? Ignore your complaints? Yes, I can very easily do that." I said.

Wendy stood behind Pet, looking at the bright red, hand-marked cheeks. She put her hand on Pet's hip, running it around her hip bone and sliding down toward her crotch, but never making the connection, just teasing Pet with what was about to happen. "Are you gonna fuck Mistress Morrigan like you should, Pet? Are you going to show her how good of a girl you can be?" My wife prodded Pet along, adding urgency to the moment.

"I'm...going to, Mistress. I will, I'm so sorry..." She said as she stepped over to me, standing before me in all her eager, pitiful glory.

"Oh, I know you are, but sorry isn't going to do much

for me now. Get on this cock, Pet. Show me how shamefully you would ride a man because you don't deserve to pleasure a woman." I leaned back, giving Pet room to mount the strap-on, but I wanted to stay upright at least for the first bit of it. The thought of how it would feel to cradle Pet's back as she rode me was far too enticing to pass up.

"M--May I take off my bra, Mistress? It's in the way of my dress." Pet looked at me with wide eyes and a worried face.

I smirked and looked over at Wendy. "Aosoth, should we let little Pet take off her bra?"

"Mmm...yes, she should...that would help things a little..." She smiled and slid her hand around the back of Pet and pulled her closer to her, Pet's ass pressed against Wendy's hips as Wendy grabbed at her breast and squeezed it hard through the lace. "I want to watch them bounce while she rides you, if they're even big enough to bounce." Wendy squeezed harder, bringing a moan out of Pet. "Mine bounce up and down when I'm showing my lovely wife how much I love her strap, Pet. She's going to be so disappointed when she sees your little nubs doing nothing."

Damn, Wendy could dish it out almost as well as I could.

"Please..." Pet looked down at me, begging with her eyes. "Please, Mistress Morrigan...Aosoth."

I grabbed Pet's face roughly, feeling the soft flesh in my fingers. "Take off your bra, Pet, like we gave you permission to, and then ride this fucking cock so hard that you worry that your hips will break, then fuck it a little harder. This is a test you do not want to fail, Pet."

She reached her hands back and fumbled at her bra for a second, pulling it down from underneath her dress and dropping it at my feet. I was not disappointed in the view, Pet had the cutest little breasts, small and soft, a cute pair of pale pink nipples adorning the milky skin. The harsh lighting in the room shone right through the lacy fabric of the dress.

"Show me, Pet. Show me how utterly depraved you are, how much you want this cock to wreck you."

Pet stepped forward and put her hands on my shoulders, digging the nails in. She wanted to get back at her Mistress a little, and I wasn't going to give her the satisfaction of me yelling at her for it. I wanted to feel her against me, her arms clasped around my back, her hips dropping forcefully with each pump of the strap-on inside of her.

I heard her whimper a little as the dildo split her open, pushing at her sensitive spots, making her whole body tremble as she did what I wanted.

"That's it, little Pet. It's too big for your little pussy, isn't it?" I said, feeling her hesitate on top of me.

"Y...yes, Mistress Morrigan...I...oh my god, I can't take it." She breathed against me as she lowered herself inch by inch until I could feel her pressed hard against me.

"Your soaked little pussy is completely bottomed out on this fake dick, Pet. You just lied to me, you said you couldn't take it." I said, staring at Pet, our eyes mere inches apart. "Why would you lie about something that I could so easily prove untrue, Pet?" I ran my hands up

Pet's shoulders, feeling her body, the heat underneath the thin fabric.

"I--I'm sorry, Mistress Morrigan, it felt so good that I couldn't think. I didn't mean to lie, I..." I squeezed her shoulders as she talked, pushing her further.

"Less talking, Pet, more fucking. Your hips are still, and we can't have that." I said, holding onto Pet firmly, communicating with her that I had her in a safe position.

"Y--yes, Mistress..." She raised her hips up, leaving just a hint of the silicone dildo remaining. "Is this..." She breathed hard and looked me right in the eyes as she took the entire dildo back into her without even flinching, "better, Mistress?"

Fucking hell. The gritted-teeth determination on Pet's face, the way she slammed herself into me, it was maybe one of the hottest things I'd ever seen. This woman loved being fucked like this, being toyed with, and she had a fucking marvelous way of showing her thanks.

"That--that will do fine...Pet..." I couldn't hide how flustered the scene in front of me made me, Pet acrobatically impaling herself on the strap-on, her big, watery eyes staring into my soul.

She put her head in the crook of my neck, "Oh my god...your hands on me and the strap-on...please...please just fuck me...oh, god..." I could feel her legs shake against my hips.

"You think you're in a place to make requests, that's so cute, Pet. Aosoth, I think letting Pet talk has lead to too many problems. Silence her, now." I said.

I had to get back into control of this scene. Pet was

outmatching me, and every impulse in my body wanted to just enjoy things with this fantastic woman, but that's not what the scene called for.

"Oh...yes...of course, Mistress Morrigan." Wendy said, bringing the ball-gag up to Pet's mouth.

The submissive pulled back just slightly and looked at it with trepidation as the red rubber ball slipped between her teeth, Pet biting down on it like a champ.

"Should have known better than to talk, slut. Mistress Morrigan doesn't want to hear all your pleas." Wendy said, pulling the ball-gag tight. It was a gag that had holes in it, because it freaked me out too much that other people were crazy enough to use solid ones.

Pet stared at me, her mouth negotiating the rubber ball, her breaths rapid and sharp.

"Now that you don't have to think about what you're going to say, Pet, you can focus all your energy on fucking me. So do it." I dug my fingers into Pet's back, feeling the situation tilt toward my control again.

I watched the sub's hips go back into motion, her small body bouncing on the toy, making sure to drive it up as deep as she could, then pulling back as she took in a ragged breath.

"I shouldn't have to remind you, but since you're so dumb, you've probably forgotten, but under no circumstances will you come while riding me." I said, having to condition myself not to come at the sight of Pet fully giving herself to me.

She moaned and looked at me with sad, begging eyes.

"That's not my fault, Pet. It's yours. Your poor body, all that fucking adrenaline you're probably feeling, the dildo filling your insides with the need for more. I know you want to come. You may play tough, but those eyes don't lie, Pet. Your little pussy can't take much more, can it? Just come..." I slid my hands down the back of her dress and placed them under her ass, feeling her flex on top of me. "You're so close, Pet. Someone like you giving up is OK, you've proven you can't endure what I have for you..."

"Guhhh..." Pet grunted into the ball-gag and pushed her hips hard against mine, burying the toy inside of her, her eyes shutting hard as she gripped me as hard as she could, the fabric of my bodysuit pulling tightly against my pussy, rubbing me just right. "Unnnggghhh-hh....fffmmmmm."

Pet rapidly tapped me on the shoulder, her eyes now filled with something other than pleasure. I knew that taps like this were a sign to stop, so I held Pet steady.

"Wendy, take out the gag, yellow light."

My wife rushed over to Pet and gently cradled the back of her head and unsnapped the ball-gag. "Oh my god, Cassidy, baby, are you ok?"

"Ahh..." Cassidy pushed the ball out with her tongue and smiled, "I'm...I'm fine, just...you edged me so fucking hard...I need to come..."

"Cassidy, of course!" I said, holding her in place, her hips motionless, "This was getting intense..."

"Sorry, I...I thought I could...hold back, but..." Cassidy looked down between her legs, "This feels too fucking good."

"Oh, I think it's me that should be apologizing..." I

looked over at Wendy. "This scene was going too fast...we were getting a little intense for our first time, huh?"

"Just...stress from work..." Cassidy started moving her hips again, her body flowing against mine. "It's been a rough week."

"Do you want to come on top of Brenda, or on Mistress Morrigan?" I said, laughing.

"Whoever the fuck you are right now..." Cassidy said, the smile spreading on her face, "because I'm going to come really hard in about five seconds."

"You are so, so hot...please, Cassidy, do whatever you need to do, baby..."

"Fuck, that's it..." Cassidy panted, her mouth hanging open, her eyes on mine as I felt her thighs tighten around my hips and the contraction of her insides on the strap-on. "God...that feels so good...can I kiss you?"

I gave Cassidy my answer without saying a thing, locking my lips with her, grateful that I could just make out with her without the baggage of the rest of the session.

Her orgasm slowed but her body was still going, the kisses between us not letting up at all as I felt Cassidy slow to a halt, her hips falling down on the dildo.

She pulled back from my mouth and let her forehead rest on my own, her breathing ragged, her winces and gasps sending me swooning. "Fuck...I wish I could have held that back...but god damn I came so fucking hard..."

"Cassidy, we got so far ahead of ourselves...you don't need to hold back at all. We are all loving this, you can come as many times as you want..." I kissed Cassidy again.

"Yeah, but..." Cassidy kissed me, another playful peck, "I really fucking like you telling me I can't."

"And I really, really fucking like doing that. I hope I'm not too scary..."

"You are fucking perfect, Brenda...be scarier."

I pushed her back, her head off my shoulder and her hands still gripping my back. "I know this is a little awkward to do with the dildo still inside you, but shall we restart the scene?"

"Mmm...yes, please. Green light."

"Green light." I confirmed.

I pushed Pet back, pulling her mostly off of the dildo, and she did the rest, letting the toy slip out of her as she put her feet on solid ground again.

"No, no, no, Pet. I can see your game now, you're so fucked up that you take something painful like being spanked or impaled for being a rotten little slut as pleasure, so, your punishment has been suspended." I said, looking at her, my expression unknowable because of the mask, which was good because I was fucking elated. "You need to earn your punishment back. I have a bit of a quest for you, Pet."

"Y--yes, mistress?"

"I want to know how Aosoth's pussy tastes, but I'm not going to degrade myself by going over there and getting on my knees in front of her and licking her pussy. That would be unbecoming of a mistress, you see." I grabbed Pet's face and looked into her eyes. "Let's see if you can figure out how to get the taste of little Aosoth's pussy on my tongue without me taking a step. Do you think you can figure that out, Pet?"

Pet looked at me, the fear in her eyes, and looked at Wendy, the glee in her eyes, and nodded her head. "Yes, Mistress."

"Good, and I want to taste you after, too. Your little cunt is naughty, but I'm sure it probably tastes decent..."

Pet nodded. "Thank you, Mistress Morrigan..."

FIVE

"GET the fuck on your knees in front of me. You've wasted enough time." I crossed my arms and scowled at Pet.

Pet did just that, going down to the position with such ease and eagerness that I knew sweet Pet was well-acquainted with finding herself in situations like this... probably more experienced than me.

Our poor subject crawled along the floor at an agonizing pace toward Wendy. I was glad for the mirror because I could make it look as if I was detached from the whole thing, but I could still watch this hot little sub eat my wife out.

"Aosoth, be good and let the little slut taste you..." I said as Pet knelt at her feet, looking up at her and waiting for my signal.

Wendy smiled, her full lips red as they always were, her face made up gorgeously, her chestnut eyes glimmering in anticipation. We shared a moment as we savored the delight of another woman tasting one of us for the first time.

I snapped my fingers and gave my signal. "Taste her."

Pet reached her hand under Wendy's baby doll dress and hooked her finger into Wendy's panties, tugging them aside, and kissed her inner thigh.

"Don't taste her fucking thigh, Pet, get your tongue in her pussy, now."

Pet looked over at me for a second, nodded, and buried her face into my wife's pussy, licking at the slick folds in front of her.

"Goddammit..." Wendy breathed as Pet lapped at her. "She's way too good at this, Mistress."

"I'm a good judge of talent, Aosoth, it's what I do. Of course, this sub is a fucking good pussy eater." I said as I walked toward her and grabbed a handful of her black hair, yanking her head away. The hair pulling seemed to give Pet a special jolt. "That's my wife's pussy, Pet. Not your plaything."

"I...I'm sorry...I wasn't trying to do it for my own pleasure...I just...she tastes so good..." Pet panted, a slick of my wife's juices glistening on her chin.

"Well, I can tell she's enjoying it, so lick her little slit a little more, Pet, as a treat from me, to Aosoth."

Pet didn't even nod as I let go of her hair, she dove back in and ate her as I walked to the side of her, looking down and watching Pet work my wife.

Wendy looked back up at me with her deep brown eyes.

"Do you think Pet knows you can squirt, Aosoth?" I said.

Wendy bit her lip as she smiled and shook her head.

"Well, you're about to, darling..." I whispered to my wife and walked around her, my fingers dipping under her babydoll to graze her nipple before walking behind the chair and taking her hand in mine. "Do it, Aosoth, cover little Pet's face in your girlcum."

"I don't know if I can...right now..." Wendy breathed, the flush spreading up from her neck.

I smiled at her and pushed Pet away from her cunt, my hand under her chin. "Aosoth can only squirt when you use fingers, so, for right now, Pet, I am going to allow you to use your fingers in my wife's majestic pussy."

Pet licked her lips, eager to continue, "Thank you, Mistress Morrigan...I'll try my best."

She slipped a hand up my wife's sheer dress, her pale, dainty fingers moving through the thatch of brown curls before slipping into the folds.

"Pet, you are not going to *try* to make my wife squirt. You are *going* to make my wife squirt. You have so, so much more to learn, and I don't even know if we have enough time to teach it." I looked down at Pet, my grin fixed, daring her to go for it.

Pet slipped her middle and ring fingers inside of Wendy, whose hand I still held, her thumb rubbing the back of my wife's hand in the most adorably intimate way.

Wendy's hips rolled, Pet's fingers sliding in and out of her wet pussy as Pet licked and nibbled at Wendy.

"Is she doing a good job, honey? Is she eating your little cunt like it needs to be eaten?" I said.

Wendy nodded and whimpered as Pet licked. "Yes, she's so good."

"And those fingers of hers, do you think she'll be able to make you squirt, my beautiful wife?"

"If she doesn't fuck it up, which she probably will, I'd say there's a good chance."

"Well, I hope for little Pet's sake she at least proves herself capable of achieving something in her pitiful little life..." I looked down at Pet, making sure she heard every word. There was no way that Brenda, the lawyer, could talk to someone like this, but the words flowed freely from Mistress Morrigan.

Pet moaned against Wendy, her hips bucking a little bit, and her back arched as she ate my wife.

Wendy let out a cry of pleasure, "Oh my god...I'm about to, I think, if she just keeps licking me there and fingering me I can..."

"Only do it if you feel like she's earned it, sweet Aosoth." I stroked Wendy's forehead, seeing the look in my wife's eyes telling me there was zero question that she was going to unleash an orgasm that Pet, that maybe even Cassidy, that poor girl, was not ready for.

"She's...oh my god, Mistress..." Wendy groaned.

Pet didn't even move, and my wife let loose. A few moments of utter silence and a look of sheer pleasure on her face and suddenly a dribble of sweet girlcum appeared all over Pet's face and hand.

"Mmm...Pet, you are so, so lucky..." I said.

Pet's face was a sticky, glossy mess as Wendy's squirting orgasm dripped off her fingers, her lips.

"Are you going to waste that on the ground, Pet, or

are you going to let me taste it? Get on your fucking feet, now." I commanded.

Pet stood up and brought her hand, still glistening, to my mouth and I grabbed her wrist and lapped up my wife's squirt from her skin and fingers. I loved how it tasted. I licked Pet's face, not caring how roughly my tongue dragged against her delicate features. She was probably amazed I had remembered the enthusiastic green check next to 'Licking (Non-Genitals)' in the pamphlet.

Wendy looked at me as I did this, a huge smile on her face.

"Did you enjoy that, Mistress?" Pet said.

I nodded. "Yes, I did. You actually impressed me, Pet. It turns out you're good for pussy eating, even if that might be all you're good for."

"Thank you, Mistress." Pet smiled and looked at the ground, blushing.

"Pet, darling, you little sub, why are you still dressed? Why the fuck did you not read my mind and understand that I need you naked right now so I can give you your reward."

"I...I'm so sorry, Mistress." Pet apologized, looking down and stepping out of her panties as she pulled the straps of her dress from her shoulders. "Is there any way I can make it up to you, Mistress?"

"No, honestly, but we'll need to deal with it, won't we?" I looked at my nails, a move I seemed to return to when I wanted to show disinterest. I'd need to pick up some new domme moves if this was going to be a regular thing.

She removed the black dress and was left in the red bra and her black panties, but before Pet could remove her bra I stopped her.

"No, I like you in that, and I think your tiny little tits look so nice in that bra."

"Y--you do?" Pet said, folding her dress up and tossing it over to the side of the room. She looked so pliable and ready, I could barely contain myself.

"Well it's better than seeing them uncovered, those shameful little excuses for breasts." I said, walking a couple steps toward Pet, putting myself directly in front of her. I already had a bit of a height advantage over her, but the boots made me tower over her small frame. "Don't tell me you actually think your tits look good, Pet..."

She looked up at me and swallowed hard.

I reached up and grabbed one of her tits and pinched it roughly, twisting the nipple in the confines of the red lace of her bra, making Pet's knees buckle slightly.

"Tell me. Don't lie to me. Don't fucking lie to me. Do you think you have nice tits?" I sneered, looking down at her, my head spinning by how turned on I was at being this dominant.

"I don't...I don't think so...Mistress, they're small." Pet's voice quavered.

I leaned in close and whispered, "But, you love it when I do this, don't you, Pet?" I twisted her nipple harder, making sure to not do it with too much force, but Wendy and I had enjoyed harshly teasing each others' nipples for a while, and if little Pet was anything like us, this was heaven.

Pet looked at me with her big blue eyes and nodded. "Yes, Mistress...I love it when you touch me."

"I'll give you that, I guess. At least you're a slut who doesn't mind if someone degrades her while they're playing with her. You're going to suck my tits now, Pet." I said. I looked down at my chest, at the zippers crossing my breasts, the line bisecting my nipples perfectly. I thankfully had pasties on underneath the suit, because getting my nipple caught in a zipper would be the wrong kind of pain and torture. "You need to get them out, Pet, I'm not going to do it for you."

SIX

PET REACHED up and hooked her finger in the silver loop of the zipper pull, but before she could start revealing my breast, I grabbed her forearm sharply, placing my thumb in the hollow of her wrist. It wasn't a dangerous hold, and I'd made sure my grips and grasps were always forceful but safe, but this move was one of my favorites, and one of Wendy's too.

"Aosoth, little Pet thinks she gets to pull my zippers down with her hands. Can you imagine someone so ignorant?" I stared at Pet, holding my eyes open, my face as stern as I could get it.

Wendy got up from her chair and walked behind Pet.

"I--I don't know what you mean..." Pet stammered, trying to make sure she didn't fuck anything up again.

"Well, Pet, you're going to put your hands behind your back, right now. And my dear wife is going to show you an admirable amount of restraint when she gently places handcuffs over your little wrists." I smiled.

Wendy produced a set of metal cuffs, their silver chrome coating shining in the red light, and fastened them over Pet's thin wrists, giving them a little pull as she stepped back to ensure they were secured. Pet whimpered a little, but I could see the excitement in her eyes as she was bound by my wife.

"She's ready now, Mistress Morrigan." Wendy said, walking back to be behind me so she could observe the scene.

"Yes, she's ready now. And she still has to reveal my breasts by pulling these zippers down, and all she can use is her soft little pink mouth." I said.

Pet looked at my chest and nodded, and I watched as her full pink lips opened and clamped down on the small, silver pull of the zipper. Her teeth gripped it as she began to tug, her tongue pulling along with her mouth. Watching the determination in her eyes, her tongue manipulating it, the silver sheen against her white teeth, it was hard to not lose my focus and swoon at how fucking hot Pet looked.

I put my hand behind Pet's neck and pushed her closer to me, forcing the pull through the small space and revealing my nipple pasty and a hint of the areola, the pinkish brown showing through the gap as she continued pulling with her mouth. She finally pulled the zipper to where it was fully opened, and then looked up at me.

"Now the other one. Do not remove the pasty yet, you'll do that after you've proven you can undress me with the honor I deserve."

She leaned up and took the other zipper in her

mouth, tugging and tugging and pulling it down to the base, the pasty showing.

I stroked the back of Pet's head as she undid the second zipper, looking up at me with those big doe eyes. If I weren't married, Pet, Cassidy, whoever, would be the kind of woman I fell for, hard. Wendy was the exception to my standard type, and maybe that was a good thing, but back in my dating days I simply lost my mind for girls who looked like they spent their days haunting a foggy isle somewhere.

"Now, Pet, I'm sure not even you're dumb enough to not see the predicament we are in. There is tape covering my delicious nipples, Pet. Can you offer a solution?"

She nodded, her face so close to my chest, her breath warming the exposed skin.

"The solution is quite simple, Pet. You need to lick my pasties off with that eager tongue of yours. If you even think for a moment about using your teeth to pull them off, I will put you in a cage and Aosoth and I will leave right now." I cradled Pet's neck, holding the back of it.

Pet's tongue poked out of her mouth, and she ran it along the top edge of the pasty, making sure to be slow and methodical. She licked up to the top and back down, her warm, wet tongue slathering the nipple pasty, making sure it was coated with her efforts.

"That's it...good girl...good Pet. Your tongue is nimble and wet, Pet. It's like you were made for this." I said. I loved reeling a woman in with praise, because it made the next insult or degradation sting that much more.

Pet's tongue was almost all the way up to the top

again and my nipple was fully erect underneath, waiting for her touch, the anticipation driving me wild. I watched the tip of Pet's tongue slide to the top edge and I could tell she was going to be able to pull it off just using her tongue. I didn't expect that to be the case, but I had to hide my amazement. Pet's sure licks left my nipple coated in her saliva, hard as it could possibly get in the anticipation of her sucking and licking it once it was fully exposed.

And suddenly, she pulled the nipple pasty up and over the tip, leaving my nipple exposed, hard as a pebble, and absolutely fucking aching for touch. The wet tape drifted to the ground, and Pet eyed my nipple with a hunger that made me quake.

"Ah...fucking finally." I said...and maybe that was Brenda saying it, not Mistress Morrigan, because after all this domination and watching Wendy get off, I was losing my mind for any kind of stimulation.

Pet's tongue darted out of her mouth and she licked my nipple. The contact was pure relief as she circled her tongue around it.

"Guh...that feels good, Pet."

Her tongue swiped over it a few more times before she started to suck, her soft lips locking around it, the suction gently pulling it into her mouth.

"Bite it, Pet. Bite my nipple, gently." I cooed.

"M--mistress...I worry that's a trap..."

"It's not, Pet, when I tell you to do something, you do it, I am a woman of my word. I demand to see my wishes fulfilled." I pushed her head against my breast, her lips pressed into it.

Pet opened her mouth and gently closed her teeth on my nipple.

"Tighter, Pet, please, do something well for once."

She closed down harder on it, biting at it gently, tugging and sucking at my hard, erect nipple. She increased the pressure slightly, giving me time to get used to the feeling.

"Right there...good pet, good girl...you like the taste of your Mistress' nipples, don't you?" I said, the swirl of pain and pleasure making my whole body throb.

She let my nipple fall from her mouth and looked up at me with wide eyes and a slick chin. "I do, Mistress, it makes my little pussy ache to think that I'm tasting it..."

"Aosoth, do you think Pet talks about how much her pussy needs attention to much?" I said, looking back at Wendy.

Wendy nodded. "She does, Mistress Morrigan, she's so fucking preoccupied with it."

"You know, Pet, I would love for Aosoth to show you a lesson in modesty, but we don't have all day." I looked back at my post-orgasmic wife, whose tits were fully visible, and gave her a smirk about the modesty line. "So, because our time is limited, Pet, I suppose I'll just have to stoop down to your level and please the greedy little pussy you won't stop talking about."

"Th...Thank you, Mistress Morrigan..." Pet looked at the ground as she said this.

"Look at me. Look at your Mistress in her eyes when you thank her. When you are grateful. Thank me properly, Pet."

"Thank you...thank you, Mistress Morrigan. I'm so

grateful that you're willing to teach a filthy slut like me manners." Pet said, her eyes gleaming, the arousal in her voice palpable.

"And I will please your pussy, Pet, right after you please mine." I sneered. "On your knees."

SEVEN

PET NODDED and kneeled at my feet.

"Good, Pet, very good." I took her head and gently pushed it against my pubic bone, the thick latex dulling the sensation but not removing it. "Do you feel how hot my pussy is, Pet? Do you feel sufficiently ashamed that you've gotten your Mistress turned on this much?"

"Yes, Mistress Morrigan...I feel your heat, Mistress...it feels good on my face." She pressed her cheek into my pubic bone. "You smell good...Mistress."

I pushed Pet against me harder, the pressure giving me some relief. The one thing I already didn't like about being a domme was that I had to restrain myself from taking pleasure, from enjoying it, because I was supposed to be above it all. Maybe I'd change that for future sessions, make my subs worship me properly.

"Do you want to taste me, Pet? You shouldn't be allowed to, but I'm going to make an exception." I said.

Pet's tongue ran along the inside of the seam where my thighs met my pelvis, and she moaned softly into my crotch, her voice muffled by latex and pussy. "Please...I want it, I want it, I need it." Pet was crazed, and that's exactly where I wanted her.

"Then pull the fucking zipper down you dolt and eat my pussy, and at least act like you know how to do it." I jolted my pelvis forward against Pet's face, getting a yelp of pleasure from my overloaded sub.

Pet took the small, metal pull in her mouth and pulled down, her teeth biting into it and her tongue guiding it down until it was fully opened, revealing my pussy, shaved bare and wet to the point that the latex was dripping with my slickness. The latex held so much of the heat and arousal in that the mere caress of air against me almost caused me to shiver in pleasure.

And when Pet started dutifully tonguing my pussy, those shivers most certainly arrived.

"Oh...Pet, your tongue is so warm..." I said, looking at her big blue eyes, staring back up at me as she lapped at me. Pet had her bound hands pressed against her ass as she knelt in front of me, bouncing ever so slightly on her shapely calves as she licked me. She was damn good at eating pussy, but I had to will myself not to come. I wasn't sure if dommes were really allowed to come before their subs, but I was also not going to just stop down this whole exhilarating scene to check the fucking rulebook.

She alternated between swirling her tongue in tight little circles around my clit and sucking, slurping on it like she had my nipple, the sharp sensations sending me into a tizzy of pleasure.

"How does my wife's pussy taste, Pet?" Wendy fired from afar.

I looked down at Pet, my eyes narrowed, focusing on her timid gaze as she kept her mouth attached to my pussy. "Answer her, Pet. Fucking answer her."

Pet looked up at me, her face slick. She removed her lips from my clit and spoke. "Your wife tastes so good, Aosoth...she tastes amazing..."

"Do I taste better than Aosoth?" I said, putting extra venom in the question. There was literally no correct answer for this, and that's exactly why I subjected this poor sub to it.

"No, Mistress...you both taste delicious."

I smirked and nodded. "You are the absolute worst fucking liar I have ever met in my goddamned life, Pet. I will take your apology after you make me come with that tongue of yours, if you even have the ability to do so."

Pet grumbled a little and looked back down at my pussy, and my heart sank. Fuck, had I messed up my first session as a domme?

"Yellow light" I said with a pained half-smile. "Cassidy, is that OK? I don't want you to be upset...I'm not sure if I'm allowed to get off before you, but..."

Cassidy looked up at me and a smile spread across her face, "Oh my god, maybe I got a little too into being the frustrated sub, I'm absolutely elated to be able to get you off first, Brenda." She adjusted her kneeling position and twisted her shoulders around, some much-needed stretching in this little break.

"Oh...ok, I just...I wanted to be sure. I've never dommed someone like...this before, professionally."

"Holy fuck, this is your first time? I thought you were just doing a guest spot. This is...phenomenal." Cassidy giggled and laid her head on my thigh, looking up at me sweetly. "Can I ask a little favor before we get started again?"

"Yes, totally." I said, taking a step back from Cassidy to give her some room.

"As much as I love having you all over me, and your wonderful wife all over me, I could use a little towel-off."

I smiled and looked around, but Wendy was already making her way to the box of fresh linens in the corner of the room. She got out a damp towel from the warmer, a very nice touch on the part of Club Crescent, and walked over to Cassidy. "OK if I do it and not Bren?"

Cassidy nodded enthusiastically. "Of course!"

Wendy ran the towel over Cassidy's face, cleaning up all the makeup, all the juices. My heart fluttered, watching her take care of Cassidy, making sure to be careful as she rubbed around her eyes. There were definitely multiple ways to be aroused, to swoon over something, and seeing my wife be so gentle and nice to a woman who we had just spent the last hour being utter monsters to, was a nice counterbalance to the intensity of the night.

"I'll massage your jaw a little, I know mine can get worn out when I'm..." Wendy looked at me then back at Cassidy with a giggle, "I don't know why I was about to censor myself there, it can get worn out when I'm eating pussy, which is what you're about to do"

"Mmm...thank you...it's strenuous, but I don't mind it."

"I am so, so glad you don't mind it, because I fucking

need it..." I ran my fingers along my vulva, the pressure and tension in my body nearly uncontrollable.

Wendy rubbed Cassidy for a few more seconds and gave her another quick swipe with the towel, then stepped back. "There, good as new!" She leaned down and kissed Cassidy, who returned it enthusiastically.

Cassidy looked back up at me. "Ready?"

"I am ready if my lovely little sub is ready." I smirked.

"Oh, I am...so ready." Cassidy looked at me with greedy eyes.

I grabbed a footstool that was next to me so that I could give my beaming partner a better angle, and because I needed to get off NOW. If anything, our little cooldown only turned me on more.

"Green light?" I said.

"Green light." Cassidy confirmed.

I propped my foot up on the stool, my boot hitting the metal with a satisfying thud. "Then get the fuck over here and get your tongue inside me, Pet."

EIGHT

CASSIDY RETURNED to the position she had been in earlier, and began licking at me, my wetness making me absolutely slick. "You're so wet..."

"Stop fucking talking. If you're using that tongue for anything other than licking my pussy I'll slap you so hard you'll see stars."

"Y-yes...yes, Mistress..." Cassidy returned to my clit and lashed at it a couple times before pulling my labia into her mouth, sucking on my flesh, which I could take a lot of, thank you very much, and she knew it.

It was beyond difficult to not turn into a heaving orgasmic mess as Cassidy ate me out. I had to act like she was getting me off, but I was mad about it...even if that couldn't be further from the truth.

Her tongue snaked along the edges of my opening, teasing me, keeping the pleasure from overwhelming me but also pushing me further. It was an insane feeling, and I couldn't believe that I had the wherewithal to not let go, not just let the orgasm rip through me.

"Stop fucking teasing me, Pet...put your tongue in me and get me off, now!" I snapped, channeling some of the overwhelming horniness into playful anger.

Cassidy moaned a little at the harshness of the order, and finally, her warm, soft tongue slipped into me as she thrust into me with her face. Her tongue snaked into me as she fucked me, her face pressing into the slick latex, and I was losing it.

As I came, I tried to hold as still as I could. I knew moaning or screaming how fucking amazing she was, or how the orgasm she was giving me was one I'd remember for years down the line, would break my character, so I just clenched my jaw and closed my eyes as the orgasm filled me entire body with fireworks.

I came hard, but I was impressed with myself that came in silence, Pet's tongue dutifully pleasing my pussy through each second.

My orgasm ended, and I was left feeling exhausted and thrilled. My knees buckled slightly, and I caught myself on the stool I was propped on, backing away from Pet.

"That was fine, Pet. The services of your tongue are no longer needed. If I weren't going to need it some time later I'd elect to just cut it off now, but I'm feeling kind this evening." I pulled the zipper up to cover myself again, and I was still so sensitive that I could have gone for another round, but it was now Cassidy's time.

She sat up from where she was, looking up at me. "Thank you...Mistress Morrigan...can I get the next part of my reward now?"

I smiled. "What makes you think I have something planned, Pet?"

"Y--you said that if I got you off, you'd return the favor, and you've said you're a woman of your word, Mistress Morrigan." Pet fluttered her eyes, the whole moment dripping with melodrama that nearly made me laugh at how over the top it all was.

"Ahh, yes, my head must have been clouded when I made such a shameful promise, but, I suppose I have an obligation to your pitiful little cunt, don't I?"

Pet nodded, "You do...if it's no bother, Mistress."

I rolled my eyes and walked over to Pet. "It is quite the bother, Pet. I'm going to despise every single moment of making you come, because you do not deserve it at all, but I know you'll just keep bugging me about it, begging me for it, until I fulfill your disgusting desires..." I grabbed Pet's chin roughly again and forced her gaze toward me. "Won't you, my filthy little Pet?"

Pet whimpered. "Y...yes...I can't stop thinking about you making me come..."

"How do you want me to do it, Pet? I'm sure someone as far gone as you can only get off in specific ways, so we might as well pick the quickest one to rid myself of this onerous fucking obligation." Onerous...damn, my law career was helping out my Domme career quite a bit. I wonder if there was a link between lawyers and masochists...hmm.

"You said you'd touch my little pussy..."

I let out a deep, heaving sigh. "Be detailed, Pet. Of course I'm going to touch your fucking pussy. With what and how hard? Don't make me spell this out."

"I'm sorry, Mistress." She whimpered.

"Just tell me already so I can be done with you, Pet. Your pussy is all you're good for, so you should know exactly how you'd want someone to fuck it, right?" I stomped in playful aggravation, again loving the sound the solid heel made on the stone tile.

"Your fingers...if you wouldn't mind."

"I would mind very much, but that's irrelevant." I put my fingers up in front of Pet's face, my nails freshly manicured, trimmed down, and filed smooth. "I pay so fucking much to keep my hands manicured and perfect, and now, Pet, you're asking me to tarnish all that hard work by putting my delicate fingers inside of you? The horror, Pet. You're more fucked up than I could have even imagined. Your Mistress putting two...three fingers inside of you?" I said.

"Mistress, I'm so greedy and shameful that I want four inside of me..." Pet drawled, not at all being subtle in telling me that she wanted me to go all out. And Pet was so delicious that I was more than happy to comply.

I got behind Pet and bent down. "Stand up, you disgusting, filthy girl." I pulled her up, careful to give her time to raise herself and get her bearings. "Wen---I, I mean, Aosoth, uncuff her, I need to strip all of these disgusting clothes from her before we use her up."

"Right away, Mistress." Wendy took the keys to the cuffs and released Pet from them, her hands free for the first time in the last twenty minutes. I wanted her free because I wanted to see her naked...I wasn't going to leave this magical night without seeing just how good she looked underneath it all.

I slipped Pet's dress over her head, seeing how beautiful she was without anything covering her, finally for the first time tonight. Her breasts were so nice, her nipples were perfectly perky, and I had the sudden urge to suck on them until they were red and erect. But Mistress Morrigan couldn't have that kind of fun, at least not right now.

"Are you ready for this, Pet? Are you ready for your shameful reward?" I held Pet's shoulder with force, keeping her in position.

"I am, Mistress," Pet said, hiding a smile. At the start of the night I would have called it out and made her pay for it, but at this point, exhaustion was starting to set in, and I was nearing my limit of domination.

But, not before I gave sweet Pet the release she'd been begging for.

NINE

I LOOKED at Pet in the mirror, her beautiful, milky skin showing in all of its glory.

"Please...Mistress, can I please lie on the table, please?" She said.

"I suppose that will let a scamp like you get off easier, won't it? I bet you do the best work in your pitiful little life on your back, Pet. Go, lay down." I pointed toward the padded table at the other side of the room.

"Thank you...thank you so much Mistress..." Pet scurried off toward the table, climbing on top of it and getting on her back, her head supported by the large headrest at one end, and her hips elevated by the curved end of the table, making for a beautiful view.

"Aosoth, darling...stupid little Pet was dumb enough to fall into our trap again..." I said, looking to Wendy. "I cannot believe she just put herself on that table without seeing the stirrups that you're going to strap her into..."

Wendy stood up and padded her way over to Pet, her

bare feet making cute pattering sounds on the tiles. "She is very, very dumb, Mistress Morrigan. If there's one constant to this night, it's how utterly stupid little Pet is."

I joined Wendy at the foot of the table. "It's such a shame that our night is about to come to a close, because this table has the ability to spread the legs of our lovely little sub wide, Pet. I could have strapped you to this all night, could have spread your legs open, could have had my way with you in so many different ways."

Wendy pulled one of the ankle stirrups tight, securing Pet's left leg before walking behind me to get her right. "She doesn't deserve that, Mistress. She should feel lucky she gets any of your attention."

"That's quite right, my love..." I looked down at Pet with more disdain.

Pet squirmed against her restraints, which was useless, because her ankles were held tightly in place by the straps. I couldn't help but be aroused at her being strapped in so tight.

"Oh, Pet..." I said, moving the back of my hand down her flat stomach with my nails dragging along the skin. "It's really a shame...if you weren't so depraved, you could have been beautiful. You could have made a woman very happy. A sweet, pliant little slut of a wife who attends to her partner's needs in noble, upstanding ways." I turned my hand over and ran my fingers down Pet's lips, feeling the wetness against my fingers. She was beyond ready for this, and I couldn't wait to get to it, but I knew teasing for a little while longer would make things that much better.

"Do you have any idea what a real relationship is like,

Pet? Any concept of what love and lust and compassion mean to people other than yourself?" I pushed the first finger inside of her, feeling the hot warmth against my fingertips, her smooth walls drawing my finger in, making me feel just how much she wanted this. "Your wife could be doing this to you right now, Pet."

Pet whimpered.

"No, really, I mean it, Pet. Imagine how much better this would feel with someone who cares for you doing it, instead of some domme you paid to take care of your greedy, selfish, disgusting needs. If you want the second finger, tell me how much of a bad girl you are."

"I--I'm a bad girl..." she whimpered again. "I'm a very, very bad girl and I'm sorry I don't make you proud."

"Mm...not good enough, Pet. More."

"I'm...I'm so bad, Mistress. I don't deserve anyone who would love me, because I don't know what love is...all I want to do is get off, and I can't even do that without being an utter degenerate!"

"Pet...you know sometimes I think you're almost smart, when you say things like that." I slid my middle finger into Pet, not meeting much resistance at all. Her chest shivered at the new entry, and that sneaky smile appeared again.

I let the smile stay there this time. "Do you want the last two fingers, Pet?"

"Yes..." She breathed, "I want the last two, Mistress... I'm sorry that I'm being greedy..."

"Your wife would never do something this depraved, would she, Pet?" I slid the last two fingers inside, packed into a tight bunch so that my thumb was the only digit free.

"No...no my wife would never...she's too good for this...she would never...touch me like this." Pet gasped as she spoke.

"Oh, but it feels so good, doesn't it? My fingers filling you up, stretching you out? Your little cunt is so accommodating, Pet." I sneered, watching in amazement as this small woman took my efforts without breaking a sweat.

Pet nodded, her eyes were fluttering as if she was losing herself in the moment. I took my other hand and smacked her on her thigh, "do not close your eyes, Pet. You need to see how a real woman pleases you more than your wife could..."

I could tell Pet was starting to get too close. Her hips were pushing into my hand, forcing my fingers to go in deeper.

"That's enough, Pet..."

Pet whimpered in disappointment and stopped her movements.

"You're moving your hips like you want my whole hand inside your little pussy..." I said. That line surprised even me, like Brenda didn't exist for a moment and Mistress Morrigan had complete control. Wendy and I had always maxed out at three fingers, and we hadn't been bold enough to even approach the idea of fisting, but...

"It pains me to admit that I do want it, Mistress...my slutty little pussy would swallow your fist..."

Wendy gasped next to me, but then smiled and looked back to me. I felt my confidence bolstered.

"Please..." Pet begged, her body so wound up with arousal that it seemed like she was up for anything.

And in this moment, Mistress Morrigan was up for anything as well.

TEN

"MY HAND...MY whole fucking hand inside you, Pet. It's all you'll ever fucking know...you'll never feel anything better than this. This is the peak of your pitiful existence, Pet, so remember it well."

"I'm such a filthy creature, Mistress, it's an honor to be destroyed by you..."

Pet gasped as I brought my thumb in to join my fingers, slowly working up to the second knuckle. This was scary but exhilarating, and I hoped that Pet wouldn't mind that I was taking this very slowly.

"Do you feel that, Pet?" I said. I looked down at Pet, who had her head propped up in order to look down at me.

"Y...yes...I feel it..."

"It feels so wrong, doesn't it? Do you feel sufficiently shameful about actually enjoying having yourself stretched out like this?"

She nodded, biting her lip.

I started to press into Pet harder, and her face

contorted as my fingers went inside, but not in discomfort, I don't think, because Pet would have stopped things, even if she wanted this. She was desperately wet, but I was worried. This was a lot, for anyone, even if Pet...even if Cassidy did it every night, something about it felt so daring.

"Aosoth, little Pet isn't wet enough for my fist. Find the lube and bring it to me right fucking now." I said curtly.

"Y--yellow light..." Cassidy whimpered, looking up at me. I pulled my hand back and looked up at her.

"Is it ok? Cassidy, I don't want to hurt you."

"It's great! I just wanted to tell you I definitely don't need the lube." She smiled, her eyes wide and eager.

"OK..." I smiled back.

I turned to Wendy and kissed her hard on the mouth. She was my anchor in all of this, and I wanted her to know just how much I appreciated her. "I think Brenda is worried she'll hurt you, even if Pet and Mistress Morrigan are very sure you can take it." Wendy kissed me on the neck.

Cassidy laughed, her stomach slick with sweat. "If it'll make you feel better and more sure, by all means..."

"Thank you...maybe next time I'll be more bold."

"Oh...you will." Cassidy winked at me.

I looked at Cassidy, at the look on her face, so sweet and excited that it took all I had to not go up there and kiss her and hold her in my arms, and never let her go. But Cassidy, and Pet, wanted to be ruined. And so, I was going to ruin her.

"Green light?" Cassidy said, eager to get back into the scene.

"Green light." I said, my gaze narrowing. "Aosoth, coat this poor thing's slit in lube. If she wants me to debase myself by fisting her, I better not need to expend any effort getting my hand in there."

"I'll prepare her, Mistress..." Wendy picked up the pump-topped lube and squeezed out some onto two of her fingers. Pet looked up at me and Wendy brought the cold gel down onto Pet's pussy, who squirmed against the coolness.

Wendy stepped back, her eyes locked on how deliciously ready Pet was. I took a breath. I was really going to do this.

I bundled my fingers again and pushed into Pet. It was easier this time with the lube, but I still felt the need to be careful. Despite her enthusiasm, Pet looked so delicate to me, and as much as we threw around words like 'destroy' and 'ruin', I obviously did not want to hurt this woman.

Pet moaned softly as my knuckles entered her, stretching her open. I stopped my efforts for a moment to look at what was happening, the scene so mesmerizing. "Oh...look how easy this is, Aosoth...this horrid little creature is so ready."

Wendy watched me intently, and I'm sure the amazement was on my face, even under the mask.

"Fuck...yes...do it...fuck...." Pet begged, her body twitching in anticipation.

"Do you think she's ready, Aosoth?"

"If she wants to be broken by your whole fucking fist,

I'd say yes. Do it, Mistress...destroy her." Wendy said, the anticipation in my wife almost as palpable as it was in Pet.

I pushed in further slowly, feeling Pet's shifting against me, seeing her breathing sharply. Just when I thought I would need to stop, she relaxed more and allowed me in deeper. She moaned, a low, guttural moan, a primal reaction to such a breathtaking act.

And with that, I pushed in further, until my entire hand, the hand of Mistress Morrigan, was inside Pet, up to the wrist. She was going crazy with lust. She had to be, because the sheer feeling of the warmth against me, the tightness, the fullness, it was so fucking strange, but it clearly satisfied a deep need inside of Pet.

I have to admit I sort of loved how it felt. It was no doubt dangerous, and clearly not something everyone could do, but with women as willing and eager as Pet, I felt that this could be a new favorite for me to do if they asked for it.

"How the fuck can this make somebody feel good, Pet? This is perverse, even for someone as low as you." I said. There was no way around it, it felt incredibly weird to do, but strangely sexy at the same time. Wendy and me had played around with larger toys before, but this was on a whole different level.

I pumped my fist into her, careful to not go too fast or too hard. Her eager pussy dripped onto my wrist and forearm, and I could feel her body pulsing against me. I'm fairly sure I enjoy fingering a woman more than others, so to have my entire fist inside of one was magical. Something yearned inside of me to have Wendy try it with me one night when I was feeling particularly flexible.

"You're vile, Pet. I bet you love the feeling of my knuckles dragging against those slick walls, don't you?" I said, allowing more evil into my voice, more aggression, since I didn't think anybody wanted to be fisted gently.

"You love that my little cunt is eating your fucking arm, Mistress Morrigan..." Pet said. It was a hell of a time to pick to be as bratty as possible, I'll give her that.

"It is a new sensation, I'll admit. Few women are as debauched as you, so if you pride yourself on being a tragic little whore who doesn't care about how twisted her desires are, then I suppose I admire you very slightly."

As I felt Pet accept my hand more, I got more bold. I pulled out of her and twisted my hand around, with the knuckles up, and went back into her. The lube and her wetness coated my hand, I don't know if I'd ever felt so much wetness from one woman as she took on this feat of endurance. And the sound...my god, the sound of my hand entering her, the shudders and moans, the low whine from Pet as I gave her exactly what she desired, was heavenly.

"Come for me, Pet. Feel how powerful my hand is inside of you. I own your little pussy, Pet."

"Oh...Mistress...oh, my god..." Pet groaned, "I--I can't stop myself."

"Come for me, you little fuck, right now, right fucking now!"

If Brenda had squirted earlier...what Pet did was an order of magnitude beyond that.

"Fuuuuuuckkkkkkk." Pet arched her back, and I nearly lost my balance in an effort to keep my hand placed comfortably inside of her. Warm fluid dripped onto my wrist and sprayed out against my forearm as Pet had what I could only classify as a religious experience.

She shook and spasmed against me as her body tried to work through what had just happened, her head tilting from side to side. She had no words to describe her state of being, and that was good. Maybe less of a religious experience, and more of an exorcism.

"You're fucking disgusting, Pet. So vile." I said with disdain. I was trying to muster any acting I had left in me, because I was beyond tired and beyond gleeful that I'd just fisted a woman for the first time. What's more, I had even more of a desire to have it done to me.

"Y-yes...I am...so sorry..." she sputtered, "you've cured me, Mistress."

"Good...that means it's time to pull out, then."

"No...please...just keep it there a little longer." Pet closed her eyes, draining the last bits of pleasure she could from this experience.

"You're lucky you're cute, Pet. You can enjoy my hand for ten more seconds." I said.

Wendy laughed and reached down to pet Pet's head, stroking her hair softly, like the good Mistress she was. Pet reached her head up and rubbed against my wife's hand, getting all she could from both of us.

"Mmm...fuck..." Pet rolled her hips a little, riding on my hand. This woman's capacity for getting fucked was truly phenomenal.

Pet let out a big sigh, her body going limp, the energy

she had from the night of pleasure now depleted, "that was so fucking good, oh my god, that was...so fucking good. That rearranged me."

Now knowing that Pet had fully satisfied herself, I had a moment of pain that our wonderful session was ending, but it was for the best.

"Scene over?" I said.

"Yeah..." Cassidy laid her head back on the table, her hair soaked with sweat. "That's all I can take..."

"I'm going to...take my entire hand out of your pussy now, ok?" I said, laughing a bit.

"Oh, yes...yes, do that..." Cassidy looked down at my wrist disappearing inside of her. "Oh my god...you actually...put your hand inside me..."

"I did!" I pulled back little by little, trying to make my hand as small as I could on the way out.

"That was...you two..." Cassidy wiped the sweat from her brow, "you are...where have you been all my life?" She laughed, which made extracting my hand much more difficult.

"Just in the suburbs..." Wendy said, her own hand back on Cassidy's head. "You'll have to visit us some time..."

I looked over at Wendy, and the idea of getting together again, being together with Cassidy outside of the Club Crescent setting, felt like such an odd thing to propose, but I wanted it so bad too.

I slid my hand out of Cassidy and felt just how wet my palm and fingers were beyond how soaked my wrist and forearm were. I grabbed a towel from the linen cabinet and wiped myself off.

"You were so, so fucking cute, Brenda, asking about the lube." Cassidy said, leaning forward and unhooking the closures on her stirrups.

"I'd never done it before!" I replied with glee.

"I would have stopped you if I needed to, but you're just...such a good fucking partner, Bren." She rubbed at the welts on her ankle from the buckle. "I was...not sure of you two when I came in, but...fuck...that was the best session I've had in months."

"We aim to please..." Wendy said, grabbing a towel and putting it over Cassidy's stomach. Our guest took the towel and wiped the sweat from her body, her legs still spread wide open.

I went to Cassidy, putting my hand on her thigh and leaned over and kissed her. "That was an experience I'll never forget."

"Me either."

Cassidy pulled herself up from the table and stretched. "I need some dinner, that took all the energy I had." She toweled herself off more. It was so oddly adorable to see Cassidy now in the room, the confident kind of woman who enjoyed being fisted and didn't mind someone's wife watching while it happened, when she had played Pet so damn well.

I watched Cassidy stretch for a moment as she worked her back. The sex was the best part of this experience, but just getting to know Cassidy was incredible. She was smart, witty, confident, and just as horny as me and Wendy.

"Would you...maybe want to get dinner with us... after you fist me?" I said, my mind firing off a thousand impulses. It's quite something to want to do in the spur of the moment, but I felt like I couldn't wait to experience it. "I mean, I know I'm a domme and this is, like, outside of the scene, but..." I felt my heart beating in my ears. This could very well ruin things for me as a domme, as it was rather improper to ask for your clients to perform sex acts on you outside of the scene, but I felt with Cassidy I had at least a little wiggle room...which is more than I could say that I had with her a few minutes ago.

Cassidy smirked at me. "You liked doing it that much to me?"

I nodded and looked over at Wendy, who seemed as excited as I was.

"Is your wife OK with it?" Cassidy looked over at Wendy.

"Oh, my god, I can't think of anything hotter to watch, if I'm being honest." Wendy said.

Cassidy turned her attention back to me, her face taking on a bit of evil glee that she hadn't been able to exercise during the scene. "You think you'll be able to take it?"

"Only one way to find out." I sat down on the table that Pet had vacated mere minutes ago and awaited my new sensation.

ELEVEN

"YOU'LL WANT to take the bodysuit off, for sure." Cassidy said, taking the bottle of lube from Wendy. "Especially if this is your first time, being as free to move as possible is going to be super important."

"Yeah, definitely." I said, unzipping the suit and pulling it off my shoulders. I was coated in sweat from exertion, but I didn't realize just how hot I was until I began taking the thing off.

"Are we doing this as friends, or am I going to be your temporary domme?" Cassidy said, her eyes hungry for me, glad to feel that the tables had turned.

"I would like a more...friendly fisting for my first time, if that's alright with you." I pulled the bodysuit off of my hips and down my legs, then tossed it to the side of the room. The sweaty heap of latex hit the ground with a strangely satisfying *schlorpp*.

"You get it the friendly way one time, but next time I do it to you, I'm gonna make you beg for it, slut." Cassidy winked at me.

"Mmm...coming for my job, I see." I giggled as I got back into position on the table.

"Oh...I thought I told you that I domme too, just in... private practice, I suppose." Cassidy dribbled lube into the palm of her hand and rubbed her fingers in the slick puddle.

"I knew she wasn't just some amateur coming off the street and acting like that." Wendy said, keenly watching Cassidy's preparations for my destruction.

"Oh, no, I have...quite the client list. I've actually fisted two actresses who you would be absolutely astonished to know they were into that..." Cassidy grinned madly.

"Who?" Wendy said, her eagerness for sex perhaps only outweighed by her thirst for celebrity gossip.

"If your wife can take all of this, maybe I'll tell you over dinner." Cassidy approached me. Even though she was considerably shorter than me, and her frame was much smaller, she appeared positively gigantic now that she was in power. "Ready, Pet?" Cassidy pursed her lips and held her gaze to mine.

"Fucking hell, I don't know if I could get more ready after hearing you say that..." I said, lying back on the table and perching my feet on the arms extending out from the sides. I didn't think I could take the ankle straps, not this time at least.

Cassidy knelt down in front of the table, positioning herself between my legs. "So, I'm not going to mince words here, this feels good as fuck, but it's unbelievably intense. Do you two use toys to do any stretching or anything?" Cassidy teased my labia, warming me up a bit. There was something about her disconnected, professional tone about this that drove me even more wild.

"We have some pretty big strap-ons we break out every once in a while." I said.

"By 'pretty big' are we talking ones you can buy in a store, or ones you have to order on the internet because no sane company would put them in a store?" Cassidy smirked, dripping lube at the top of my vulva, the warm liquid streaming down my skin.

"If you're asking if I've fucked Brenda with a tentacle strap-on, the answer is yes..." Wendy pulled a chair up so that she would be right next to the action.

I gave Cassidy a hapless grin. I *did* really love that weird fucking tentacle.

"Oh, this should be nothing for you then..." Cassidy took her index and middle fingers and probed me. I had no doubt that she was telling the truth that she dommed professionally, because the way she applied pressure in just the right way and spread me open was the work of a veteran.

"Let's wait until you actually have your fist in my pussy before we say it's nothing." I said, laying back and trying to open myself up more.

"God...damn..." Cassidy leaned down and kissed the top of my vulva, then ran her tongue through my pubic hair. "I bet next time you ask me to do it without lube too...I love it when women are this fucking soaked..."

I rolled my eyes to the back of my head as the passion from Cassidy overtook me. She was phenomenal at this... maybe even too good. No, strike that, nobody can be *too good* at sex, at least I hope not.

"It feels so good already." I adjusted myself so that I was pointed at a more upward angle to allow Cassidy to do this as deeply as she could.

"I've barely even started, Pet." Cassidy kissed the inside of my thigh and pushed a third finger into me.

"This is so, so fucking hot. Cassidy, are you OK if I masturbate while I watch you two?" Wendy said, her face blushing, her forehead beaded with sweat.

"Honestly, I'd be a little disappointed if you didn't, because this is going to be fucking hot." Cassidy massaged her fingers into me, coaxing me more and more. She knew how to control a room, that was for sure.

I watched Wendy as she walked over to her purse and pulled out the clit-sucking vibe that she kept with her at all times, slumbering in its small case, ready for when Wendy needed a little extra.

"Are you going to enjoy watching your wife come while I have my fist inside of you, Brenda?" Cassidy licked the top of my vulva again, leaving more saliva behind, lubricating me more.

"You're goddamn right, I will." I said.

Wendy got back to her seat and opened her legs, then applied the small vibe to her clit, the buzzing and sucking sound rather familiar to my ears. I'm serious, Wendy fucking loved that thing.

"Alright..." Cassidy slid the fourth finger into me and grabbed my thigh with her free hand. "I think you're very ready for me to go all the way, but I want to make sure you feel the same way."

"Please...fuck, yes, please, Cassidy, put your hand

inside me." I gasped, the anticipation almost too much for me.

She gripped my thigh to spread me open as much as possible, and I felt Cassidy's fingers pushing into me. Fuck, the stretching felt so phenomenal.

"Good girl...you're doing such a good job..." Cassidy said, working her fingers up to the last knuckle.

"Oh my god, please keep talking..." I said. I grabbed my breasts and pulled at my nipples to enhance my sensation as Cassidy filled me more and more.

"What should I talk about? How warm you feel?" Cassidy's fingers curled, pushing against my walls, increasing the pressure. I couldn't believe how overwhelmingly good this was. I now totally see how Cassidy could get into something like this.

"Mmm...yeah...yes..." I said, my body straining but accepting the pressure.

"You're very warm, my little Pet. Asking for something like this was a bold move." Cassidy pushed her fist forward, further into me. It was such a different feeling than usual, I had no choice but to pay attention to every change, every way her hand pushed and stretched me.

"Fuck...Cassidy, that is so good...oh my god..." I reached down and put my hand at the base of my stomach, pressing so that my muscles tightened even more.

"You're dripping." Cassidy chuckled, and I felt my wetness along my thighs. "You were made for this kind of treatment, Brenda."

"Don't stop...fuck..." I took my hand down further and grasped Cassidy's wrist as she pulsed her muscles, not moving in and out as much as just making her fist... bigger somehow. "Push it in...god...fucking...I..."

For someone as loquacious as me, someone who is paid handsomely to talk to people all day in both my professions, I hope you understand how exhilarating it was to be left completely speechless.

"Your beautiful wife is going to come for me, Wendy. Are you watching?"

"Of fucking course I am!" Wendy gasped. I was too far gone at this point to be able to look up at her, but I imagined the mask of amazement on her face. "Fuck...I'm coming...fuck..." Wendy panted, the vibe sucking her to bliss.

"Then you better join her, Pet." Cassidy said.

When I heard her laugh under her breath, that was the moment I was sent off. These were the kinds of things that really did it to me. Yes, all the hard fury of BDSM was fun and all, but those little moments when a person realized just how far they'd gone, just how much they were doing, just how much they were sharing themselves with someone, that kind of thing always sent me over the edge.

And, if that sent me over the edge, whatever Cassidy was doing to me sent me a mile past it. I couldn't even see the edge, the person I was pre-orgasm, as my body seemed to collapse around Cassidy's fist.

In a fury of sound and sensation, I pushed down on Cassidy's hand, getting deeper than she had been, the pressure going so far as to be right at the limit of what I could take. I felt myself contracting against her hand, my body reckoning with the massive presence. And you're goddamn right, all three of us squirted tonight.

I returned to reality slowly, my senses needing time to catch up from being teleported to wherever Cassidy had sent them.

"Good girl...god, Brenda, that was impressive for a first time..."

I opened my eyes as much as I could and saw Cassidy looking at me over the rise of my stomach and thighs. She looked eager enough to go another round with her other hand, but I knew even thinking about that would break me in more ways than one.

"That...fuck...Cassidy...I'm..."

"You actually got her to be quiet for more than a few minutes, Cass, I don't think I've been able to do that since we met." Wendy said. I didn't need to look at her face to know that the warm smile that I loved so much was there.

"OK, the pulling out part...it can be tricky, but just relax." Cassidy said. I felt a little extra pressure as she started her extraction. "Breathe, baby...breathe for me, Pet."

This woman could make me come by reading the phone book, I was sure of it.

I calmed myself down, centering my energy like I was in a yoga class and not having a gorgeous woman remove her fist from my vagina. Cassidy pulled back gently, the aftershocks of the pressure would have been arousing on their own if my body was not so very tired at this point.

After a few more deep breaths, I felt her hand slip out of me entirely, my body yearning to refill the void as soon as possible.

"Wendy, dear..." Cassidy said. "Would you mind getting us some towels?"

RESTRAINT

ONE

TAKING on a resistant submissive is a hell of a challenge. Not everybody just wants to bend over and take it, rather literally I may add. No, you see, for some people, the thrill of going down with a fight before plunging into pleasure is the exact thing they desire.

So all of that is to explain just how Nina, a high-powered Hollywood agent whose days are usually fueled by rage and bluster ended up tied to a chair in a play room at Club Crescent, her hands and feet bound, a silk ribbon cinched around her mouth, allowing her to breathe but not much more. Because she wouldn't *fucking* accept her punishment.

"If I take the gag out of your mouth, are you going to start being a little bitch again, Nina? Or are you going to comply with my demands?" I said, sitting in a chair across from her, my legs crossed, fishnets forming a delightful looking pattern across my thighs.

Nina grunted and heaved from behind the gag, trying to move her hands and feet to no avail. She wasn't going anywhere unless I allowed it. Her eyes were steely and crazed, the intensity probably serving her incredibly well when dealing with clients, but when she was my client, and I was in a position of power like this, they lacked a great deal of their impact. Craze and intensity is diminished considerably when I could sit across from you for the entire night and wait for you to just wear yourself out.

My combative submissive's body was the kind that you needed in Hollywood for anyone to take you seriously...at least if you were a woman. Men could and did look like the most disgusting slobs on the planet and fall backwards into success, but women had a higher barrier to entry. She was thin, but of course not too thin, body toned by Pilates or yoga or both. Her skin was smooth and shiny with a perfectly even tan, not allowed to give a single hint about her age. I guessed early forties, but with the entertainment industry, I could have been fifteen years off on either side. She had subtle curves and small breasts, breasts that were now straining against the button-up shirt she was wearing, her arms lashed behind her to give her no choice but to present them. Her dark hair, wavy and luxurious, which she was quite proud of and mentioned often, was gathered in a utilitarian bun at the top of her head to keep it out of the way of tonight's activities. It gave me no small delight to take the immaculately manicured coif and shove it into a bundle that only served to get it out of my fucking way.

"Answer me, Nina." I kicked the side of her knee, looking disinterested in her games.

"Unnngh!" Nina tried to speak behind the ribbon. "Fhuuunnn!"

I looked at my nails and held my hand out in front of my face. "I suppose I'll ungag you for the simple fact that letting you talk will let you just dig yourself in even further..."

I stood up and walked behind Nina. I caught a glimpse of myself in the mirror and thought I looked quite threatening and dominant tonight. The aforementioned fishnet tights that stopped about halfway up my thighs, a tight black patent leather skirt with a side zipper, and a black leather bustier that pushed what I had up into a nice package.

I pulled the knot out of the gag and loosened it from Nina's mouth. I then drew it away from her mouth by dragging it against her face, not caring that I trailed a line of saliva along her cheek.

"Fucker! You motherfucker! I'm going to fuck your entire life up! I'm going to make your existence a living hell!" Nina screamed the words.

"That's a shame," I said, looking over Nina's shoulder at my reflection. I slapped the bundled-up ribbon across the back of her neck. "All that indignation for someone who has absolutely no power to act upon it..." I brought my hand around to Nina's chest and grabbed her right breast, squeezing it to the point of pain. "How long will it take for you to understand that I own you, Nina?"

I pinched and twisted her nipple until she cried out in pain and fury, then released.

"Let me out of these restraints, you fucking psycho! Do you know who I am?!"

"Oh, you're in the 'special thanks to' in a couple dozen movies. Is that what you thought your life would amount to, Nina? A footnote in someone else's story?" I laughed to myself.

Nina tried to shake her arms free again but the rope was so tight that even her fitness-strengthened muscles had been rendered useless.

"You fucking... I am an important person in the industry. People respect me. I have a real job, while you're an insignificant whore!"

"How exactly can I be so insignificant when I have you in such a compromised position, Nina? Would an insignificant whore be able to control and withhold your pleasure all night..." I brought my hand to her left breast, pulling the cup down under her shirt, exposing her nipple, "you don't get to feel a thing without my permission, Nina. You only exist because I allow you to."

Nina opened her mouth and let out an angry, frustrated noise, shaking her head back and forth. She grumbled...or maybe it was groveling. Perhaps she was learning.

"Oh...now she's speechless..." I chuckled. I circled the chair and straddled her, making sure I hiked my skirt up so I could show I wasn't wearing panties. I needed her to see I was already a little wet, and she wouldn't be enjoying it for a long time. I draped my arms over Nina's shoulders, gripping the chair behind her. "Is she ready to behave?"

Nina tried to move her shoulders to push me back, but the ropes held strong. Her delicious-looking mouth hung open as she realized she couldn't fight against the restraints. I stared at her as she considered her situation, and a part of me was expecting a struggle, but when she answered it was the most calm, demure voice. "What do you want me to do?"

"Mmm...that's a good girl. We're going to try to earn you some favor now, ok? Would you like that? Would you like my disdain for you to be a fraction less than it is right now?"

"Y-yes. What is it, Mistress?" Her voice was a defeated whisper, and it felt like the most delicious kind of submission, like she knew that it was my game, and she'd lost, but she still had some dignity by trying to comply, as fanciful as that was.

"You're going to lick and suck my nipples until I'm satisfied with the job you've done. You will not stop until I tell you to stop. If you think you've been doing it for an hour, and surely you should stop, you should ask yourself 'has Mistress Morrigan told me I can stop sucking her beautiful nipples?', and if that answer is no, well...you should keep sucking them, Nina." I said with a venomous grin.

I didn't give Nina a chance to respond, I just pulled down the right cup on my bustier to allow my breast to be free. Instinctually, Nina leaned forward and clasped her lips around the pink bud.

"And, Nina, if I feel even the first hint of your teeth against my angelic, perfect nipples, I will blindfold you and suspend you from the ceiling, and you'll have to wait until the cleaning crew comes in here Monday afternoon to discover you still in that embarrassing predicament."

I ran my fingers through Nina's hair and started to rock against her thigh as she licked my nipple.

"That's right...I don't care if it's uncomfortable...I

want it...you're very good at that, Nina. Can you feel how hard my nipple is for you? See what fun things you get to do when you're sweet and obedient?" I said, starting to roll my hips on Nina's lap. "My tits are so much better than yours, I'm sure getting to experience something so beautiful makes you feel especially insignificant, doesn't it?"

My other nipple was already hard as a diamond, and I made sure Nina gave them equal time, pulling down the other side of the bustier. She made sure she lavished both of my breasts with her tongue, taking as much of me in her mouth as possible to create that wet sucking sound.

"You love my tits, don't you, Nina?" I said.

"They're beautiful..." Nina said before getting right back to the task at hand, and I rewarded her for it.

"Such a good girl...that's so much better, isn't it? Now Nina, pull your head away from my tits for a moment. I want to give you a treat."

Nina did just that, pulled back from me and looked up at my face. She looked a little lovedrunk, giving herself permission to just enjoy sex with me instead of playing her role as a combatant. I'd get that fixed soon, but first I wanted to tempt her further.

I took my right middle finger and dragged it along my slit, gathering as much sticky wetness as I could. I held the finger up to Nina's face, the skin glistening with my wetness.

"Taste me, Nina."

Without hesitation, Nina wrapped her lips around my finger and sucked off every bit of my nectar, then pulled off, running her tongue around the finger, making sure to get every bit of it off.

"Now isn't it a shame that's all you're going to get to taste of my delicious pussy tonight? You gobbled up your entire portion without even thinking about it, Nina. And now you're going to starve for it, aren't you?"

"Mistress..."

"And I am so, so wet, Nina. I can barely contain it. Treating you like the filth you are has gotten me so worked up, and you know a woman tastes that much better when she's really, really needing it, don't you, Nina?"

"Yes... Mistress..." Nina's eyes were locked on mine.

"And you could just beg and plead with me, you could take this time to grovel and apologize for what you've made me do tonight, but it would mean absolutely nothing. You've made your choices, Nina. Your poor choices." I reached between my legs and gathered some more wetness with my middle and index fingers. I held my hand in front of Nina's face, so very close to her, then pulled it away and licked the length of my fingers, tasting myself. "Oh, Nina, I taste divine."

TWO

NINA WATCHED INTENTLY, hypnotized, but then she looked away, trying to shake out of it, her eyes moving up to the ceiling and she let out a breath through her nostrils.

"Nina, darling, be honest with me..." I returned my arms to being draped over Nina's shoulders, but took a moment to be extra sadistic and dragged my still-wet fingertips along the back of Nina's neck. "Do you think your sorry little pussy tastes as good as mine?"

Nina's lips pursed and her eyes closed as I did that, the light, delicate touches enough to make her shiver, but not enough to bring any sort of release. "Probably not, Mistress."

"I didn't ask for 'probably', Nina." I drove my hips against her lap, scooting the chair an inch or so back with the force. "Yes, or no."

"N-no, Mistress. My pussy does not taste as good as yours. It can't possibly, Mistress." Nina's eyes stayed shut as she spoke.

"No, of course it doesn't," I said, looking back up at

our reflection in the mirror. I grabbed the back of Nina's head and pointed it toward the mirror as well. "Look at us, what a lovely couple. A sexy domme and a broken shell of a woman who still doesn't know her place. Should we take a picture and send it as a Christmas photo, Nina? Should we let every single friend and family member know exactly what you spend your weekends doing?"

"I don't think that would be a good idea, Mistress..." Nina said in a whisper.

"Why wouldn't it? You're absolutely stunning...especially when you're so willing and eager to submit. Don't you want your friends to know how much you love sucking my tits? Are you embarrassed by it, Nina? You seemed rather keen on them just moments ago..." I stood up from my position, giving Nina some temporary relief. "And, god, you certainly spend enough money on me that you should be proud to show off where those big Hollywood paychecks go." I bent over in front of Nina, giving her more of a show, making sure she could see what she wasn't allowed to have.

"I don't know what I'm saying, Nina. I'm quite sure your Christmas cards show up in the mailbox and find their way to the trashcan a moment later. Do you think your high-powered clients have any room on their substantial mantles to house your pitiful little greetings?" I walked over to the cabinet where I kept my gear, pondering what I would torture her with next.

"I don't have to take this shit from you, Mistress Morrigan. You're a nobody. You're nothing. I can't go anywhere in LA without someone recognizing me and wanting some of my time. You're anonymous." Nina seethed.

"A bold move from someone who was almost getting on my good side, Nina." I closed the cabinet and walked at an aching pace toward Nina, brandishing the next star of the night. "Do you know what this is, pet?" I batted it against my hand, looking down at her.

"It's a strap-on, Mistress Morrigan. Because you couldn't get real dick if you tried." Nina focused her gaze on me, trying to get back at me with more brattiness. She was good at winding me up.

Of course, I loved just being able to dominate, to make a woman bend to my will and have her thank me for every moment of my cruelty, but to be entirely honest, I think I liked clients like Nina more. They made me work for it, challenged me, wouldn't just give me what I wanted right away.

"Oh...dear, dear Nina..." I took the shiny red dildo and popped the head of it against Nina's cheek, making a satisfying knocking sound. "Were I to want to degrade myself so far as to be with a man, I would have a line of them out the door waiting for me every night. But my tastes are more refined."

Nina looked up at me and raised her eyebrows as if to say 'prove it' but instead I pressed the rubber tip against Nina's lips. I pushed it a little more, the bright red silicone almost a perfect match to Nina's sumptuous lipstick. She opened her mouth slightly, pressing her teeth into it. Not enough to actually bite it, though...Nina was an experienced sub, so she knew the danger of damaging toys, and I appreciated her for that.

"Open your mouth, Nina. Suck it. If you don't accept it, I won't hesitate to shove it down your throat and not give you an option." I said, pressing the dildo harder against her resistant tongue.

She kept it between her lips for a moment more before finally complying and taking as much of it into her mouth as possible.

"Such an amazing little worthless slut you are. Sucking that fake dick like it was real. Can you take all of it, good girl?" I said, my voice taking on a musical lilt.

"Hmm-mmmh" Nina shook her head slightly, unable to form words.

"Do you think that'll stop me from making you do it, Nina?" I smirked.

"N-n-nh-mmm"

"That's what I thought...now..." I drew the head of the dildo back out of Nina's mouth and then immediately plunged it back in, starting to face-fuck my reluctant submissive. "Show me those sucking skill you've been hiding, Nina. Just because I don't have a cock doesn't mean I don't enjoy watching a depraved slut try to navigate one..."

I let myself be a little more vicious as I drove the fake dick into her mouth, and I was pleased that Nina just sat there and took it, gagging as it went deep down into her throat but keeping herself composed and still, keeping up with it. I knew Nina was bisexual, and I sort of marveled at the experience the men in her life got to partake in when faced with Nina. She wasn't shy at all about her prodigious talents, looking up at me with half-narrowed eyes, giving me a 'this is so easy' without saying it.

"You think you're so fucking cute, don't you? You think you have all the power...oh Nina...Nina...if only you understood your position in the hierarchy..."

I pulled the dildo out of Nina's mouth, my victim resisting it by trying to suck it as hard as possible so that it emerged with a delicious sounding pop.

"Nina, be honest with me, when's the last time you sucked a cock like that? You took that on like it was your job, and..honestly, seeing how many box office bombs your clients are in, it might be your job soon..."

Nina spat the excess saliva from her mouth, dribbling it down her chin and looked at me, her eyes filled with hate, and it only turned me on more.

"Well? Don't be rude, Nina, you still haven't answered me. Tell me the last time you degraded yourself by sucking a cock. It's a simple answer, really."

"I-I-I...a couple days ago." Nina said with a smile. I wondered if it belonged to one of the mid-list stars she seemed to attract into her orbit. You know, the kind of guy you see in a movie and think 'it's always great when they show up in something', that kind? That was Nina's clientele, and perhaps inadvisably her dating pool as well.

"Did he cum in your mouth, Nina?"

"Y--yes."

"And did you swallow it, Nina?" I held Nina's chin in my hand, turning her face side to side.

"Y-yes. Mistress Morrigan, he--" Nina tried to speak, but I slapped her, cutting off what she was about to say.

"That's enough information, I don't want to hear about men anymore tonight." I held the dildo and harness in my hand, looking down at Nina. "You've gotten me so goddamn bored that I need to use you for something again, Nina. You're not going to enjoy it, but I genuinely couldn't fucking care."

I placed the dildo and harness into Nina's lap, the red rod still slick with her spit. "I'm going to put this harness on you now, Nina. I don't want to hear a single word of opposition."

I stood behind Nina and grabbed the dildo and harness, slipping them through her legs. I drew the harness up her thighs, fastening the straps against her. It was an enticing look, a gorgeous submissive sitting there with a harness with an eight-inch dildo jutting up from her lap.

"Now, Nina, I have some business to attend to, and I ask you, please don't react to this. This is for my enjoyment only." I got back in front of Nina and straddled her, sliding onto the dildo with zero effort...I was just that turned on by all of this, I even surprised myself a little.

I didn't give her any warning that I was doing this, and it seemed to surprise Nina just a bit when the full length of it was inside me, my weight resting against her, further restricting her already bound movement. "Oh... yes...I need this, Nina. I had to fuck myself because I knew you wouldn't have the capability of doing it." I rode the dildo, feeling the entire length of it filling me up before I raised off of it again, bouncing on Nina's inert hips. It was so fucking fun to just use her body.

I rode the fake dick and wrapped my arms around Nina's head. "Can you hear it? Can you hear the sound of it going into me, Nina? Do you hear how utterly soaked I am?" I grinned.

Nina just kept quiet and kept closing her eyes, as if trying to take herself somewhere else while I violated her. I wondered if she was trying to not come...because that's where I would be in this situation.

I laughed in her face. "Look at me. Eyes fucking open, and speak. I need updates on how fucking horrendous this makes you feel."

"M-Mistress Morrigan, you're so fucking terrible." Nina said quietly. It was clear this was turning her on enough that keeping up the illusion of being above it all was getting more difficult.

"Aww...does this not get you hot? This dildo that I'm riding doesn't turn you on at all?"

"No, it's disgusting...you're such an awful slut..."

"I'm your slut, though, aren't I, Nina? The one bouncing on your cock. The one getting your pants and shirt all wet...you wouldn't have me here if I was unwanted, right?" I licked the side of Nina's face, taunting her further.

Nina whimpered. "It's disgusting."

"You're so mean to me, Nina! What do I need to do to get you to stop being mean?" I pouted, jutting my bottom lip out in a deliciously bratty expression.

"Please...just stop..."

"No fucking chance...at least not until I come." I said. I leaned in and licked her again, going from the side of her neck to her nose, breathing gasps of hot air against her as I brought myself closer to orgasm.

Nina finally gave in and looked at me as I fucked the fake dick. She watched, transfixed, maybe wishing that I'd be the one fucking her instead of myself. I felt my thighs clenching up around her, my muscles tense as I worked toward that first, amazing release.

"Oh, you like the look of that, don't you, Nina? You like seeing your owner's pussy weeping for you, even if you don't get to enjoy any of it. God, Nina, I don't know if I've ever been this wet..."

Nina bit her lower lip as I drew the words out of her. "God...you're disgusting, Mistress Morrigan...so disgusting..."

"You're the one fucking paying for me, slut. You're the one that wants this. You want me to be disgusting, don't you? You want me to be utterly filthy." I laughed, feeling on the verge of a truly wonderful orgasm.

"Fuck, fuck, fuck...fuck..." I leaned into Nina's ear. "I'm about to come, Nina...I'm going to come all over your pretty little dildo and make a mess. I'm going to ruin these pretty designer clothes. You know I can squirt rather well, right, Nina? And with this dildo, at this angle...god you're going to be destroyed."

"Please...no...no no..." Nina whispered, like she was really going to take my orgasm as a personal slight.

"Even if I were to choose mercy for some reason..." I felt my body start to activate, the warmth spreading through me, "we're far past the point of no return, Nina..."

I let out a groan and started to clamp down on the fake cock, the penetration feeling so goddamn good as it filled me, the head of the dildo grinding against exactly where I needed.

"Fuck, Nina...I'm coming...oh...I can feel it...oh it's so fucking good..." I groaned again, tensing myself as much as I could around the toy, exerting my body as hard as it would go. And just like that I exploded, my hips jerking, my wetness soaking Nina's stomach and thighs as the orgasm tore through me, so fucking strong as I rode Nina. I screamed with how fucking good it felt, feeling myself making a complete mess of the other woman's legs as the liquid left my body. Hitting that spot and feeling that release was one of the most intoxicating things I could ever feel, and it was rare I had one that felt this fucking good.

THREE

GETTING my head back into the scene, I knew I had to act like Nina didn't just blow my fucking mind. I pulled off of the dildo and stood up, looking down at Nina's lap. Her $500 designer slacks were soaked through with my fluids, and the $1,000 shirt too. And dry cleaning can only do so much.

"God...look at you, Nina. Filthy. How can you live looking like that?" I said, not wanting to touch myself to cool down in order to make it seem like I was so not bothered by all of this, betraying reality.

"F-fuck...my clothes are ruined, you fucking bitch. Why didn't you listen to me? Why do you always do the opposite of what I want?" Nina said, starting to panic and looking like she might break down.

"Oh, Nina, I'm no villain here. I bet your pussy's been so wet for so long that some of this..." I pressed my finger into the soaked fabric. It felt kind of gross, honestly, but it drove the point home, "some of this is your fault, you know. I can't believe you'd blame me for ruining you when you did this to yourself."

In reality, as much as Nina faked that she was dismayed that I ruined her clothes, she absolutely loved destroying expensive clothing items in the heat of passion. There was a conspicuous consumption, financial domination part of her kink that I didn't question. She brought the two thousand dollar outfit, she didn't mind what got all over it, and I was here to get her off, so all's well that ends well. Perhaps it wasn't quite eating the rich, but fucking the rich with abandon, that I could do.

I needed to prepare to move us on, so I released the harness and pulled the strap-on from Nina's hips. I then reached behind my back and undid my bustier, letting it fall to the ground. It was nice to be able to cool off a little and feel the air on my skin. Nina looked at me, trying to look away, trying to pretend that the sight didn't stir any feelings. "I'm giving you a treat, Nina. I know you've been begging to see me naked and you're getting it. I don't know why I'm so good to you." I knelt in front of her, posing like a model, pushing my breasts together with my arms to generate as much cleavage as I could. "Look at me, Nina. Tell me how fucking beautiful I am."

"I don't need to stroke your ego anymore tonight, Mistress Morrigan. It's far too swollen to require it." Nina looked over at me with an air of superiority.

I stood up and stepped forward, getting right up into Nina's face. "I wasn't giving you an option, you rotten slut. If you want to ever get out of that chair, tell me how fucking amazing my body is."

Nina just rolled her eyes and sighed. "I would love to run my tongue across your nipples, Mistress Morrigan."

I smirked. "Oh, would you? But you won't...this isn't about *you*, Nina. This is about *me*. Now start with the compliments. Immediately."

Nina shook her head slightly. "You're so sexy and powerful, Mistress Morrigan...your tits are beautiful...and so soft and tender. And I can't believe that you would share yourself with such a filthy person." She said it with a decidedly bored tone, like an actor on the fiftieth take of a particularly tedious scene.

I slapped Nina across the face. Unlike a lot of clients, Nina didn't mind face slapping, and I have to admit doing it had a very dramatic effect. I had to train myself for far too long to be able to do it safely, though. One might underestimate the value of a stage combat course at UCLA in aiding in their dominatrix career, but it did a world of help for me.

"You can try to say it in a way where you don't sound so fucking bored, you little cunt." I slapped her lightly again, my nails grazing her chin.

"I-I...you're amazing, Mistress Morrigan..." Nina said, the light red of her cheeks giving her away.

I reached between Nina's legs and cupped her mound, feeling her soaked through panties, although some of that wetness was my own. "More. Fucking more, Nina. Tell me how beautiful I am."

"You're gorgeous, Mistress Morrigan...so strong... you've ruined me. You've absolutely wrecked me."

"That's fucking right I have," I said, giving her another light slap. "I'm going to untie you now, Nina. Can you even believe how altruistic I'm going to be? And you say I'm cruel..." I walked behind Nina and released the clamp holding the rope around Nina's left arm taut. I was shit with knots, guess I didn't spend enough time in Girl Guides, so I couldn't give my clients the elaborate knot-work that so many of them desired. But I could tie them up, just with a little mechanical aid.

"I don't get why I deserve such treatment, Mistress Morrigan." Nina said quietly.

I freed Nina's right hand and then untied her legs, throwing the rope off to the side. "You never will. Now strip, Nina. I'm tired of smelling those disgusting clothes."

As Nina got up from the chair, I could tell she was a little shaky. It was a domme's job to monitor their client's state and make sure they didn't, say, pass out in the middle of a session. Even with the most attentive dommes, it still happened, but I was happy with the fact that I'd only had to stop one or two sessions entirely after I got really concerned about a client.

"Yellow light...just checking in, are you OK?" I said, relaxing my posture, giving myself a little break too.

Nina was looking down at her ruined clothes and looked up at me, her eyes eager and bright. "What?"

"You just seem a little shaky. I think we at least need a water break."

"You're a doll, Brenda, really. I wouldn't have asked, but, it does sound good." Nina grinned.

I grabbed two waters from the small refrigerator and handed one over to Nina, who took it with grace and kindness that the character in the scene we were playing out couldn't even imagine.

“How am I doing so far?” I said as I took a sip.

“Phenomenal, as always. Pretty much breaking my hips by fucking yourself on top of me, that...that’s a hell of a move.”

“That kind of stuff I can only do when I have such an athletic and eager client, and you very much fit the bill on both fronts.” I took a towel and wiped my thighs down to cool off and clean up before we moved on.

“Well I appreciate you not holding back...” Nina said, stepping closer to me. “Are you OK with kissing outside of scenes, because...god, you’re beautiful...” Nina’s eyes were starry and seductive, and in moments like this I realized how so many people ended up in her gravity...she was charming as hell.

Some dommes, I’m sure, had major reservations about doing anything affectionate with clients outside of a scene. This was a job, after all, even if it was a fun one, and lines of acceptable behavior were perhaps more important here than in most other professions.

I respected those dommes, but I wasn’t one of them. Maybe it’s because Wendy and myself only took women as clients, or maybe it’s because ethical polyamory got us into this world in the first place, but I had no issues with being as affectionate with clients as they wanted to be, in scene or out.

“Of course, darling.” I leaned in and kissed Nina, appreciating the feeling of warmth and kindness in it. I loved making her beg for things, degrading her at every turn, but the truth was Nina was an utter sweetheart.

“Mmm...” she pulled back. “I needed that. Now I’m ready to go back in.”

"Then let's continue, shall we?"

FOUR

NINA GOT up and unbuttoned the top button of her slacks. She pushed them down her legs, letting them fall to the floor, exposing the expensive black lace thong I bought her for tonight. If this woman loved ruining her own clothes, she positively got off on ruining gifts.

I walked behind Nina and snapped the waistband of the thong against her hip. "Nina, can you imagine how this thong would look on a woman who could actually fill it out?"

I squeezed Nina's ass, digging my nails into the firm muscle. I wondered if this is what it felt like to be with an elite athlete, all sleek muscle and sinew. But in a way, Nina might have been better than that, since she had to keep aesthetics in mind along with her fitness.

"I have to imagine other women when I'm with you, were you aware of that? I think you know you don't do much for me, but I don't think you understand the depths of it. There isn't one thing I find appealing about your sorry excuse for a body. The fact that you would even think you can show it to me is enough to make me gag." I said, snapping her thong again and giving her some space to get undressed the rest of the way.

I think Nina was into the degradation, especially about her body, because she knew it was an outright lie. She was more fit than me, way more, and I'm pretty certain she had no lack of compliments about her toned, California-perfect physique in all other places in her life. But, I was happy to provide the counterbalance.

Nina hooked her thumbs in her panties and pushed them down her thighs. Her body was perfect, taut and toned from the countless hours working with trainers, not a hint of an imperfection, not even a stray pimple or scar as far as I could tell. She was strictly a no-marks kind of girl, and I was grateful for it. Leaving bruises or welts on such a pristine canvas would feel like a crime.

But it just meant that I had to work that much harder to leave the bruises and welts on her ego.

"Do you even have tits, Nina?" I said as I looked her up and down while she dropped her soaked shirt at her feet. "I mean, you have a chest, but, whatever is on there... do doctors even consider those breasts?"

Nina looked over her shoulder at me with a small smile, like she couldn't believe that she was being put down about her breasts. They were small, but astonishingly perky. I could only imagine how perfectly she filled out a red carpet dress. "My tits are so tiny and pathetic that I have to pay women like you to play with them."

I slithered behind Nina and ran my hand up her

toned stomach before resting it on her breast. I toyed with it, gently flicking the nipple with my thumb. "They're not even enjoyable to play with. There's just nothing here, Nina. Pitiful." I started to lick the back of Nina's neck, running my tongue along her neckline. "God you're begging me to put my tongue inside you, aren't you?" I laughed, holding Nina close. "Beg me. Literally. Beg, Nina."

Nina whimpered quietly before finally doing just that. "I...I want to feel your tongue in me, Mistress Morrigan...I want it more than anything...you don't even understand..."

"Oh I understand. I understand how giddy creatures like you get when a woman finally finds herself desperate enough to demean herself to give you pleasure. It's so rare, because why would we subject ourselves to it when literally any other woman would be a better choice?" I splayed my hand across the space between her navel and her pubic bone. It was a sensitive spot, and on a body as sleek and tight as Nina's, I could feel the muscles tensing under my light touch.

Nina gasped softly. "I want you...you're my only option..." she whispered, trying to play the game as best she could.

I turned her to face me and got on my knees in front of her, licking the front of her left thigh. Nowhere near anything that sensitive, because Nina loved to be edged to the limit, and then edged a little more.

Nina groaned quietly and looked down at me with a disappointed face. "No, Mistress Morrigan, not like this..."

"I have no idea what you're talking about, Nina." I looked up at Nina, taking the skin on her inner thigh between my teeth and gently pulling on what little slack I could find. "I'm nowhere near any of your horrible erogenous zones, I'm just giving you some attention that you've been begging for."

I nipped again and released her flesh, looking up at her. I placed my lips right at the point where the cut of Nina's hip, defined and firm on her body, lead to her thigh and exhaled my hot breath, looking up at her and blowing softly against her, knowing that the air would trail down between her legs and tease her.

"I don't think it's really in the cards for me to lick your sorry excuse for a pussy, Nina. Why would I waste my time on something so undesirable?" I said, lightly blowing between her legs as I spoke.

Nina whimpered a little. "I need it so bad..."

"Well that's quite funny, thinking you can make demands here. But, I'm feeling generous, Nina." I lightly slapped her ass, the firmness of it driving me a little crazy. How the fuck did someone get so in shape?

"You...you're feeling generous to me, Mistress Morrigan? But...but I'm your captive...how could you ever want to be generous?"

I stood up from my position in front of her, running my fingertips over her breasts as I rose, her body like an absolute statue. "You're not questioning me, are you, Nina? You better not be. God, you better not be."

"N-no, Mistress Morrigan, I...I'm not, I promise."

"Good...I wouldn't want to have to gag that awful, awful

mouth again. Sit on the bed. Now." I gave her a nudge with my shoulder to point her toward the bed at the side of the room, its crimson sheets still neatly tucked and perfect, since beds didn't seem to get too much use in our particular hobby.

Nina got the hint and moved over to the bed, sitting down on the edge.

I knelt down in front of the bed in front of Nina's knees, which were pushed together.

"Nina, did you not think that it might have been advisable to open your legs when I told you to sit down? Do you even know what we're here for?"

I pulled her thighs apart hard, hoping I could give her taut abductor muscles a stain before putting myself right between her knees, getting up close and personal with Nina's pussy. It was, like everything else about her, absolutely gorgeous.

"Nina, as you've been a good girl, or the best girl you can be, I have a treat for you. Can you guess what it is, dear Nina?" I cooed.

Nina's face was flushed a bit more now. "A...a treat? For me, Mistress Morrigan? I don't deserve a treat."

"Please shut up with the babe in the woods bullshit. I can tell you're on fire inside. Drop the act." I said. "Because you're too slow to answer my questions, I'm just going to tell you. I'm going to put my finger inside of you, Nina. Just one. I hope you understand this is a major undertaking for me to do even this, so please do not take this for granted."

I dragged a finger along the length of her, starting at the clit and making her shudder, then trailed downward slowly, all the way down to her entrance. "Nina, can I tell you how wet you are?"

"Y--yes..."

"Disgustingly. Good girls don't get this wet. This is vile." I parted her lips and burrowed my fingertip toward its destination. Nina watched intently, my slow and deliberate movements doing so much to make this more achingly drawn out.

I gently teased at Nina's opening before pressing into it, hearing Nina let out a soft moan. I pushed my middle finger in to the first knuckle, my short nail scraping lightly against her. She was primed and ready to pop, so I had to do this carefully.

"Does it feel good to have me here, Nina? Does it make you happy to feel a finger inside of you?" I asked, my tone taking on the sweetest notes I could manage. I stroked upward, slowly as I could, navigating Nina like I was trying to avoid cutting the wrong wire. Although unlike in the movies Nina's clients started in, an explosion here would be of a much more desirable sort.

"It feels so good to have you there, Mistress Morrigan." She breathed, closing her eyes to savor it. "I'm so lucky to have you with me."

"Nina, right now I'm looking at you and I can tell you're thinking about something. If you come while I'm doing this, there will be so much hell to pay. Do not test me." I pushed my finger in further, probing her, teasing her. Every single impulse in my body wanted me to just give her this, to just let her boil over in satisfaction, but I knew I couldn't. The bigger satisfaction was in waiting, and it's what Nina wanted, no matter what her character said.

Nina bit down on her lip to try and quiet her mouth, a soft squeak emerging. "Mistress Morrigan, I want it so much...please, Mistress, please let me have it, let me have your fingers..."

"Nina...contain yourself. I cannot even speak the consequences that you will face if you come. I assure you that it's not worth it." I picked up my pace, stimulating her more, knowing that I had to hold back ever so slightly.

Nina's face got redder as I continued, trying to stay in character but knowing it was getting more and more difficult to hold on to it. "God...fucking..." Nina let slip, looking away as she spoke. She grimaced in delight. I knew this feeling myself, holding yourself right at the point of no return, your toes on the threshold, but having the power to hold it back. Yes, it was hellish, but it made the eventual release that much more satisfying.

"I can feel you tensing. Your little pussy is trying to devour my finger. You want to come so...fucking...bad... but do not do it. Do not let yourself come while I finger your soaking wet pussy, Nina." I said. I loved this little mind game, trying to drive those primal, Pavlovian urges in someone by repeating words like 'come' and giving them explicit detail about what you were doing to them. The way it overloaded and taxed a person was so satisfying, especially once that final release was allowed.

"N--N--Mistress...fuck fuck..." Nina closed her eyes tightly, and her face screwed up in a desperate, frustrated expression. "I...fuck...fuck...I have to..."

She was right there, so I knew now was the time to bring things crashing down.

"Well, I think that's enough of that." I pulled my finger out of Nina and stood up, wiping my hand with a towel. I so badly wanted to taste her, but it would have ruined the delightful pain of the moment.

"No, Mistress, please...fucking god...I was two seconds away..."

"I know. That's why I stopped, Nina." I smirked.

FIVE

"YOU CAN'T DO this to me." Nina whined, crossing her legs tightly and squeezing, trying to keep the heat inside as much as she could.

"Oh, but I just did, Nina. I said you weren't allowed to come, and I certainly wasn't going to make it happen for you." I reached down and grabbed Nina's toned thigh firmly, "and do be careful at how tightly you're clenching your scrawny little thighs, because if you come from that, the punishment still stands."

Nina exhaled a frustrated breath. "You...fuck. I need it."

"What are you going to do to get it?"

"I need to do anything. I'll do anything to make it happen."

"My god, Nina. You should probably know by now to not say things like that when you're around me. Because when I already own you, giving me permission to do *anything*, well, that just makes me more bold." I climbed onto the bed next to Nina and played with the stray bits of hair that had fallen out of her bun. "I'm going to test your resolve, Nina. I'm going to see if you have the moral integrity to be granted the right to orgasm. How does that sound?"

"What will it be?" Nina asked, looking into my eyes. "Please, tell me..."

"I need to see if you can control yourself. To prove you're not some wild animal seeking the basest pleasures in life. I know exactly what you want, Nina, and you need to prove to me that you can behave like a human."

I sat up on the bed and straddled Nina's face, making sure to keep my vulva a couple inches away from her mouth. This was going to be hell on my hamstrings, and Nina's yoga conditioning would probably would have allowed her to do this better than me, but it was more than worth the tease.

"I'm going to stay like this for as long as I want. You will not lick, kiss, suck, or slide your tongue against me under any circumstances. If I even feel too strong of a breath, your night is over, and I'll send you home without an orgasm. No matter what I say, you will not touch me with your face or mouth." I said, lifting up a little before letting myself settle in. I so desperately wanted to just let Nina eat me out like I wanted, but, again, she was paying for the tease.

"Yes, Mistress Morrigan. I won't move."

"Speaking like that puts your tongue dangerously close to my little slit, Nina. Be careful..." I laughed. The mere vibrations from her speaking were punishing enough to me since I was supposed to be acting like I wasn't enjoying a bit of this.

Nina tried to remain as motionless as possible, but her hot breath on my wetness made me just want her that much more. I didn't let it show on my face, of course, but it was incredibly hard to just stay here when I needed her as much as I did.

"I can't tell you how badly I just want to sit on your face, dear Nina. I want to feel you inside of me. I want you to worship me." I ran my hand along my lips, knowing it would intoxicate Nina. "Nina..." I moaned, sounding frustrated, "I know what I said before, but, please, just lick me a little. Just slide your tongue between my little pink lips. I need it from you, Nina." I played up sounding as desperate as I could, trying to mirror how desperate and pressed Nina herself was right now.

I was hoping it might cause some kind of lapse, but Nina seemed to be resolute. She knew that she needed to make it through this.

“No...you...you said not to, I'm not falling for it.” Nina seethed.

I stroked Nina's forehead lightly as she tried to keep herself composed, looking down at her as I teased her face. "Nina, please. I need you to do it. Imagine how wonderful I taste...think about how good it will feel for me..."

Nina whimpered. She was being such a good girl. "No...Mistress...please, I'm going to...I need you..." Nina said quietly. Because I couldn't make this night go on forever, I didn't lash out at Nina for the couple of times she did graze her mouth against me, but, god, it made me want it so much more.

I lowered down a little, pressing myself ever so slightly against Nina's face. It was an absolutely devilish thing to do, but even through that, Nina didn't react. Her nose pressed into my clit, but she didn't budge. "I can't take this anymore, Nina. Just please...please fucking lick me. It'll be so easy to do it. Your tongue is right there. Just press it between my wet lips..."

Nina whined a little as she gripped at the bedsheets for dear life. "No...I can't...I'm trying so hard not to lick you...please, Mistress...don't do this..."

"God...you're no fun at all..." I pulled up and swung my legs over Nina's face, relieving her from her torture. "I can't even get you to eat me out...what is wrong with you?" I said, standing at the side of the bed. Nina just stared at the ceiling. "Look at me when I talk to you, Nina!"

"You're...so cruel." Nina said quietly as she turned toward me. "You're an awful human being."

"When sluts like you break out the insults like that, do you think you're the first one that's said that to me? Do you think that will hurt me in some way?" I laughed.

I looked at Nina, still naked, laying there. I was getting to the point of exhaustion with the edging, but I knew this had to keep going, my coup de grace of playful cruelty.

"So, Nina. You were so well behaved that I can't help but think that maybe I could let you come. But then, I had a thought that...I didn't need to do that at all, did I?"

"Mistress...fuck...you can't..."

Without words, without snappy dialogue, I walked over to the side of the room where my street clothes were nicely folded. I took the rain jacket that I'd brought pretty much for the purpose of this next stunt and slid it over my arms, then cinched the belt at my waist.

"I can, Nina. I think that's ultimately what you never realize, you dumb girl. Every single thing you say I can't do, or I shouldn't do, it just makes me want to do it more. So, I can leave this night without letting you come, and, that's exactly what I'll do."

I gave Nina a limp wave and walked over to the exit door. I pulled it open and looked around as if I were checking for things left behind, really playing up my dismissal. I flicked the light switch next to the door and left the room, plunging Nina into complete darkness.

"No, no no... Mistress Morrigan, don't go..." I could hear Nina from the other side of the door. It was so tempting to go back in there and finish all of this off, but I knew the wait had to drag out a little longer. I heard Nina's heavy breath behind the door, as this was just the door that lead to the dressing room, it wasn't soundproofed like the main doors of the playrooms.

I heard a long groan and an angry sigh, which told me what I needed to know. She was so frustrated, she needed me there. And now I'd get to come back in there like the savior that I was. In due time.

Nina was losing her mind, there in the darkness. After being taken to the edge and denied, I knew the feeling, her body felt like a rubber band wrapped around a thousand times, so much energy contained in her just waiting to release. But she was a good sub, she knew she couldn't release it until she was given permission.

I waited it out behind the door for about two minutes, wanting to let her ache in all of this, let it all really sink in.

SIX

I OPENED the door and saw Nina lying on her back on the bed, sheets pulled in every direction, pillow pressed against her stomach. She was really so far gone at this point.

"Nina...you pitiful thing. Why are you still laying on this bed?" I said, pulling the rain coat off and tossing it against the wall.

"Please let me come, Mistress Morrigan...please don't leave me like this." Nina looked like a stray speck of dust falling onto her body would be enough stimulation to make her come.

I took my familiar position at the edge of the bed, sliding easily between her legs. "I should, Nina. I should leave you like this, and I should tell you to come back in two weeks, with the explicit direction that you are not allowed to orgasm until you return, but..." I took my fingers and spread her lips slightly. Her vulva was almost dangerously hot to the touch, or maybe that was just my perception. I'm not sure if I'd ever seen a woman who was so good at denying herself this, at holding back. "You're a good girl, aren't you, Nina?"

"Y...yes..." Nina stammered. "I'm your good girl...I'll always be your good girl..."

I ran my finger along her wetness, her body tense under me. "Then I suppose I'll let my tongue release you. I'm going to eat your pussy now, Nina. And you have full permission to orgasm. No holding back." I slid my hands under Nina's thighs and dug my fingers into the hollows of her hips, drawing her toward me.

I'm a married woman, so it may have been uncouth to admit this, but tasting Nina in that moment may have been the best a woman has ever tasted to me. I'm sure Wendy would have had the same opinion were she in my position.

She was so ripe for it that she became a geyser the moment my tongue drew across her. Nina let out a guttural growl of release and went wild under my tongue, bucking her hips toward me. Tempted and teased this much, few women would have any choice but to squirt, and Nina was no different. She started coming within ten seconds of me going down on her, her thighs shuddering and flexing against my shoulders.

I moaned softly against Nina's sopping wet vulva. Her whole body felt like she was ready to pop at any second, the flood of her fluids overwhelming. Squirting was fun but this was on an entirely different level, I could barely keep up with how much Nina was putting out.

"Fuck...Mistress Morrigan...yes...oh my god...fuck..." Nina grabbed my hair and pulled on it a little harder than she should have, but she had earned it.

I sucked on her clit gently, letting the juices fill my mouth. She tasted so good, even after I lapped up what seemed like a liter of her. I looked up at Nina's face, and she looked like she was going to break down any second, like her next orgasm was so intense that it was on the edge of pain, the pressure and need for release too strong. I knew Nina could have multiples with ease, and today the second followed the first by about five seconds. No squirting this time, though. Damn.

With most other women, I would have stopped here. One only has so much in them, even when they're having this much fun. But I knew she had the endurance, and I knew she'd appreciate it, so I just kept tonguing her, tasting her, my face and chin messy and sopping wet, me not giving a fuck about it

"Fuck fuck fuck..." Nina hissed, still holding my hair with one hand and clenching the bedsheets in the other. "Mistress..." Nina whined, the feeling too good for her to be able to handle it.

The moment struck me that I was beyond turned on by all of this release, so my hand found its way between my legs. I might as well give myself a little treat for all this hard work, right?

Nina was right back to moaning as I took her over the edge for the third time. She squirted a little bit this time, the fluid dancing across my tongue as I slid my fingers into myself and thumbed at my clit, bringing me to the edge as I pressed my face into Nina for one last go. She came a fourth time during my orgasm, this one very weak, and I moaned into her, my second orgasm matching the intensity of the first sans waterworks.

I finally pulled back and got on my knees, sitting next to Nina on the bed and looking down at her as I panted a little, taking my time to recover. She just laid there, her face completely dazed as she breathed deeply, the relief of coming all of those times taking hold.

We sat in silence for a bit. I liked to do this so that reality could catch back up with us. Being returned to your everyday life after being so thoroughly tested was a potent shock to the system, so any kind of stimulus or movement was too much in that penumbra of our bodies adjusting, our sense organs recalibrating.

After thirty seconds, I laid my head on Nina's leg, enjoying the firmness of her taut muscles.

"Nina...these aren't supposed to be as good for me as they are for you, but, my god I enjoyed that." I laughed a little.

Nina put a hand in my hair. "Yeah...I...I knew you'd be great, Brenda. God, you really put me through my paces...god you are so fucking soaked...I didn't know I could squirt that much."

"Oh, my dear, that is one thing you don't need to apologize for, I love it. Being able to make a woman do that takes skill and dedication, and I'm...quite happy I can be so dedicated." I grabbed a towel from the bedside table and dabbed Nina's prodigious fluids off of me.

I slid my hand on top of Nina's thigh, feeling the heat and sweat. "That was a workout and a half..." I said, my body feeling incapable of doing much more than collapsing. Somehow, I managed to crawl up in the bed next to Nina, our spent bodies melding like warm clay.

"Yeah I guess my spin class instructor will once again

wonder how I can miss so many classes and still look so damn good..." Nina laughed to herself. "Now that I think about it, I could make a billion off the idea of BDSM as exercise."

I rolled my head toward her, my energy fully spent. "From what I know of Pilates, they already have a bit of a corner on the market with their ropes and straps...but a little leather would certainly promote sweating..."

Nina and I drifted off for a bit, enjoying the exhaustion and satisfaction we'd both earned. Sleeping in Club Crescent wasn't exactly prohibited, but it was certainly abnormal...and this was in a place where people were regularly whipped for pleasure. A little nap wouldn't hurt though, right?

MIRAGE

ONE

LOS ANGELES IS a city of illusions of all sorts. This city was built on the idea that with enough ingenuity, effort, and of course money, they could make anything a reality. I guess that's sort of grandiose way to say that renting the use of a lingerie boutique for a night so you can deliver an elaborate BDSM roleplay experience to a client who was willing to pay for such a realistic setup is actually cheaper and more accessible than you may think. A few hundred dollars to the owner of The Purple Bodice, plus the promise that none of this would make it onto the internet and an assurance that we would walk away buying an armload of corsets was all it took to make this dream happen.

Tonight's unlucky client was Katy. She spent her days in PR, where it was her job to look cheery for clients and make the best of everything, so it made sense that she would enjoy a little contrast. This one had more of a setup than me and Wendy's usual romps in that it came with a bit of a story. Whether this story was pulled from

Katy's real life wasn't my place to ask, but something this specific had to originate from somewhere real, didn't it?

Katy was coming to the Purple Bodice as a customer, unsure if she was willing to wear the daring outfits that she fantasized about but was never bold enough to try. Why she felt the need to be degraded and humiliated while doing this instead of just going into a store and giving it a go wasn't my problem. But, making her feel like she had walked into the viper's den was.

"I think that's her." I said to Wendy as a set of headlights swept across the small window in the door. We had to pick a small, out of the way shop like this because most other lingerie stores were in strip malls or had windows that left no question as to what was inside. In the hushed, dark confines of The Purple Bodice, we were free to do whatever we liked.

My wife took her place in the scene, where she would be playing a shopper who just happened to get caught up in all of this. I, of course, would be the owner and proprietor of The Purple Bodice, here to show Katy why it was such a mistake for her to doubt my feelings about fashion.

Katy entered the shop, and as instructed, locked the door behind her. This small detail broke the immersion just a little bit, but we certainly didn't want a random customer to waltz in while she was being spanked...well, we could do that, but that would be engaging a whole different handful of fetishes we weren't here to entertain tonight.

Our client was the kind of woman you see and wonder just how she was blessed with such a stunning figure. Blonde, average height, but with a sculpted frame and tan skin that made her look...well, a bit like a shorter version of myself if we're being entirely honest. I guess I'm a bit particular to being attracted to women as stunning as me.

I played my best version of a bored and distracted shopkeeper while Wendy milled around, evaluating the wares, the only sound in the room the metal hangers clinking on the racks.

"Umm...hi..." Katy said with a sheepish wave.

Since I was already looking down at a magazine, I decided I wanted to make her work for this a little more. I didn't give her a bit of attention, and made a point to flip to the next page to ensure she understood I hadn't heard her.

Katy stepped further into the room. "Hi, uh...are you...open?" she asked.

"Oh...I didn't notice you." I said, a disaffected expression on my face. "I suppose if you need someone in charge, that would be me."

Katy bit her lip in anticipation. "I was told...umm...I heard this store was very discreet. That I could buy lingerie in private here..."

"Yes. This is that store." I swept my eyes over Katy and smirked. "But if you think any lingerie is going to do anything to improve that wisp of a figure, I'll just say right now that you're utterly incorrect. We can't really work with someone who gives us nothing."

"Excuse me?!" Katy gasped. I could see the first hints of arousal starting to appear. For someone whose job was literally being the person everyone pays attention to, this passive attitude seemed to work wonders for her.

I stood from my stool and straightened myself up, just to emphasize the height difference between us. "I'm just being honest. Some women aren't meant to be attractive, and, it appears to me that you're one of them. I'm sure that's difficult to hear, but I shouldn't be the first person that has told you that."

For someone as beautiful as Katy, I'm quite sure this was absolutely the first time she'd heard this kind of assertion lobbed at her, but I made it my mission to put women in their place when they wanted to be there.

"You know...you can't speak to me like this. I'll leave and take my business somewhere else." she huffed, sticking her nose in the air and crossing her arms over her chest in defiance.

"Oh yes, you can go to a mall store, a place that'll sell you some ready-to wear bullshit that will rip the moment you try to wear it a second time, brought to you by a miserable looking clerk who wants to make a hefty commission. You are more than free to do that, but it won't make you look any better." I stepped out from behind the counter and approached Katy, then put my finger under her chin, directing her face toward mine. "But I said whatever I had wouldn't make you look better, not that I'd refuse to sell it to you. You're free to throw away as much money as you'd like here at the Purple Bodice." I gave her a toothy smile that probably appeared positively vampiric.

Katy's face grew flush, and her eyes went wide. I knew exactly the buttons to push. I walked back behind the counter to show Katy further dismissal.

I turned toward Wendy, who had stopped pretending

to look for clothing to gawk at me verbally accosting a stranger in my store.

"Ma'am, I am...so sorry she is treating you like this." Wendy said. She placed her hand on Katy's forearm, comforting her but also making her first contact with her. Wendy was always so touchy-feely. "You can't talk to someone like that!"

"This is my shop, so I very much can..." I said, tapping my pen on the desk, looking between the two women. "Now, see...I'm sorry, what even is your name?" I peered at Katy with boredom.

"Katy...and you're bein--"

"--OK, Katy." I switched my attention over to Wendy after cutting Katy off and gave my wife a sly smile. "Now, you see, Katy...a woman with...assets like this fine customer..." I reached out and swept my hand under Wendy's breasts, feeling the weight of them in my hand, salivating at the idea of them even though I got to enjoy them every day. "A woman like this, she can fill out a piece very, very well...in ways you couldn't possibly imagine."

Katy watched in silence, her eyes still wide as I gave her the spectacle of Wendy's tits being grabbed so brazenly.

"But you? It's hard enough for any woman like to look good in anything, really, and our clothes are no exception." I turned my attention to Katy, cupping her much smaller breast, making extra effort to swipe my thumb across her nipples, which I could feel were already straining against her thin bra.

"You can't...fuck, you can't touch me like that!" Katy yelped.

"I can't?" I grinned, cradling her left breast in my hand, continuing to rub circles around her stiff nipple with my thumb. "Your body seems to be telling me I can, Katy. And, I'm not doing anything sexual, just..." I pinched her nipple sharply, "sizing you up, that's all."

"This is...this is inappropriate...I'm a customer..." Katy said, her voice shaky.

"You have the ability to knock my hand away, Katy, and yet I see you're not doing it. That's rather interesting, isn't it?" I narrowed my eyes, continuing to stroke Katy's nipple. "You can also leave, which I've already suggested you do, but yet, here you are."

"What are you trying to get out of this?" Katy asked. I could hear the faintest hint of a moan at the tail end of her question.

"Nothing. I'm trying to convince you to leave my store and never return. I don't need customers, Katy, especially not little stick figure women who would slide out of a corset in a second." I finally relented, removing my hand from Katy's breast and picking up the pen I was playing with before. "So choose, do you want to waste your money with me or not?" I turned to Wendy and flicked the end of the pen against her large breast, making sure to strike her against her nipple. "And you, whoever you are, don't answer for Katy, this isn't your business."

Katy's mouth hung open. "You are unbelievable! Do you talk to all the women in your store this way?"

I walked out from behind the counter and approached Katy, reaching down and cupping her ass, giving her cheek a hard squeeze, hard enough to show the contour of pain. "Only petulant little sluts that need to be taught a lesson..." I grabbed her even harder and dragged my lips up Katy's neck, the heat from her body beyond enticing. "Now, Katy, would you like to put something on to see how pitiful you'll look in it?"

"Fine. Show me...the best thing you can find in here for a woman who...has curves like mine." Katy's voice had softened considerably, and her eyes looked positively glazed over.

"Curves?" I chuckled as I went into the small back room of the shop. "I'd say you're lucky if you have right angles, Katy. Wendy, dear, show Katy your tits so she knows what curves look like." I shuffled some boxes to make it sound like I was rummaging for something that would fit Katy in the far back of the stockroom, when in reality her first costume was already laid out for me, ready to go. "And if I hear a goddamn word of protest from you about showing your tits, Wendy, I will spank you into next week."

I heard Katy's sharp gasp as she witnessed Wendy's breasts in the flesh for the first time.

"Oh my god..."

I stepped out from the back room holding an impossibly cute and sexy black lace bodysuit. It wasn't much more than a swimsuit made of lace and mesh if I was being honest, but I knew it would look irresistible on Katy's slight frame. It was also so, so small, I was amazed it would fit anyone. But maybe because I had a more athletic build and Wendy's body was blessed with luxurious curves, I just wasn't used to seeing things so slight.

Wendy was leaning against the counter, her shirt off, a red lace bra holding back her large breasts but doing absolutely nothing to hide her hard, dark nipples. "See, Katy? Aren't her curves gorgeous?" I said, placing Katy's outfit on the counter.

"You know I have a boyfriend..." Katy said, trying her best to ignore Wendy's tits as she walked up to her. This was another wrinkle of the roleplay that I loved diving into. Even though in reality Katy had never even come within a mile of being intimate with a man...and, rightfully so...she wanted to play a woman who would be 'converted' to enjoying women. That reluctance and trepidation, when it finally ceded to giving into one's passion and one's true nature, if I could bottle the power of that energy I'd save the world.

"Why do I care who's plugging your tired little pussy, Katy?" I said, smiling at Wendy, admiring my wife's tits as she kept them on display. "You can at least appreciate the aesthetics of a beautiful woman, can you not?"

Katy nodded.

TWO

"THEN FEEL HER TITS, Katy...go ahead, I can see you wanting to do it so bad..." I pushed my hand between Katy's shoulder blades and led her forward, getting her right in front of my wife.

"No! You can't--" Wendy stammered in mock protest.

"Don't act like you dislike getting those huge things felt up, slut. Please..." I pushed Katy forward more, feeling her resist, so I pushed harder. She played a scared straight woman with shocking accuracy.

Katy reached out and gingerly placed her hand on Wendy's chest, then she reached up and placed her other hand on her, really feeling her tits, her palms flat, her fingertips gripping Wendy's soft skin, feeling the weight of her heavy tits in her hands.

"I...I'm sorry, I don't mean to...she's forcing me." Katy whimpered.

"No, it's alright, I understand..." Wendy stared at Katy, her eyes half-closed as she enjoyed our guest's massage.

"You see, Katy? That's what a real woman feels like. Do you feel how big her tits are? How soft they are in your bony little hands?" I kept my finger placed at the exact spot on Katy's back, just above her bra strap, needling her, pressing her to be closer to Wendy.

"What are you...what do you want from me?" Katy gasped, her palms still on Wendy's chest.

"Nothing, really, I'm just fucking with you to make you lose your mind...and maybe convince you that you're not straight, but we'll get to that later. Take your hands off of her gorgeous tits, now." I released the pressure of my finger on Katy's back.

"You...I hate you." Katy hissed as she removed her hands from Wendy.

"Oh, no...my heart is bleeding...as if I fucking care what you think about me." I laughed, shaking my head at the ridiculousness of being told this. "Get naked, you need to put on your first disappointing outfit." I walked back behind the counter, and Wendy took a step back to give Katy some space.

"So, I just get naked?" Katy said. "And...in front of you both?" She looked back and forth at us, her eyes pleading for us to not let her do this.

"Katy, I know you're dumb, but you can't be this dumb, can you? How else do you expect to put on lingerie if you don't get naked?"

Katy glared at me. "I'm not used to putting on something like that with...other people here. You know, people watching."

I shook my head at her, then nodded at Wendy. "I do

not fucking care. Get naked or leave, those are your choices."

Katy bit her lower lip. "Maybe you two can, like, turn away?"

"Absolutely not." I smirked.

Engaging with voyeur fetishes was a particular favorite of mine. As someone who didn't mind being watched, obviously, it gave me a certain spark to find someone who enjoyed it as much, maybe even more. But Katy wasn't content with the simple thrill of being seen in such a way, she said that she liked to play into the embarrassment of it, the panic of feeling exposed and vulnerable. In her emails with us when she was setting this up, Katy had said that her ultimate fantasy would be to have to walk completely naked through a crowded luxury hotel lobby and have to go down on the Maître d', but my production skills and ability to ask favors didn't quite reach that point...yet.

Katy kept looking up at us as she undressed, her face blushing a deeper shade of red with each piece of clothing removed. She was selling the hell out of this, but I suppose everyone in LA had some bit of the acting bug rub off on them just by proximity.

"Please, I'm...so embarrassed, please stop looking at me." Katy said as she unbuttoned her blouse.

"I'm watching your every move, dear. Every single thing you do." I said, my voice deep and sultry for the first time in the evening, but definitely not the last.

"You don't...why are you like this?" Katy asked, looking at Wendy to save her from me as she took her top off. Her white lacy bra was clearly one size too large for her, the gap showing her nipples freely. I genuinely hoped Katy wore properly fitting bras in her everyday life, because an improperly sized bra was a hell that I wanted no woman to endure. But, I assumed this bit of costume was to amp up the embarrassment, the feeling that she looked awful in her clothing no matter what. For someone as stunning as Katy, I'm sure this was a treat to feel the opposite side of the equation.

"I'm like this because of women like you, Katy. Women who think they have the right to wear my beautiful creations despite not having the proper canvas to display them." I scribbled onto my pad of paper, as if I were making detailed notes about Katy's appearance...in reality I was just drawing loops and lines, trying to distract myself from the growing tension in me at the idea of seeing Katy naked, finally.

Katy turned her back to us as she undid the clasp to her bra and dropped it to the ground, her naked back in full display, but not showing what was underneath. "This is...please...I can't..."

"Turn toward us, Katy, right fucking now." I drummed the pen against the countertop. The amount of control I was getting just from this damn pen was pretty amazing, and I noted that I should use writing implements more often in future scenes.

"Ohhhh fuck..." I heard Wendy breathe out a deep sigh, the sight of Katy's nude form being shown to her in its entirety.

"Wendy, dear...shut the fuck up and take a step away from her. She's to be seen, not touched. Ever."

Katy stood in front of us, her top half fully exposed.

Her breasts weren't that small, in fact I knew she was precisely a 30B, which meant they looked about the same as my 34C size on my broader frame. Her nipples were very small and dark pink, utterly delicious with not much areola to speak of. The more I looked at her, the more gorgeous she was.

"God, it's worse than I thought..." I looked her up and down, sneering at her body. This required some major acting from me, of course.

Katy looked down at the ground.

"Do you even need to wear bras? I mean, when you're working with absolutely nothing, I don't see the point in trying to dress them up if there isn't anything worthwhile to cover." I said, my tone steady despite the hunger to devour Katy increasing. Wendy was more feral, I could already tell, but she was also my darling sub who knew not to get out of line.

"I guess not..." Katy mumbled, keeping her eyes trained to the ground, the embarrassment of all of this really sinking in for her.

"Those little pink gumdrops are the only thing you have going for you, Katy. And, god, you look eager for someone who says she's hating this so much..." I said, salivating at Katy's perfect, stiff nipples.

Katy brought her hands up and cupped her tits. "Don't call them that...they're my nipples. They're just...a part of my body."

"I know exactly what they are. I was complimenting them, Katy. I know it's not something you probably ever get, but you should be thankful when a woman praises you."

"Well, I'm not thankful...they're...I can't stand people looking at me." she said. "This is all...god, it's so much."

I leaned back on the counter, hinting at my cleavage by running my pen along the portion that was exposed due to my partially unbuttoned shirt. "Now the pants, Katy. And do not think you're allowed to leave your underwear on...or think you can argue with me that you should be able to keep them on. I want you naked, without protest, quickly."

Katy reached down with one hand, still trying to cover her breasts with the other as did so, and undid the button of her pants.

I held my finger in the air to get her attention. "Hands off your tits, stop fucking covering up."

"God...damnit..." Katy said, huffing and getting extra bratty. Fuck yes.

"If you don't follow my orders I'll kick you out of here as naked as you are right now and lock up behind you, so please, don't test me, Katy."

Katy gave me an eager look, knowing that I would love to do just that for her, to engage her deepest fetishes by putting her out in the middle of Los Angeles topless, but for now we'd have to keep ourselves to the secluded confines of the Purple Bodice.

"This...you know..." Katy unzipped her pants, her bare body now exposed to Wendy and me, aside from one last piece of clothing. "God fucking damnit, why am I letting you do this."

"You're beautiful, Katy..." Wendy said, trying to comfort the frightened doe.

"Shut up, Wendy. Patronizing little whelps like this does nothing. Stop lying to her." I barked.

"If my boyfriend knew how you were talking to me..." Katy shivered and flicked eye contact back at me in split-second moments, nailing this whole shy act.

"He'd what? What would your horrid little boyfriend do about it, Katy?" I said, keeping my eyes locked on her flitting gaze.

Katy slid her panties down, finally completely nude. A nicely manicured light blonde triangle of pubic hair rested above her delicious looking lips.

"Nothing. He'd do absolutely nothing. Because he's... pathetic." She said.

"Pathetic, just like you, isn't he, Katy?" I said.

"Yes..." Katy shuddered.

"Has he even made you come before? I know you're not much to look at, but you should at least be allowed to experience orgasm every once in a while, Katy."

"You can't...you can't ask..."

"I would really suggest just answering her, Katy. Messing with her is going to only make it worse. So please just tell her if your boyfriend has made you come." Wendy said, putting her hand on Katy's hip, dangerously close to grazing her pubic mound. I was envious that my wife once again got to touch the naked flesh of our subject before I did.

"No...he has not, and he probably won't, either...he doesn't know what he's doing..." Katy's voice trembled. "Please don't make fun of me..."

"Well, I think we're far past not making fun of you, but I do feel bad for you, Katy." I picked up the bodysuit and tossed it to her, and she nearly didn't react in time. "Not bad enough to not want your money, of course. So, try it on, let's see how awful this looks."

Katy stood on a wooden stool and slid her feet into the outfit and worked it up her long, athletic legs. "This feels so...I'm not used to wearing this type of thing..." She pushed her hands through the top and threaded her arms into the holes, then slid the material up her irresistible body.

"That's quite clear, and you shouldn't be used to it, because you're not the kind of woman who will ever be really able to show herself off." I stepped out from behind the counter and circled Katy.

The bodysuit fit Katy so, so well. Every stitch seemed to enhance her beauty, from the way the back of it pressed against her tight, perfect ass, to how the thin mesh coated her firm breasts, making them appear even more delicious than they surely were. I was elated that Katy would get to take this home, because any woman who got to witness her in it was in for an unbelievable treat.

"God, it's like trying to fit something over a tree branch." I said, groaning, grazing my finger along the seam on Katy's ass. "Even me, the finest tailor perhaps in this entire world, cannot salvage beauty from nothing."

"Please..." Katy shuddered as she felt me touch her, a grin creeping across her face as I did so.

"Look at yourself in the mirror, Katy, go." I nudged her, pointing at the large three-paneled mirror against the wall of the shop.

My subject complied, and I could tell it took a lot for

her to not burst into glee when she saw just how damn good she looked. I knew Katy was a woman who understood her looks set her apart from the vast majority of people, so I hoped she could put that aside.

"I think it looks...really...really OK, Katy." Wendy said, standing behind her, putting a hand on Katy's shoulder.

"Not much to work with, but let's try." I moved in front of Katy and squatted, bringing my eye level to the thin bit of fabric that covered her pussy. "Of course this starved little thing is threatening to eat this fabric, isn't it?" I pulled the crotch of the bodysuit up, tensioning the fabric between Katy's lips, creating sharp pressure that I knew would cause her heart to race. "This delicate bodysuit can barely contain your puffy pussy lips, Katy..."

Katy exhaled deeply and closed her eyes as she felt the tension of the bodysuit on her cunt. I loved being on the receiving end of the pleasure that comes from having this exact move performed, so seeing her delight at it made me that much more ravenous for her.

"That...god...that hurts, Morrigan, please..." Katy panted, clearly trying to convert the pleasure radiating through her body into panic.

"How do you expect me to size this if I can't tell just how much your pussy wants to show itself to the world, Katy?" I pulled harder, a little worried whether or not the thin fabric could withstand such force, but because I could tell it was setting Katy off, I didn't want to hold back.

Katy whimpered, her hips bucking just enough to let

me know I was hitting a sensitive spot. I brought my hands to her hips and dug my nails into her ass.

I gripped, hard, making sure to give her the pain she wanted. The smell of Katy was overwhelming this close to her pussy. I wanted to taste her, to make her moan my name right here and now, but that's not what she paid me for.

"How...how are you...so evil..." Katy started.

"Hush, pet. It's time for the second piece." I said. I released my hands from her, the red indents from my nails clearly visible, then I gave her ass a swift hard spank.

"You can't...fucking hit me like that!" Katy stamped her foot on the wooden stool.

"Oh?" I stood chest-to-chest with Katy, staring her down. I slapped her again, letting my hand linger so I could feel the sensory pleasure of the delicate lace stretched across Katy's beautiful ass. "I can't?" I slapped her again, getting a yelp out of her before she reset herself into playing the utter brat she loved to be.

"I am so fucking mad at you...and you have to pay for that. For being so mean to me, for putting your hands on me, for not knowing how to treat someone with a figure like mine..." Katy looked over at Wendy, her hands out, pleading. "Please, Wendy, I...you've seen this behavior, she's cruel, and sadistic, and...I'm right to fight back against this treatment, aren't I?"

Wendy looked at Katy with sympathy in her eyes. "Oh...oh my goodness. Katy, she's...she can't speak to you this way...can we...can I get you some help?"

"Yes, please!" Katy looked over to me, her face pink

with rage...OK mostly with complete arousal, but she sold it well.

"I know exactly how we can diffuse things..." Wendy said. A moment later, she slid her hands around the back of Katy's neck, the black leather collar pinched between her fingers. Before Katy even had the chance to turn around, Wendy was already drawing the buckle tight, the plush inner fabric cinching around Katy's neck perfectly. She let the silver chain drop from her hand and swung the other end to me, which I caught, the leather loop of the leash falling right into place at my wrist.

"Good girl, Wendy. I was waiting for you to finally collar this mouthy brat." I gave Katy the most utterly evil and disdainful smile I could.

THREE

"NO!!! What in the...what the fuck???" Katy pawed at the collar as if it were permanently affixed to her.

"Katy, hon...trust me, the best way out of this is through. Just let Mistress Morrigan do what she needs to..." Wendy said with a saccharine tinge as our evening started to get finally dark as the three of us wanted. "On the bright side, you're definitely going to come tonight... whether you want to or not, honestly."

I applauded Katy's shock and panic at the presence of the collar for adding to the scene. The truth of it was this moment was heavily scripted, because I didn't fuck with anything around the neck without ample rehearsal, but Katy made it feel almost real.

I tugged at the leash, drawing Katy closer to me. "Are you ready to behave, Katy?"

Katy scowled, but still appeared utterly helpless as she felt the pressure of the leather and chain against her neck. "God...fucking dammit. You can't keep doing this to me...fuck."

"I think I've proven I can and I will, Katy, but I guess whatever fantasies you need to entertain for yourself..."

Katy leaned forward and spit on my chest, just below my throat. I looked down at the spittle, my expression turning utterly dreadful.

"Oh...you don't know what you just did." I said, slowly and with a threat and gravity that it took a while for me to perfect.

"Katy! What the fuck?" Wendy said. She walked toward me and put her hands on my shoulders, "mistress, Katy didn't mean it...here, let me clean you..."

Wendy leaned down and licked the glob of spit from my chest, staying there for an extra couple of long licks at my throat for good measure. I kept my eyes locked with Katy's the whole time, still selling my anger.

"Thank you, Wendy, you're a very good girl. Katy here could learn a thing or two from you if she wants to leave The Purple Bodice alive tonight..." I said.

How fluid play became a favorite of Wendy and me, I wouldn't know, but licking up the spit or silky girlcum from someone's body was fucking irresistible to me.

Katy looked stunned at the way Wendy was submitting to me to try to appease my wrath, and I knew we had her, finally.

I reached up and pet the top of Wendy's head. "You see, Katy? Good girls know their place. They're not doing dumb things like spitting on their Mistress, they give us the care and love we deserve..."

"You're not my fucking Mistress!" Katy snapped.

I tugged on the leash, hard, causing Katy to stumble forward toward me, nearly toppling off the wooden stool.

I gripped Katy by her hips to stabilize her, a real moment of panic in her eyes.

“Yellow light...shit, are you ok?” I looked down at Katy’s feet as she regained her balance.

"Yes...just...yellow light’s a good idea." Katy looked up at me.

"Katy...do you want me to release the collar?" Wendy asked.

"No. Just...let me have a moment."

“Sorry, I didn’t remember you were on the foot-stool...new space and all." I said, feeling a sudden drop in my stomach as I scorned myself, and not in a fun way, for not being absolutely careful with my wonderful client.

"It's alright...no harm done." Katy rolled her ankle around a couple of times and planted her feet back on the ground firmly. "By the way, you two are so...fucking good at this, holy shit." Katy grinned, a major blush spreading across her face.

"It helps when we have a client that's so game to play along..." I reached out and stroked Katy's hand. "You look divine in that bodysuit, by the way."

"I know!!" Katy slid her hands down her body and grasped at her breasts. "I will definitely put this one in the rotation for my girlfriend."

"Very, very lucky girlfriend..." Wendy said, biting her tongue playfully at Katy.

"You two will have to meet her sometime." Katy winked.

"God, yes." Wendy was already running through scenes in her head, I could tell.

"Well, ladies, let's refrain from fantasizing about Katy's girlfriend and get back to the scene, shall we?"

Katy tossed her hair to the side and drummed her fingers at the tops of her thighs, dispelling some nervous energy. "Alright, yes, green light."

"Green light." I smiled.

I pulled the leash, a little more gentle than usual to ease Katy back into the scene. "Did you just say I'm not your Mistress?" I leaned forward and dragged my canines along her neck. "Katy, I fucking own you for tonight..."

"God, you...you can't just do things to my body like that. That feels...really fucking good." Katy gasped as my teeth hit a tender spot along her neck, making her shiver.

"Oh, yeah?" I licked at the very base of her neck, the hollow of her collarbone. "Bet your awful boyfriend never gives you this kind of attention."

Katy scoffed. "I'm...sure he can, just..."

"But he never will." I tugged at the collar, tilting Katy's head to the side so I had better access to her neck.

"No...no, no, no..." Katy huffed and acted as if she was turning away from my affection. This girl was easily a top-tier client, and I would have done this for free, and probably would before too long.

"I know how unsatisfied you are with him, Katy...the way he gropes at you with his rough hands, so lacking in subtlety or care. I bet when you're in bed with him, he makes you get on all fours, rams you from behind for about ten seconds, leaves you full of cum and falls asleep, doesn't he?" I said this as I laid more and more kisses and touches along Katy's body, overwhelming her senses by having a beautiful woman touch her while she talked about a horrid, albeit fictional, man.

"You have no fucking idea how it is between me and... him." Katy moaned and shuddered as I teased her neck and collarbone with my lips.

"Tell me what he does to you, Katy. Tell me about what it's like to have sex with him. I am not giving you the option, I want an honest assessment." I looped the chain around my hand an additional time, increasing the pressure. "And don't leave anything out."

"God, he...fucking...gropes my breasts, you know, just grabs and squeezes, he thinks...it feels good, but he's too rough. Then he...ohhh fuck, Morrigan, that's..." Katy's chest was heaving, actually heaving, this was getting her so worked up.

"Stop delaying, Katy. Tell me how lacking he is when he fills your tired little cunt with his pathetic cock..."

Katy groaned and writhed under my grip. "He fucks me...like, just, slams his cock in and out of me...and he does it for maybe a minute before he blows his load in me..."

"Like you're just a warm hole to him, right? Like you don't matter at all..." I looped the leash again, more tension, subtly pulling down on Katy's neck.

"Yes! Exactly!" Katy yelped, a high-pitched noise.

"Well, pet, how does it feel to have a Mistress touch you?"

"Fucking...awful!"

"Katy, I can see it in your eyes..." I grinned. "Just be honest."

"It feels so, so fucking good, Morrigan! So much better than my boyfriend could ever...ever hope to give me."

"Katy...tell me you need it from me. Tell me how much you need my touch..."

"Please...please, Mistress...please..." Katy got the hint I was giving her by pulling the chain down and leaned across the desk, her taut ass on display.

"I'm not doing anything to you, what the fuck do you take me for?" I pulled the chain sideways, telling Katy I still had control and tension even if she was leaning over. "Wendy, inspect Katy's little slit, see if there's anything worthwhile happening with it."

"Yes, Mistress!" Wendy walked to the opposite end of the desk and grabbed Katy by the hips, digging her fingernails into the thin, tight bodysuit. She kneaded Katy's ass like she was working on dough in the kitchen, making Katy sigh in a way that was music to my ears. Despite Wendy's friendly and soft appearance, she had the muscles and dexterity of an expert chef, and she reminded me and the other women we pleasured every single time that there was a beast hidden under the marshmallow exterior of my love.

Wendy moved her hands downward, using her left to pull the bodysuit to the side and her right to touch Katy's pussy. The moment Wendy came in contact with it was instantly recognizable in Katy's face.

"How is it, Wendy? Is it as used up and sad as I imagine it is?" I tapped the pen on Katy's shoulder.

"You...are such...a cunt..." Katy's voice was tight.

"You haven't seen the half of it, Katy." I tapped at her

shoulder with the pen harder. "Speaking of cunts, Wendy, I need your report on Katy's, right fucking now, stop delaying."

"Yes, Mistress...she's...well, I can feel how aroused she is...I don't know what her boyfriend was like, but I know that Katy is more turned on than she's been in a long time."

"Well I expected that...has the relentless pounding from his horrid dick completely ruined her, or do you think there's something to salvage?" I said.

Katy whined as Wendy played with her clit. "Ohhhhh fuck, god...no, there's...oh...it's still pretty good... just...really needs to be taken care of..."

"Oh...I can hear she's wet, Wendy..." I unbuttoned my shirt an additional button, exposing more of my bra. "Now be a good girl and kiss Katy's little pussy so she can remember the sensation while I destroy her after you're done..." I watched Katy's face as Wendy teased her and got her closer to true satisfaction.

"Katy, please lean across the counter, grab the other side of it here, give sweet Wendy room to work." I tapped the edge of the counter to tell Katy what to do.

"This is so...fucking embarrassing..." Katy laid across the wide counter, her delicate fingers closing around the edge.

"Is this slut presenting herself sufficiently to do what you need, Wendy?" I said.

"Yes, Mistress." Wendy grabbed Katy's ass and held her open, then sunk her head down to eat her out from behind.

"Katy, don't make a goddamn sound while she does

this." I slammed my hand on the desk just a few inches from Katy's face.

Katy whimpered in a high-pitched tone, then closed her mouth.

Wendy ate Katy with expert skill, lapping at her with urgency that she usually reserved for me. She was using all her strength to keep Katy in place as she devoured her. I imagined how delicious Katy was, and felt a little left out as I watched Wendy enjoy her so much. But, that's the occasional downside of a domme, I suppose.

"So, Katy...I'll let you ask Wendy to finish you off, or you can go home to your boyfriend who is going to fuck you as brutally and unsatisfying as ever...because, of course, you're...not a lesbian, right?" I chuckled as I appreciated the irony of asking such a silly question while a woman was fully eating her out. "If you don't enjoy women, what Wendy's doing to you shouldn't excite you at all, should it?"

"No..." Katy was getting even more into this scene now that we were really pushing it with this level of degradation and humiliation. "She...god...I mean..."

"This should be rather unappealing to you, should it not, Katy? A beautiful woman, face pressed into your tight little ass, her tongue sliding between your lips, hitting the spots she knows so well because she has them too...but if you're not into women, this should be awful..."

"It is...fuck..." Katy gripped the counter harder, her body shaking, her breathing quick. "I'm straight, I swear."

"Quite hilarious, Katy, that you still think that's remotely true." I smirked. I ran my hand down Katy's back, enhancing her pleasure. "Wendy...Katy has five seconds to ask you to make her come, and if she doesn't do so, I need you to stop immediately."

Wendy didn't lift her head up from between Katy's thighs to acknowledge me.

"Fuuuuck...please...make me come...make me...I need...fucking fuck!"

I tapped my hand on the counter and tilted my head with an exaggerated pose, even though neither woman in the room could see me...I knew they could hear the intent. "God, I think she said something, but I have no idea what it was...and now she's down to three seconds, Wendy..."

Wendy redoubled her efforts, burying her tongue into Katy.

"Fucking god dammit Wendy please, fuck...make me come!!!"

I looked down at the counter to see Katy with a crazed, desperate look on her face as Wendy knelt behind her, not holding back at all.

"Wendy, dear...I think she's the strong, silent type, and I guess she just doesn't need to come...unless she uses this one second left..." I toyed with Katy's hair, teasing her further.

"No, wait, no!!! Don't stop!!! Oh fuck!! I'm so fucking close!"

I sighed heavily. "What a missed opportunity, Katy...a real shame." I pulled at the chain to assert that I was in charge, as if there was a question. "Wendy, I'm sorry you couldn't make Katy come, I know you really looked forward to giving this little creature the release that...by all accounts, I really thought she craved, but I guess she's too straight to get pleasure from even your expert tongue."

"That's disappointing, Mistress..." Wendy leaned back, her face flush and glistening from her relentless work on Katy.

"Well, life is disappointing sometimes, dear, please get over it. Wendy, stand up, Katy, stay right where you are."

Katy complied, her face pressed down on the countertop, her chest heaving. Wendy stood up and unhooked her bra, tossing it to the side.

"Katy, stand up straight, please." I said, tapping the counter to punctuate my order.

Katy followed the instruction and pulled herself up, battle-worn and gleefully exhausted, a half-lidded smile on her face.

But the moment Katy straightened her back out completely, I smirked. "Now lay down again, Katy. Same position."

"Why do you need me in this position?"

"You really are fucking dense, aren't you, Katy?"

"What?!" Katy's eyes were wild. "What is it?"

I stood next to Katy for a good ten seconds, completely silent and motionless, before tapping her lightly on the ass. "There wasn't a reason, I just wanted you to follow my orders like a good little pet. Up now, you have more punishment in store."

"Fuck you...fuck you, you fucking monster." Katy seethed as she stood up.

I jerked the leash, making sure the pathway between Katy and me was clear this time. My sub tumbled toward me, landing against my firm chest. "You wish you could fuck me, Katy...you wish..."

"What is wrong with you? This is insane, why...why can't you just make me come..."

"Because you have not earned it." I slid my free hand across Katy's breasts. "We need a costume change... Wendy, get the second one, the...elaborate one." I looked at my wife with excitement in my eyes, knowing we were approaching the climax of our night.

Oh, but climax was far from what would be happening to any of the three of us, not while there was so much more pleasure and pain to deal out.

"You do not deserve at all what you're about to put on, Katy, I want you to remember that. And please, strip down, remove that bodysuit I worked so hard on, and the one you've disappointed me in." I snapped, eliciting a Pavlovian reaction from Katy.

"You fucking bitch..." Katy was amping up the bratti-ness, and I was living for it. The second half of this little encounter was going to be more intense, and her being sarcastic and a fucking chore to deal with was only going to make things that much better. I don't know if Katy used other dommes, but whoever she did play with out there was beyond lucky to have such a versatile woman enhancing their fantasies.

"And I was about to take the collar off, too, because I thought you learned how to behave..." I kept tension on the leash but didn't tug as Katy pulled the bodysuit down her body.

"Why would you ever take it off...I like this. I love

wearing your collar..." Katy pouted as she stepped out of the bodysuit.

I caressed Katy's ass and kissed her on the shoulder. "Don't fucking try that on me, you cretin. I know what you're doing." I followed the sweet kiss up with a bite. "Stockholm syndrome doesn't work for Mistress Morrigan, I'll make sure you hate me the entire way..."

FOUR

"YOU'RE SO FUCKING EVIL..." Katy spit on my chest again, the feeling hot on my skin.

I stared at Katy and didn't react to the saliva on me. I unbuttoned my shirt the rest of the way and unclasped my bra from the front, discarding everything on my body other than the skirt I was still wearing.

"Do it again, bitch." I smirked at Katy.

Thank god, she took the bait, spitting on me again, the saliva landing just above my nipple.

"Do you enjoy spitting on your Mistress? Are you going to try to do it to her face now, Katy? I can tell you really hate her and want her to be humiliated and punished."

"Fuck you." Katy spit and hit my chin. I had to contain myself to not smile at the playfulness of it.

"Not yet, but close..." I pulled the leash and drew Katy's head to the spot on my breast where the spit was still lingering. "You've made me dirty, now clean me up, slut."

Katy sighed, "God dammit. Fucking hell."

"This collar stays on forever if you don't do as I say, Katy. I don't care how much you despise me. Clean me."

Katy slowly moved her tongue to my breast, lapping up her own spittle, the warm wetness of her mouth contrasting the cool, tacky feeling of the saliva on my chest. It was an incredible relief after having to be so above it all for so long. Katy's mouth was nimble and strong, tickling the very center of my being with her deft work.

"Ohhh god, you're finally learning...thank you, slut..." I slid my free hand behind Katy's neck and toyed with the leather of her collar. "Keep it up, pet."

Katy did keep it up, moving from my breast up to the second location at my collarbone, licking at that as well. It was obvious to me Katy had experience doing this, which wasn't shocking at all considering who she was. The skill with which she pleasured me was surprising, however.

"Such a good pet...one more spot..." I gently pulled the collar from behind, directing her to my chin.

I held my mouth open, the last traces of Katy's indignity on my face, and Katy rewarded me in a way I'd been yearning for a sub to do for so long.

She spit into my mouth, hard, following it up with a toothy, utterly psychotic smile. "Fuck you, Mistress."

"Mmhmm. I see how it is, you little fucking brat." I swallowed, the warm spit coating my throat as it went down. I shoved Katy back to the counter and released my hold on her leash. I swiftly smacked her pussy, hard, drawing a growl from her. This sunny, unassuming PR woman who spent her entire life being a cheerleader was now a feral beast that had very little chance of being tamed. "I'll keep slapping this useless little thing until it goes numb, Katy."

"Fucking try..." Katy jutted her chin at me, a taunt that electrified me.

"You just have no sense of self-preservation, do you?" I slapped her pussy a couple more times, feeling the heat, feeling Katy melting from the pain and the lingering pleasure. I slapped again and held my hand in place, feeling her wetness under my fingers.

"No! No, I don't!" Katy snapped as she bucked against me. Katy was ready to bite my head off, her body tensed and electrified, looking as savage and sexy as a person could. "You're not going to break me, you won't..."

I grabbed Katy's chin and held her face an inch from mine. "You're already broken, you just don't know it yet..."

Katy snarled. "You fucking cunt! God dammit..."

"Hush, pet...open your mouth wide..."

Katy shook her head and tried to pull back, but I had her face tight in my hand. I put my index finger into her mouth, pressing on the tongue.

“Come to think of it, Katy, I never asked...have you eaten pussy before?”

Katy shook her head vigorously and tried to protest but I pressed on her tongue further.

I nodded my head slowly. "Mmm. I could tell...but you’ve thought about, haven’t you?”

Katy made a weak attempt at protesting and I laughed, shaking my head at her. I pressed my fingers to the roof of Katy's mouth, and the pressure forced a moan out of her.

"I need you to not lie to me. You're only making this worse."

Katy tried to move her tongue but couldn't, not while I pinned it to the bottom of her mouth. So, instead she resorted to giving me a reluctant, wide eyed nod.

I slid my fingers around in her mouth. It was an odd sensation to feel someone that way, the soft flesh contrasted with the sharp, solid teeth. In any other situation, I guess other than at the dentist, touching someone like this would result in getting bitten, hard. But I relished in the permission and trust Katy gave to me to do this to her. I turned my hand over and hooked my index and middle finger at the bottom of Katy's mouth, pulling it down toward me. I gathered some saliva from my mouth and let it drop against Katy's tongue. It felt so dirty and so right.

I withdrew my hand and rubbed Katy's lip with my fingers, smearing my saliva against her lips. She closed her mouth and swallowed, wincing at the indignity that she loved.

I moved in toward Katy and kissed her, slow and hard, sliding my hands to her neck. Katy had said that she loved choking, but that was a bridge I wouldn't cross. But, a little extra pressure on the neck probably wasn't too much of a risk.

"Do you think a woman who hasn't been thoroughly broken and told her place would have allowed something like that to happen?" I said.

"I...uhh, Mistress Morrigan, don't mean to interrupt, but I have the outfit." Wendy said, coming out from the back room holding a large black box in her hands.

"Good, took you long enough." I looked at Wendy and grinned. "This horrid wretch needs something put on her, I'm getting sick of looking at her disappointments." I stared Katy down as Wendy walked toward the counter with the box.

"I don't want to try something else on, I want to leave, I want to..."

I grabbed Katy again, going lower than the chin hold I usually used, putting my ring and pinkie fingers against her jugular. "You're going to tell me you want to come, don't you?"

"N—no...no."

"Katy, you must realize by now lying only makes this worse, right? Just fucking admit it."

Katy breathed heavily, my hand on her throat keeping her in an uncomfortable but not dangerous spot. "Ok...yes...I do. But I'm...not a lesbian..."

"Katy..." I knelt down and spread Katy open with my fingers, then licked at her. She tasted so fucking sweet and incredible. Wendy was truly lucky to have experienced it before me.

Katy moaned theatrically in response to my licking, overreacting to my presence. "Fuck...god...fucking damn stop!"

I stood up and faced Katy down again. "Katy, if you weren't into women you wouldn't be getting so goddamn wet, would you?"

Katy pouted, the cogs turning in her head to come up with a snarky answer. She smirked and looked me in the eyes. "Yeah...I...maybe it does make me wet, Mistress."

"Ooh...and she's even calling me Mistress now,

Wendy..." I tapped Katy's lips with my fingertip. "I knew we'd break her."

Katy's eyes went wide, and she turned toward Wendy then back at me. "You mean...she...she's..."

"Oh my god, Katy, there is no way you're so dense that you didn't think I was in on this from the first second. Do you think you'd get to see my tits if I wasn't brought here to help destroy you?" Wendy rapped the box against the counter.

"I...I trusted you..."

Wendy shrugged, "Yeah, and I've trusted a lot of people who ended up fucking me. Hey, at least I get to do it to you literally..."

My wife and Katy, the consummate thespians.

Wendy grabbed at the top of the box and lifted it. "So, we were looking at this corset to start, and..."

Katy gasped as she looked down into the box. The flame-red corset was quite a sight to behold, as were the accessories.

"So you like it?" Wendy smirked, pushing the box forward.

"I...do, it just...it looks so small..."

"Yes. It is too small. But what's a couple of cracked ribs between friends, right?" I trailed my finger along Katy's ribs to emphasize the evil I was projecting.

"Please...I won't be able to breathe..."

"That's the point, slut." I didn't even give that one room, instead grabbing the box by the corner and drawing it closer to Katy. "Put it on. Now."

"I should call the police..."

"Oh give me a fucking break." I pressed myself

against Katy. "Nobody can save you, Katy, except yourself. You want to say something, but you know this is all you need right now...you know how much you crave what I can offer you. So I have this corset, and you're going to put it on. And I'm going to make you come harder than you've ever come in your insignificant life once you squeeze yourself into it."

"And you'll let me go after?"

"We'll see...maybe we'll just keep you forever. Would your sad little boyfriend even notice if you never returned to him so he can use you some more?"

"I...god, Morrigan, no! I want...I need this..." Katy sighed. "I...god..."

I smiled, a smug, cruel thing that I'd practiced and refined over time. "Then put on the corset."

"Yes, Mistress."

Finally, music to my ears.

FIVE

KATY PICKED up the corset and held it against her frame. It was devilishly small, but it was one that Katy owned and used all the time, apparently. We even put it on her and had her run around our house for a few minutes when we did our initial consultation to prove that, yes, she could breathe while she was packed into it. Ok, yes, I also fingered her to a delightful orgasm while she had it on just to really prove it to us...I'm a very thorough researcher, you see.

"This is going to be so goddamn uncomfortable, I don't know how you expect me to come..." Katy slid the corset over her head, wiggling through the already small garment until it came to rest just above her hips.

"That's absolutely not my problem...just remember you don't get your freedom until you come." I said.

I snapped my fingers. "Wendy, bind our slut in this corset, and don't stop pulling it tighter until you hear something pop."

"With pleasure."

"Pop?! That's a bit...dangerous." Katy winced and bit her lip.

"Pop, break, snap...shatter. Any or all of them will do. I've broken your mind, it was only a matter of time before I demanded it from your body as well."

"You're fucking cruel, Mistress." Katy pouted.

"You're about to see just how cruel, you worthless little thing." I stared down at her, a look of disgust on my face as Wendy moved behind Katy and began lacing her corset, pulling tighter and tighter on the strings.

"Wendy, please. You don't have to go along with her evil..." Katy said, sucking in her cheeks as the corset cinched around her.

Wendy yanked the string like she was trussing a chicken, causing Katy to stumble backward and nearly lose her balance. She leaned against the counter and had to breathe deep to avoid toppling.

"God..."

"How do you I'm not the more evil one?" Wendy tugged the strings tighter, the fabric and boning shrinking down more.

Wendy genuinely was the more evil one, it's why she let me domme. Who knows what kind of trouble the two of us would get in were she allowed to run free all the time.

Wendy yanked on the strings, making Katy whimper. "God fucking dammit, Katy...don't you realize it doesn't matter how hard you try to convince me to stop, it's going to happen anyway?"

"You two are..." Katy heaved, her breath now more shallow. "Fucking insane..."

"Do you think that's the first time we've heard that?" I dragged my fingers along Katy's labia, teasing her while Wendy continued to work on the corset.

Katy coughed and moaned.

"It's ok, you don't need to speak. You don't need to breathe, either, if you fancy just passing out right here."

"I fucking...I will...I will pass out."

"Oh well." I slid my finger roughly against Katy's slit, then brought the finger up to her, glistening from her arousal. "Taste it."

"No...no..." Katy stammered.

"Katy, you need to follow my orders. I need you to taste how turned on you are so I can prove to you that you're loving every second of this torture." I placed my fingertip against Katy's closed mouth.

"Ok..." Katy opened her mouth and took my finger in, her lips soft and yielding as they wrapped around it.

"Such a good girl..." I teased, and I mean I truly teased, pulling my hand away from Katy at an achingly slow pace, letting her take her time cleaning herself from me. "God your mouth is warm...and soft."

"Thank you..." Katy was fully blushing at my words.

I tilted my head and sighed, running my hand down the corset and down Katy's thighs, letting my finger travel toward the back. "Oh...so nice and tight. Wonderful work, my love."

"It's so fucking uncomfortable" Katy spat.

I placed my hand against Katy's stomach, pressing in. "Make no mistake, it could be worse, slut."

Katy grunted in discomfort at my hand pressed down against the tight corset. I then pulled my hand back and smacked her stomach. She groaned and squirmed.

"Does it hurt?"

“Of course, it fucking hurts!”

"Wonderful..." I looked at the box. "Wendy do we have something to cover Katy's bottom half?"

Wendy picked up a small box. "These panties...are so... very small. I looked at her size chart, but they were all out, so I had to go two sizes smaller. I don't think they'll fit. At all."

Now these...these were a surprise for Katy.

The poor girl looked at them and her eyes went wide. "Mistress...there's no way..."

"I know...putting these on, the seam will probably press so hard against you, it'll...well, you'll get to find out, won't you?" I smirked.

Katy had to suck in a breath to fit into the tiny pair of underwear, but after a bit of shimmying they did go on.

"Look at that..." I rubbed my hands along the lace, feeling just how impossibly tight they were on Katy. They'd be awful to have on for a whole day, or even a couple of hours, but for a few minutes...

Katy groaned in pain and discomfort as I ran my hand against the seam. The poor dear would definitely feel this for a while.

I placed my hand against Katy's hip. "This looks incredible, pet...I'm actually starting to think you might be somewhat attractive, once you're clad in a thousand dollars of high-end lingerie."

Katy tried to suck in her stomach, the discomfort turning her on more and more. Her nipples were hard, perched at the top of the bra cups. "It's...ugh...so tight...so fucking painful. I need to come so goddamn badly..."

"Then do it." I said.

"Wh...what? All of this and you're not going to get me off?"

I clicked my tongue. "God, Wendy, she's still so mouthy..."

Wendy stood beside me. "It's almost impressive."

"I'll give her credit where it's due, I suppose...and if you want to come so badly, just rub yourself against the counter. We're not stopping you, Katy."

This was why Wendy and I had laid a thick tablecloth over the counter before all of this started. Another of Katy's impressively voluminous list of kinks and fetishes was to rub herself against objects to get off, something I was very excited to watch.

"What...this is ridiculous...how is this not fucking against the rules, how do I make myself come when I'm all tied up?" Katy said.

"Rules? Do you think there are rules for what we're doing to you?" I shared a laugh with Wendy. "I already said I'm not going to help you." I tapped Katy's ass. "Fuck yourself against the counter or just stay here forever, your choice."

Katy let out an indignant whimper and sighed. She pressed herself against the counter, sliding her stomach and pussy along it, the tightness of the corset and panties making her movement more labored and tense.

Watching Katy's ass flex in the overly tight panties was a sight to behold, and made me so turned on I decided I simply had to start touching myself as well. Could you blame me?

Wendy rubbed Katy's shoulders. "Oh Katy...I bet that feels amazing even if you feel like you're being crushed right now. It's going to take you so long to come, and we're both going to watch every second of it..."

"It...it doesn't feel amazing at all...this...this will take hours..." Katy rolled herself against the edge of the counter, a movement that I think she had practiced and perfected over many years of sexual frustration.

I put my fingers in my mouth and sucked on them, getting them good and wet, and then slid them down my panties to start touching myself. "Oh my god, Katy, you really do want to make a mess on this table, don't you?"

"Fuck...off..." Katy grunted, rapidly batting herself against a hard edge, her body growing hot and pink as she gathered her energy and held back her orgasm.

"You are going to ruin those panties...that fabric is going to get so wet..." I was rapidly approaching orgasm myself as I watched Katy fuck against the counter in desperation.

"I don't...care...about the fucking panties...I just need to...fucking come..."

"Fuck, then just come, bitch..." Wendy grabbed Katy's chin, staring into her eyes. "What the fuck are you waiting for? Two beautiful fucking women are watching you degrade yourself, and I ate your pussy way longer than I should have. You should have come the moment your sad little slit touched the edge of that counter."

"I..." Katy moaned and slid along the edge, her body in pure overdrive. "I...want..."

Wendy shook Katy's face, pressing down against her cheeks with her fingertips. "Are you too afraid to do it in front of two gorgeous women? Are we intimidating to you, Katy?"

Katy looked back and forth from me to Wendy and back at me again, a crazed, desperate look in her eye. "God...you two..."

I walked around behind Katy and took her hips in my hand, holding her still while she tried to grind on the edge of the counter. I pressed her from behind, enhancing the pleasure. I slid my hand down the front of her hips, over her panties, and felt that she had completely soaked through them to the point that it felt like the thin fabric wasn't there. Katy didn't reduce her fury of grinding, smashing my fingers against the counter in a way that would definitely bruise, but I didn't mind it at all. I wanted to make Katy come harder than she had in her life, so if that meant taking a couple of knocks to the fingers, then that's the sacrifice I had to make.

"F---fuck---fucking hell...." Katy gasped.

"Oh my god is she finally doing it? Are you finally coming, Katy? Took you fucking long enough..." Wendy said with evil glee.

Katy gasped, her eyes rolling back, a guttural moan coming out of her mouth.

"Oh, fuck..." I tried pulled my hand back, but I was pinned against the counter, my fingers smashing into Katy's wet folds.

Wendy was not so forgiving. She grabbed Katy's face again, that evil sweet look again on her face. "You're not really coming...you're faking it, Katy...I can tell."

"F--fucking hell...you can...what?"

"She can definitely tell you're lying, pet..." I said.

"I'm...not...I'm fucking...coming...." Katy moaned.

"She's dry as the desert down here, Wendy...I guarantee you she's not coming..." I said, hoping suspension of disbelief would cover the very obvious sounds of her wetness slapping against my fingers.

I had never, ever felt a woman dry hump something and be that wet...Katy really was a treasure of a sub, I couldn't have dreamed for better.

Katy pressed herself against the edge harder as her orgasm peaked, her entire body locking up. I'm pretty certain something actually did pop inside of her, but she seemed to be OK, so who was I to deny her from having such forceful pleasure.

I held Katy tight, pressing her hips down against my fingers and holding her up as she bucked and came a second time right after and finally, thankfully, came to a stop.

I stepped back and Katy stumbled backward from her hunched position, falling against me, but I was ready to catch her. "Ohhh....my god...holy shit..."

"Mistress...it's still going..." Wendy whispered.

I nodded and smiled, putting my hands against the front of the corset and feeling her body shaking and pulsing.

I held her from behind, then kissed the small of her back. "I want to go down on you so bad still..."

"I would literally dissolve..." Katy laughed. "Thank you both...so...so much, this was insane..."

As the moment settled to something more calm, I

noticed that the red panties were cutting into Katy's asscheeks in a way I didn't like. "Umm, Katy, I think the underwear needs to come off..."

"You might need to cut them off, they're so fucking tight..." Katy laughed a bit to herself, enjoying my embrace, utterly blissful.

Wendy grabbed a small pair of curved trauma scissors from the bag we always kept close for just this reason. A standard flimsy first aid kit from a department store was only the start when it came to BDSM preparedness: you needed something akin to what an EMT would bring to a call. Gauze, iodine, forceps, tweezers, smelling salts, stethoscope...and the worst part of it all was you couldn't even use them for fun reasons. But, safety first, as always.

My wife slid the scissors under the waistband and cut at the sides of the panties, causing them to fall apart. Katy breathed a sigh of relief as they fell from her hips, a big grin on her face.

"God they were so...tight...fuck it was good."

"I know...but your wonderful ass does need some blood flow, dear." I gently massaged Katy's thigh and ass, making sure the stark red lines where the elastic cut in on her skin wasn't something more concerning, but they didn't look to be more than slight scuffs.

Katy winced and I backed away.

"I'm fine, don't worry...just a little sensitive. That was really nice. Fucking incredible."

I leaned my head down and kissed Katy's cheek before standing up.

"Katy, you were an unbelievable scene partner..." I said, recovering my shirt from the clothes rack it was tossed over. I decided to leave my bra off, as there was an almost complete certainty that Wendy and I would need to fool around in the car once we sent Katy on her way.

"Three years of improv classes will do that for a girl... Wendy, can you..." Katy pointed to the tightly-cinched straps holding the corset in place.

"But you look so good in it!" Wendy quickly moved behind her and gently pulled at the pink laces. As an added bonus, my lovely wife planted a sloppy kiss on Katy's shoulder as she did it.

"Katy, I don't want to be too forward, but, if you ever want to do something like this again, and you don't want to go through the...official channels and actually buy our services, I would do this for free any time. Right babe?" I looked over Katy's shoulder at Wendy.

"I almost want to refund her right now for the gift she gave us..." Wendy got to the top of Katy's corset, and the tension around the woman's midsection finally released.

"I might take you up on that..." Katy pulled the corset away. There was something so irresistibly sexy about the way something would emboss someone's skin when they wore a corset like this, or anything that tightly binded them. I could still see every last junction and line of the boning pressed into Katy's skin, outlined in pink.

"Your girlfriend, should she be so inclined, is also welcome to join us." I said, helping Katy get the corset back into the box.

"Oh, god...I don't think either of you are ready for Emma yet." Katy laughed as she pulled her shirt over her still-sensitive body. "But I'm sure she'd love you two..."

INDUCTION

ONE

"SHE WANTS TO BE...TORTURED, and, I don't think I can do that to her." Hanna said, looking over at myself and Wendy, and then at Kira. She patted Kira on the knee and gave her wife a weak smile.

"Well, Hanna, I would say you've made quite the step to fulfilling Kira's wishes here if you've come to Club Crescent. Not only are you OK with your wife being here, but...you're here too, which is...an interesting choice." I smiled, watching Kira's movements. She was quiet, but of course she would be, she wanted to look as submissive as possible when confronted by the woman who was possibly going to show her wonders beyond her imagination. In case it wasn't clear, that person was me.

"It's just...the pain, the...I don't even understand the impulse." Hanna furrowed her brow and tugged at a lock of her dark hair. "Why would somebody want someone to hurt them on purpose?"

"There's pain," Wendy stepped into the conversation,

and I was grateful because her more soft tone sounded less severe than mine, "but it's done here in a controlled way. In a safe way. BDSM isn't about harming the person in your care, it's about exploring all forms of sensation, feeling how the body reacts to it, and creating a little scene that allows people to work out their anxieties, their fears, their hangups, in a way that lets you explore them freely as long as everyone agrees to it. And, as a plus, you get to have some amazing sex as a result." My wife could teach classes on this, and I've told her she should. Maybe one day she could even write a book about all of our little escapades...

"Kira, you've been quiet since we sat down here. Is everything OK?" I said.

Kira looked up at me after fixing her gaze on the table for the past three minutes. She looked nervous as hell, but finally mustered up the courage to look up at me and smiled slightly. "Yes...I want to...feel something more. I love normal sex, and I love sex with you, Hanna," Kira squeezed her wife's arm and then turned back to me, "but...I want to be controlled, I want to be put in my place. I just want to be used sometimes, if...that's OK."

"If that's what you want, baby, that's what we can do." Hanna leaned over and kissed Kira and the two shared a loving moment. I think when people imagine BDSM, they imagine anger, strife, and cruelty...and, yeah, of course there's plenty of that. But it was also an expression of love, of care. You wouldn't do things like this to someone safely if you didn't care for them. The restraint to explore pain and pleasure, to not go too far, but make sure you're going as far as you can, that was something special. And right now, I saw that desire in Kira to feel all of that.

"Now, I want to be clear on what's going to happen in the room." I said, splaying my hands on the desk, using my lawyerly rhetorical tactics to their fullest, "When we go in there, I will be performing sex acts on Kira, and chances are she will be doing the same to me. We will be having sex, is that OK with both of you?"

Kira nodded gently and looked over at Hanna.

Hanna let out a little nervous giggle. "Yes, that's... that's OK. Is it...ok with your wife that you'll be having sex with another woman?"

I looked over at Wendy with a smirk. "Wendy, dear, do you have even the slightest problem with me having sex with someone who is not my lovely wife?"

Wendy shook her head, and laughed. "If I had a problem with this, we would have been done a long, long time ago."

"Excellent." I turned back to the other two women. "Now, are you familiar with a safeword at all?"

"S--Starburst. That's my safeword." Kira spit out, eager to move along.

"Starburst it is." I smirked at how enthusiastic Kira was for all of this. People like that always made the most interesting clients at the very least.

I glanced around, observing the room. We were in a small consultation room at Club Crescent, the decor in here much more friendly and calm than the more... extreme aesthetics of the rest of the building. This was the last moment of true reality before Kira and Hanna plunged into this, and I sort of admired the fact that they got to experience it for the first time.

"And Hanna, you will...be in the room, watching Kira and myself?" I said.

Hanna looked over at Kira who smiled warmly and nodded, squeezing her arm.

"I--I think that's what she wants. And if she wants that, then, so do I."

"And are you alright if Wendy is in the room with us as well? She's not going to try to put the moves on you or anything, and you have just as much of a right to the safeword as Kira does. But, I will say, she is quite the conversationalist." I grinned at my wife.

"Think of me as...color commentary, I'll be there to make sure you know what's happening...and to tell you that, no, Mistress Morrigan isn't going to hurt Kira. Well, not more than she wants to be hurt." Wendy gave Hanna a look, warm with a hint of mischief, something my wife was an expert at.

Hanna let out a nervous laugh. "No, I don't mind that at all. It's going to take me some time to get used to all of this, but, you two seem nice."

The energy in the room felt right to start, as Kira was champing at the bit to get this underway and Hanna seemed persuadable. I got out of the chair and motioned for Kira to do so. "Kira, you'll come with me. I'll let you use the dressing room while I get dressed in the main room, and when we are both ready, I will invite our observers to join us in the room...at a healthy distance."

Kira stood up and took my outstretched hand. She

was shaking, but I was pretty certain it was the result of good anxiety, not bad. Somewhere under that shy and unassuming facade there was a woman who felt like she just won the lottery, and here I was, the one who was drawing her lucky numbers.

TWO

"AM...AM I allowed to come out?" Kira's voice didn't carry much over the fans that had to work overtime keeping these kinds of rooms cool...and to drown out the sound from adjacent cells.

"Yes, Kira, you may join me now." I said, making my final adjustments on my costume. Tonight I went for a more subdued look...well, as subdued as a dominatrix could be, that is. It was a red leather dress that clung to my curves well and featured a zipper that ran from top to bottom, meaning with one sure tug I could be naked in moments. Combine that with some medium-grid fishnets and some understated black Mary Janes, and, well, it was very nearly an outfit I wouldn't mind wearing outside of Club Crescent.

"OK, um...so, I'm going to come out."

"Kira, you will join me in the main room. I need you to follow my orders." I said, introducing the first spark of command-giving into the evening.

I heard her take a deep breath before answering, "Yes, Mistress."

I smirked and went over to the door, waiting for Kira to exit. And, finally, she did.

Kira was dressed in a simple white corset and white lacy underwear, along with sheer tights that stopped just above her knees. It was a bit of a default submissive choice, and a little too Alice in Wonderland for my tastes, but I wasn't going to call her out for it. Now, if she showed up for a second session in such boring gear, well, Mistress Morrigan would possibly need to have a word about the dress code in her dungeon.

She was still nervous, and she seemed self-conscious about her body from the way she crossed her arms in front of her stomach. In reality, just about anybody would when they saw the mirrors on the walls and how on display they would be in one of Club Crescent's elaborate playrooms. And this one was the smaller of the chambers, with the least visible and vaguely threatening equipment. Her wavy blonde hair went halfway down her back and was cinched into a simple ponytail, and a blush was spreading across her freckled chest. And maybe it was the corset doing a magic trick, but I was quite shocked that her breasts were at least a cup size larger than I thought they would be.

"You're quite beautiful, Kira, you know that? I'm saying that as Brenda, not Mistress Morrigan...I really mean it." I said.

"Th--thanks. I like your costume, it...looks great." she smiled softly and tried to make eye contact, but ultimately found the floor much more interesting. Ahh, the nerves of a first-time sub.

"Are you ready for our audience, Kira?" I said, stepping close to her, but not wanting to cross the threshold of touching her.

"Yes, Mistress. I'm ready to play." she said with a small grin.

"Excellent."

I walked over to the intercom, as for rather obvious reasons cell phones weren't allowed at Club Crescent, and pressed the button. "Wendy, can you and our guest please join us in the play room?"

The silence as we waited for the two of them to come in was awkward, but there was no way to avoid it. Making small talk in the moments before beginning a BDSM scene was quite difficult, as nobody really wants to talk about the weather when their mind is preoccupied with what it will feel like to be bound and gagged.

And so it was that Kira and I just stood there and waited, making awkward glances at the wall or the floor. After what was probably less than a minute, the door opened and our spectators entered the room. Wendy and Hanna filed in, and from their happy state, I could tell Wendy had probably spent the time when we were getting ready on working her charms on Hanna. She was rather charming, after all...how else would one land such a magnificent woman as myself?

Kira was doing the best to be as submissive as possible. The corset she was wearing put a huge emphasis on her waistline, and I'm sure she had quite a hard time breathing. I made a note to myself that removing it would be an early objective.

My wife and Hanna settled in on the couch on the far side of the room, leaving Kira and myself in the middle. There was more silence, but as our little drama began, it wouldn't last long.

"Ladies, we are beginning the scene now. All rules about contact, consent, and kinks are going to be strictly followed by all parties. This is not a place for ambiguity or questioning...if you feel uncomfortable and want things to ease up, say 'yellow light' and we can pause things and discuss. We will re-enter the scene when all parties agree and confirm with 'green light'. A safeword, in tonight's case 'Starburst', is an instant stop without questions. If you feel the safeword is not sufficient, there are three stop buttons located in the room." I indicated the glowing green buttons mounted by the doors, and one in the middle of the room shielded under a plastic cover to prevent accidental presses. Yes, pointing them out did make me feel like a flight attendant. "These buttons will immediately turn all lights in the room on, cut the power to all outlets that could be powering a sex toy, and will alert the management office immediately." I turned on my heel, snapping forward with military precision, a bit giddy that I was finally getting this long speech down without hesitation. "In short, we are safe, we are under control, and we are going to have a wonderful fucking time tonight. Sound good?" I turned toward my rapt audience.

Hanna nodded emphatically. Wendy was grinning

ear to ear. And Kira had her gaze locked to the floor and was nodding just slightly, with her arms still crossed.

"Well then, Kira...shall we give them a show?" I asked.

Kira nodded this time, more sure of herself.

THREE

I SLOWLY STEPPED FORWARD, coming up to Kira, who was looking at me. I gently caressed her face with my right hand, feeling the smoothness of her skin and her faint blush as she heated up. "Why are you even here?" I said, making sure it was clear my tone had darkened considerably now that the scene was underway. "What right do you think you have to be in front of Mistress Morrigan?"

Kira opened her mouth and started to say something, but I gently pressed my thumb into her lips, making a shushing noise. "No, no. It was rhetorical, my dear, because I'm not looking for an answer from you. You wouldn't be able to provide a sufficient explanation anyway, I'm afraid. You're too scared, too skittish..." I ran my hand down her stomach, feeling the fine lace and embroidery under my fingers, stopping when I felt the warmth of her stomach, "...you're terrified at what's about to happen to you, aren't you, you little sweet lamb?"

Kira's eyes had widened at my touch, but she was

trying her best to stay calm and collected, nodding ever so slightly in assent. I pressed my lips close to her ear and whispered. "Good girl, very good. You should be terrified. Because I'm going to eat you alive..." I pressed my body against hers, feeling the softness of her chest against my more thin frame. This initial verbal dressing down was always a good indication of how much further I could go, and gauging by Kira's reaction, I still had plenty of runway.

I walked behind Kira and ran my hands down her shoulders, sweeping my hands over the tops of her breasts, the extra softness feeling delicious to press and prod and hear the slight gasps emanate from Kira's mouth. "You do have very nice tits, though, Kira...you should be proud of them." I ran my fingers along the edge of the corset, knowing I was close to Kira's nipples, trying to coax arousal out of her to diffuse some of the nerves.

"Thank you, Mistress Morrigan."

"Kira, you don't get to speak unless I ask you something. That's how this is going to go tonight."

"Yes, Mistress, I'm sorry, Mistress."

"Now I see that your lovely wife is watching us, and she seems to enjoy the view...Kira, dear, can you please ask your wife how she approves of the evening thus far?" I said, nuzzling my chin against Kira's neck. I wanted to lull her into a false sense of softness, maybe even make her think this would all be far less harsh than she had imagined...but, of course, then she would leave the room disappointed, so I wanted to give her these moments before I started really clamping down.

Kira turned her head, looking back at me. "Mistress... am I allowed to talk?"

"To your wife, yes."

"Kira, honey..." Hanna said, getting up from the couch and slowly coming over, her voice timid and filled with concern, "are you ok?"

"Yellow light." I held my hand up and looked at Hanna sternly. If there was one thing you didn't want to do to a dominatrix, it was fuck with her protocols. But I could also tell this woman was genuinely concerned for her wife, so I let the facade slip a moment later. "Hanna, dear, if you want us to pause the scene, I need you to say 'yellow light', so that I know that what you're doing is not role-playing. I say this for your safety and mine."

Hanna bit her lip and looked down, then back at me. "Y--yes, you're right. Um..." She took a deep breath. "Yellow light. I don't want to interrupt you, but..." Hanna swept a stray strand of Kira's hair behind her ear, "you're... OK with this? What she's doing?"

"Hanna, baby, yes..." Kira leaned forward and kissed her wife, the two sharing the moment. "I am so, so into this. I'm playing a role, I'm being submissive, I'm being scared, I'm exaggerating it. It's like a little play, or a TV show." Kira looked over her other shoulder towards me, "I know that if it gets to be too much, Brenda, Mistress Morrigan, whoever, will stop if I say so." Kira put her hands on Hanna's chest and gave her a pleading look, "so please, baby, trust that I'm fine. I'm having such a wonderful time already."

"Alright." Hanna sighed, then nodded at me, "I'm... sorry for the intrusion. I'll watch you two from over there, now, and..." She looked back at Kira, "you let me know if anything goes wrong."

"I will let my Mistress know, because she is in control tonight." Kira said, the slight bit of bratty energy given back to Hanna was a clue at another angle I could play.

"Umm...sure, yes, you're calling the shots, Mistress Morrigan." Hanna sat down next to Wendy and eased back. "Umm...ok, I guess, green light from me?"

The three of us returned with our own green light signals, and I got back into my posture.

"Now...where were we...oh, yes...Kira...you were going to tell me how you were feeling about tonight." I returned my hands to their position over Kira's shoulders, my fingers grazing her breasts once again.

"I'm feeling good, Mistress. I like what's happening."

"Are you enjoying what I'm doing to you?"

"Yes, Mistress, I'm...I like it very much."

"Then why aren't you doing what I told you to do?" I tightened my grip on her shoulders, going from soft to hard in an instant just to show her I could. "I told you to tell your wife how it feels, not me. I would advise you to listen closely to my orders, little lamb, or tonight is going to be far more brutal than you could even imagine." I loosened my grip and resumed gently swiping my hands across Kira's chest. "Now, Kira, I will give you another chance to follow my goddamn instructions."

"I understand, Mistress Morrigan...and I'm sorry for disobeying your orders. I'm very sorry."

"What I want from you," I pressed myself against Kira and wrapped my hands around her midsection, feeling her soft stomach under my fingertips, "is to tell your beautiful fucking wife how you feel about what I'm doing to you. Tell Hanna the feelings I'm stirring in you, Kira."

"Hanna...my love, I...I really, really like what this is doing to me. Mistress Morrigan...is so, so beautiful, and, she...she knows how to use her hands."

"Yes, Kira, I do...now tell Hanna how lovely she is, and how wonderful she is to turn over care of such a wonderful creature as yourself into the loving embrace of Mistress Morrigan..." I said, sliding my hands down to Kira's sides, gripping her at her hips.

"Hanna, I...I love you so, so much. I want you to see how...how wonderful this makes me feel. You've given me something, something I never knew I wanted."

"Now Kira, don't be coy..." I slid my chin along her shoulder, kissing her lightly, "you've known you have wanted this for a long time, haven't you?"

Kira nodded, biting her lip. "I...I have, I wanted this for, god, as long as I can remember. I want...to be a good little toy, I want to feel a woman take control of my body..."

"Because you're a pathetic little slut, aren't you?" I said, repeating the motion along Kira's shoulder, but this time grazing my teeth against her skin.

Kira gasped, and nodded again. "Yes...I am a pathetic slut..."

"And now that you have this thought working its way through your head, it's all you can think of...your little pussy is weeping already, isn't it?" I moved my hands from Kira's hips to her ass, gripping her, increasing the tension.

"Y--yes...I...I need..." Kira's words caught in her throat, but she had to continue.

"You need...what? What do you need?" I said.

"I need...Mistress Morrigan...to fuck me."

"Very, very good..." I let Kira's ass go, then brought my right hand up and slapped Kira's ass firmly. Kira squeaked in surprise, and then moaned softly, clearly enjoying the impact. "We're not even close to giving you that yet, but it's good to know you'd like to get fucked, Kira...it's good to establish an objective."

I took Kira by the shoulders again, this time spinning her around so she faced me, our bodies almost pressing up against each other, the slight pressure of her chest on mine enough to set off sparks of excitement. "Knees. Now. You're enjoying this too much."

Kira smiled softly, her lips just curling into a wicked little grin before dropping down.

FOUR

KIRA KNELT in front of me. I was already considerably taller than her on our feet, but the height disparity here was even more staggering. "You're obedient, I'll give you that, you sweet little lamb." I swept my thumb across Kira's lips, drawing out a bit of saliva to brush along her cheek.

"I've...had some training in obedience." she said, grinning a little too cockily. I loved seeing how the brattiness of a woman like this came out in a setting like this, but I couldn't have it yet.

"Did your little wife take you to a dog school? Did she teach you to be leashed and bound, and to only come when asked?" I said, walking in a circle around Kira, establishing dominance.

"N--no...Catholic school..." Kira drawled.

"Oh my god, baby, is this what this is about?" Hanna said from the sidelines. I was going to admonish her for breaking protocols again, but I thought this could play as part of the scene. Maybe letting them talk would help ease things along.

Kira nodded and turned towards her wife, grinning a little too devilishly for the moment. "It is. You have to admit...I'm having fun with the memories of awful head-mistresses at least."

"Yellow light." I said, not wanting things to spiral. "Just so we're clear, these awful headmistresses were awful in an...ok way? Not something that would probably better be discussed and worked out with a therapist or a lawyer?"

Kira realized what I was saying and laughed a little, "Oh, umm, yes, just the standard amount of dogmatic trauma, not something worse."

"Good..." After realizing how awkward I had made everything, I brightened my expression and clasped my hands while looking around the room. "Green light?" was met with universal agreements.

I straightened my back and pressed my hip against Kira's shoulder. "Now, Kira, sweet lamb, tell me what you like most about being obedient."

Kira was quiet for a few moments, considering what she could say. "It makes me feel safe, Mistress Morrigan." she said finally, a softness returning to her voice.

I brushed her cheek softly again and nodded, then circled in front of her to stand over her. "Why on earth do you think you're safe, Kira?" I dragged my nails along Kira's chest slowly, giving her another peek at pain, "this place is not safe, especially for little sluts who go down on their knees the moment they're asked."

Kira swallowed and let her eyes close, reveling in the

pain of my nails dragging over the tops of her breasts, and I could see that this was her little window into the darker pleasures of this.

"You like it, don't you, Kira? This pain, the sensation of it, the knowledge that I could make it hurt so much more in an instant if I so chose..." I pressed my nails in harder, my fingers leaving a light red trail from the scraping. Not enough to draw blood, but enough to make her think it was a possibility.

"I...I do." Kira said. She opened her eyes again to see the damage, then looked up at me. "It...it makes me feel..." she struggled with her words for a moment, "alive?"

"And more pain, Kira...would it make you feel more alive? I need you to admit how depraved and wanting you are before I give you one more moment of stimulation."

"More, please, Mistress Morrigan. Give me more... make it hurt so bad. I...I'm a pathetic little slut...and I want it."

"Oh, my little Kira...you are so very obedient. I wish all my submissives were like you. None of you are special, but you are...preferred, I suppose." I broke my attention from Kira and looked back at the couch. Wendy was, of course, watching with rapt attention, but I was heartened to see Hanna was as well. Those nerves, that apprehension, it was more or less gone now, and I liked to think that Hanna was trusting me with her wife's safety. But, this next part was going to test just how open she was.

"Hanna, dear, do you mind if Wendy acts as my assistant for a short while?" I said.

Hanna blinked for a second and turned her head.

"Umm, yeah...go right ahead." She was blushing, giggling a little bit, and I swore I saw a smile.

"Good. Wendy, darling, get me a chair and Box C-1, please."

Wendy practically jumped from the couch, eager to finally get to participate in things. "Yes, Mistress Morrigan, of course."

"Wh...what's in Box C-1?" Kira said, looking around a little but being smart enough to not turn her head too much, as she was quite correct that doing that would draw Mistress Morrigan's ire.

I reached down and grabbed Kira's jaw, holding it gently, but any pressure around the face was beyond powerful. "If I wanted you to know what was in the box, little lamb, I would have said what was in the box, wouldn't I?" I looked up, still holding Kira's face, and saw Wendy was still over by the cabinet of toys and implements. "Wendy, since Kira here seems to think she can ask her Mistress questions, please provide me Box G-2 as well."

Wendy stifled a gleeful laugh, because she knew what was in store for Kira...and maybe also because she knew Kira had no idea.

FIVE

"IS THE CHAIR COMFORTABLE, KIRA?" I said, tracking Wendy as she returned to the couch.

"N...not really...it's...cold..." Kira gripped the steel seat underneath her, bracing for what would come next.

"And now, Kira, do you believe you deserve comfort?"

"No, Mistress." Kira's breathing had changed. She was on edge, her nerves returning in a heartbeat, but with something else, too, a spark of excitement.

"Very good." I nodded and picked up Box C-1 from the small table beside me. "I have a present for you, Kira... well, it's more of a present for me, really." I handed the square lacquer box to Kira, who accepted it with eager hands. "Open it."

Kira's fingers shook slightly as she pulled at the box, the sound of the metal tabs opening was musical, albeit ominous. She opened the lid and peered at the contents. "Oh..."

"Do you know what you're looking at right now, Kira?"

"I...I think so." Kira's eyes were searching the contents of the small box, the thin silver chain spiraled in the middle connecting the stars of the show.

"So tell me, Kira. A good girl wouldn't know what something like this was just by glancing at it, but something tells me you're so far gone you identified it in an instant. I think you've done your research, looked at things like this late at night while your dear Hanna was asleep...I venture to even imagine your little hand was between your legs while you did it" I took a step closer. "Answer, sweet Kira. What are they."

"They're nipple clamps."

"Very good..." I patted Kira's cheek, "Now, Kira, we're going to use these, and you're going to enjoy them. This is not optional." I snatched the box back from Kira, teaching her that I was in control once again.

"Mistress Morrigan, what..." Kira said, still bracing.

"Kira, I'm wondering why you're not already preparing yourself for your punishment. If I'm going to use nipple clamps on you, what needs to happen before I can do that?"

Kira blinked for a second and swallowed. "Mistress Morrigan, you...want me to..." She nodded slightly and slowly brought her hands up to her chest...

"Kira, if your tits aren't out in the next five seconds, I will knock you out of that chair and make you forget that pleasure was even an option." I ended the sentence with a stomp that echoed through the room.

The energy in the room flipped, and I heard Hanna grumble, about to say something, but then a moment later I saw Kira give her wife a look of admonition. This was fine. This was what Kira wanted. And to my delight, the look seemed to calm Hanna down once again.

Kira reached for the clasps on the corset, which were already strained, and began unbuckling them. It was a cheaper piece of lingerie, not really field tested for any serious BDSM, so the clasps were the cheapest possible, awkward and bent, a small struggle to release each one.

"Kira, if you are delaying this on purpose, this is over. You are falling behind my schedule, you're doing a shit job at being obedient. Take it off. Now."

Kira sped her movements up, and I could tell she was frustrated with it, so I decided to not push more, as much as I wanted to move things along. After a few more eternities, Kira finally pulled the corset away from her chest, her body marked with red lines and indentations from the suffocating ribbing. The corset did do a good bit to push her breasts up nicely, but either way they were utterly gorgeous, and my next target.

"Oh, Kira...it's a shame you have such pretty nipples..." I rubbed my thumb in a circle around her areola before pulling the nipple down until it popped out from under my thumb, a good bit harder than it was before. "They are going to be so very red and sore after we're done..."

"I'm ready, Mistress." Kira said, a hint of pleading in her voice, a bit of hope she wouldn't need to ask.

"That's cute. And it would be an important piece of information if you had any say in when I did this to you..." I took her right breast in my hand and gave it the same treatment as the left. "In fact, that reminds me, we have a second box to open, don't we?" I gave Kira a cold, seductive smile before turning to the second black lacquer box, about the same size as the one for the nipple clamps. I held the box in front of her, and because of what happened with the last one, she instinctively reached out for it, which gave me a perfect opportunity to slap her hand back.

"What are you doing, Kira?" I said as she placed her hands on her knees, getting more giddy with every moment.

"Mistress Morrigan, please..." Kira was holding back whimpers now.

"Do you think you should open this box?" I said, slowly lowering it, making Kira feel the distance. "You don't deserve the satisfaction." I thumbed the latch and pulled the box open, then withdrew the secret object.

"Oh..." Kira was positively bursting to get this moving, which made me want to edge and tease her even more.

"I knew a needy little slut like you would salivate when you saw a ball gag...it's almost too easy." I grinned.

Kira leaned forward a bit, making a pleading gesture. She was close enough that I could slip it on now, but that would be too easy.

"Yellow, again, I'm sorry." Hanna said, standing up from the couch. "This is...isn't this a little dangerous for a first time, choking her?"

I turned toward Hanna and put the box down, still holding the ball gag in my hand. "It won't choke her, Hanna dear, it's perforated to allow normal breathing." I held the device up in the dim lighting, so Hanna could see the holes punched through the tough bite-proof rubber ball. "Wendy over here has worn one for...three, four hours at a time before?"

"One time it was six..." Wendy said, smiling to herself at the memories of that marathon session.

"I'd be more than happy to put it on myself to show you I can breathe normally, Hanna, I don't want this to be scary, but I assure you it's safe."

I was about to demonstrate the proper use of the ball gag when Hanna must have decided she had another way to leave me speechless.

"Put it on me." She said, looking at me with wary determination.

"Are...are you sure? That's not my job to put you in such a thing, Hanna..." I said, looking for permission from Kira, but her face was beaming.

"I won't trust that it's safe unless...I try it, so, let's try it."

"Very well. And you want me to put this on you while the scene is still paused?" I looked over Hanna's shoulder at Wendy, who was looking a little too excited that there was a glimmer that Hanna was going to be more of a participant than an observer.

"Yes...I'm not ready for...all of that, if I'll ever be."

"Perfectly reasonable, Hanna. Now, please, open your mouth."

SIX

I SLIPPED the rubber ball in Hanna's mouth, careful not to be too harsh or forceful with any of my movements as I fastened the strap around the back of her head, securing the buckle.

"Can you breathe, Hanna?" I asked, putting my fingers between the strap and her cheek, making sure it was secure but not too tight.

Hanna tried it for a moment, taking in a deep breath and exhaling with seemingly no extra effort. Of course, she couldn't smile, but I saw something soften in her eyes.

"Yeahh...I can...bweeev" Hanna said, trying to navigate around the ball but failing.

"You can almost speak coherently with it in." I smirked. "You can take it off when you would like, it's just a belt buckle closure behind your right ear."

Hanna stood for a few more moments, working the gag in her mouth, before reaching back and releasing herself.

"See? Perfectly safe." I said.

"You're right, and..." Hanna looked at the gag in her hand, "I think I'm...understanding the appeal."

"Oh?" I said, now quite on edge about how this could turn...it was always fun converting a skeptic to your side.

"Not...not the whole thing, but...can I...help you? With...doing things to Kira?" Hanna stumbled through the sentence with great difficulty, her nerves no doubt jangling, but the look Kira gave her in response was beyond fantastic.

"Baby, really? You...oh my god...I would love that." Kira beamed. If she previously looked like she had won the lottery, she now looked like she'd won the whole world.

"I...want to try."

"I'd love to have you help, Hanna. Really." I said, reaching out and grazing my hand along her forearm, which was wreathed with at least a dozen colorful tattoos.

Hanna nodded, looking at Kira, furrowing her brow. Hanna looked like the kind of woman who contemplated things a lot, and I have to admit I found that brooding quality rather appealing. In fact, women like Hanna were usually more of the type to find themselves in my dungeon as opposed to the more cheery, carefree Kiras of the world, but Mistress Morrigan's torture took all kinds.

"If you are going to help, I do have some stipulations. One, you'll need to tie your hair back...getting a lock of that caught in a belt or a strap could ruin the mood quite quickly. Second, you'll need to tuck your shirt in... bondage gear isn't just tight for aesthetic reasons."

"Or I could just take the shirt...off?" Hanna said, as if it was a wild, uncouth thing to say, completely ignoring the fact that her wife was topless and eagerly awaiting to have her nipples clamped by a dominatrix in a red leather dress.

"You certainly could do that as well..." I said, again glancing at Wendy, who I knew wanted to bound from the couch and shower Hanna in love and assurance, but she seemed to also understand it was best for Hanna to come to this on her own.

Hanna nodded, then, with a slightly shaking hand, undid the top few buttons of her flannel and then removed it entirely, tossing it back towards the couch. I couldn't help but take in her appearance. She was toned and tightly bundled, her black sports bra stretched tight against her firm chest. The art gallery on her arm continued across the rest of her torso and onto the other arm, and when she reached up to tie her hair back, her triceps flexing in the dim purple light of the room, I had to firmly remind myself that I was here to devote my energy toward Kira, not her absolutely mouth-watering wife. Unless, of course, things took another unpredictable turn...

"Umm...alright, we are...moving along!" I said, regaining my composure and trying my best to not tip my hand as to my current frazzled mental state. "Another thing, Hanna, you must follow my instructions exactly, ok? If I tell you how to do something to Kira, I need you to do it exactly how I tell you. I won't play any mind games with you while we're in the scene, I'll reserve those for Kira. Mistress Morrigan will be entirely forthright with you to make sure we do this safely."

Hanna nodded and smiled a little, her charms coming

through even more now that she seemed to be more comfortable with all of this. "Sounds good, let's...do some really weird things that I'm going to try to be normal about because I know it'll make Kira happy." Hanna chuckled.

"Green light?" I said, scanning the room.

SEVEN

"WELL, Kira, as you see, things have gone so poorly that I needed to bring assistance to handle you. Do not take this as a sign you are somehow beyond my abilities." I said, stepping toward Kira and beginning the scene. "This is my assistant...Hanna?" I said, kicking myself for not establishing if she wanted to use a code name.

"That's me..." Hanna said, a little cheery before correcting herself, "Uh, I mean, yeah...slut...I'm...here to help."

So maybe the acting part was going to be a little more tough to bring Hanna around to.

"I like my assistants quiet and dutiful, Hanna, so please, keep the chatter to a minimum."

"Yes...yes Mistress Morrigan."

I gave Hanna a nod as she looked toward Kira. "Now, Hanna, please secure the gag around Kira's dirty mouth. I don't want to be bothered by her screams and moans while we torture her pretty pink nipples." I looked over to Hanna and nodded. "Go on, I'll check your work."

Hanna reached behind Kira and buckled the strap of the gag tight, a little more rough than I might have gone with. "Like...that?"

"Not too bad..." I said, inspecting Kira's mouth, tapping on the ball with my nail. Kira looked practically orgasmic just after the first few moments of having the ball impeding her mouth. "She'll be quiet, alright, but, maybe a little uncomfortable..." I reached back and corrected the strap, loosening it one notch. "We need our little sluts seething in pain, not suffering in discomfort, don't we, sweet lamb?"

Kira grunted in assent, and I leaned forward and kissed her, pressing the ball into her mouth slightly with my tongue, just to let her know that the pressure could increase. I personally loved this move, and from Kira and Hanna's reaction, it was a crowd favorite as well.

I turned away from Kira, trying to hide my own excitement as much as possible. It was only the start, but this was already so, so much more intense than I anticipated, and it was only going to get more intense from here. All of this slow burn had me so desperate to come that I was basically torturing myself at this point, but I knew I had to be more calm and giving than I would have been with more experienced subjects.

"Hanna, dear, please hand me the nipple clamps. I want to apply them to Kira and move this along...she's been sitting there unharmed for far too long." I motioned toward the black boxes on the table.

"Yeah...of course..." Hanna fumbled for a moment, the two boxes on top of one another. She picked up Box

C-1 and pulled the clamps out. She handed them over to me and I held them, the metal cool in my hand.

These particular clamps were perfect for a beginner...which is why they were labeled C-1, for Clamp level 1. No screws or springs here, just a set of tweezer clamps, a simple U-shaped wire with rubber-tipped tongs and a bulbous end at the bottom, where two small silver moons dangled. A small plate could be moved up or down to increase or decrease pressure, and on the off chance that an overeager dominatrix pulled them too hard because she was thinking about what it would be like to sit on the face of said submissive's wife...well, the clamps would just fall off harmlessly instead of causing damage.

"Thank you, dear. Now, you see here, these little plates, I'll just move these to adjust the amount of pressure being applied. If we go too far, and they're causing our dear lamb Kira more pain than we like, you just slide the plate away and release." I placed the rubber tips against Kira's left nipple but took pause. "Hanna, be a doll, and please get Kira's nipples hard enough to put these on. They're pitiful right now." I looked up at Kira with a half wink, both of us eager to see Hanna take a more active role.

Hanna gave her own half grin, then approached her wife and bent down to her breast. Hanna took her left nipple between her fingers, gently at first, then pressing the flesh between her index finger and her thumb.

"Mmm...you like that babe?" Hanna said, biting her lip as she played with Kira's nipple.

"N...no...please...it's...awful...I don't like any of this..." Kira added a theatric whimper.

"Oh, really now?" Hanna said, then leaned down to suck on Kira's nipple, gently, her lips barely grazing Kira's flesh. Kira bucked and whimpered as her wife worked her, Hanna clearly getting the hang of it. "You seem to really fucking like it..." Hanna sucked Kira's nipple forcefully, leaving it hard and glistening with her saliva. I was impressed.

"Hanna, that's enough, the subject is more than prepared." I said. I could tell Hanna was frustrated by the sudden stop, but she thankfully stayed in her place.

"Very good, Kira..." I said, placing the tongs of the clamp on either side of Kira's erect nipple, the soft rubber tip gripping the reddening flesh. I slid the plate up, letting her feel the initial sensation as the clamp bit in. "These will keep poor Hanna from being tempted to suck those nipples for a while at least..." I moved the plate closer to her nipple, about a half a millimeter at a time, increasing the pressure. This was delicate work, but nipples were also rather resilient, and every woman had a different level of sensation, so I was willing to go as far as Kira wanted.

"That's halfway, Kira...do I need to go tighter? Do you need to be punished more?" I said.

"Mff...mmmm..." Kira said, nodding, her eyes pleading for more, the pain evident, but she wasn't ready for it to stop just yet.

"Oh...so you do need more..." I pushed the plate up a little higher, and didn't leave the choice to Kira any further. I didn't want the things going numb tonight.

"Mmm...that thing I said about them being difficult to suck on when they were clamped..." I lowered my head to Kira's breast and dragged my tongue against the pinched bud. "I'm pleased to report they're still rather easy to lick."

"Fuck..." Hanna said, perhaps astonished by my expertise.

I smirked and bit my lip a little, "Oh, Hanna, I didn't mean to leave you out, my dear assistant...please, see how easy and accessible Kira's nipples are to licking..."

"Well, umm, yeah...ok." Hanna knelt and brought her head to Kira's breasts and slowly circled Kira's nipple with her tongue, slowly and sensuously.

"Good, now...keep it up...but Kira, I will warn you, you are not allowed to come until I say so, no matter how good this feels." I looked up, and the expression on Kira's face was beyond delicious. Her eyes were so full of want, but she also knew better than to push this boundary.

"Hanna, you're going to make the poor girl pop, let's give her a rest." I said, putting my hand on Hanna's shoulder to control the tongue lashing.

"I...ok...right..." Hanna looked at me, her face flushed red with desire, and she seemed to realize how close she was getting. I felt for her...this was a tough balance for everyone, especially in a room where there was already such a lot of emotional and erotic tension. But she was learning.

"Would you like to apply the second clip to our little lamb, Hanna?" I said, holding the rose gold clip in my hand, chain laced through my fingers. As I asked and waited for Hanna, I tugged the chain just a little to give a jolt of stimulation to Kira just to remind her that I was still focused on her.

"Yeah, ok...that sounds..." Hanna blinked, "that sounds fine, Mistress Morrigan."

I nodded and gave Kira the most tender look I could. She was absolutely beside herself with bliss, but I could tell she had so much more capacity to take even more. "And do you mind if I prepared Kira's nipple for the clip?" I said, running my finger over the nub. It was already more than hard enough to apply the clip, but I honestly just wanted the release of being able to do something instead of running through all the fantasies and possibilities.

"No...no I don't mind."

"Good...I will tell you just like I tell you with every step in this process, just in case." I lowered my head, taking Kira's breast in my mouth, taking her nipple between my tongue and my teeth, pressing the soft skin against the incisors. "She might take a bit to get ready..." I said, giggling as I enjoyed the taste of Kira's skin and the way she melted under my care.

"She might...might need to have her pussy rubbed before she's completely ready..." Hanna said.

I looked back at my neophyte assistant with a cocked eyebrow. I should have lashed out at her, told her to not tell me what to do, turned this back into the darkness that it needed to be, but with how nervous Hanna was being, and how far she had already come in the short time we'd been here, I was willing to let it slide to please her as well as Kira.

"And you would like to watch me do that to Kira, wouldn't you, Hanna?" I said.

Hanna bit her lip. "Y-yes..."

EIGHT

"NOW, Hanna, as you may or may not know, the pussy is a sensitive spot on our sweet lamb Kira..." I said, kneeling down behind Kira, my arms snaked around, opening Kira's legs, "it's almost impossible for me to play with it, it could be too much for our poor little slut." I tapped my fingers on the top of Kira's thigh, playing with her before I made my strike. "But if I did something like this..." I swept my hand down and pressed my index and middle finger against the crotch of her panties, feeling the heat and dampness under my fingertips. The sudden force caused Kira's ass to tighten and her body to shake, and the impeded moan she managed to let out told me that edging her had been very worth it. "I could make poor little Kira come in about five seconds if I wanted to..."

I massaged Kira with my fingers, keeping the pressure firm and unceasing, "it's just a shame she's not allowed to come no matter how good this feels...how much she absolutely loves that her beloved Mistress Morrigan has finally started paying attention to her begging little slit...

how much she enjoys that her wife is seeing her get fucked like this without even a thread of jealousy or judgment."

Hanna looked on in a daze of arousal, biting her lip, her hands clenched against her side. "That's...fuck." Hanna said, looking back to Kira and seeing just how much she was being brought to the brink, how close she was to the edge. Seeing this awakening within Hanna was catnip for me, but I knew I shouldn't push it too far.

"Hanna, our subject is ready for the second clamp... more than ready based on how disgustingly soaked she is. Now, were you watching while I put the first clamp onto Kira's nipple?"

Hanna nodded. "Y...yes. I was paying...very close attention." Hanna said, almost as if she were proud to have done something right.

"Good." I pulled my hand away from Kira and wiped my fingers against her thigh. "Do as I did, place the tongs on either side of her little pink nipple, then press the plate up until our little lamb squeals...then go just a little further, Hanna, I promise it won't hurt much more, but she'll thank you for it later.

"Uh...yeah...alright..." Hanna walked toward myself and Kira, my hands still feeling the tight, warm muscles of the shivering sub's inner thighs. She picked up the other clamp and placed it on Kira's nipple, her hands shaky and unsure, but when the metal clamp held true, she seemed to calm down. "So just...push up?"

"Yes, Hanna, gently. Watch how Kira's nipple reacts to the pressure, how it gets more red, how the skin around it blushes. The pain of it makes your body crave the pleasure that much more, the endorphins and adrenaline mixing to make a cocktail more powerful than any drug..."

Hanna pushed the small plate upward, as slowly and careful as I had, telling me she indeed had been observing me intently. "Like that?" She looked at Kira, whose eyes were shut tight and her moans muffled.

"You can push just a little harder, Hanna...but yes, that's good. Very, very good. Our little lamb is over the moon with how this feels on her depraved little body..."

With the last small adjustment, Hanna yelped against the ball gag and patted her feet on the ground in ecstasy. "Right there will do, Hanna. Now, do you see the chain that connects these devious little clips?"

"Yeah." Hanna nodded.

"Grasp the chain in the middle, and walk back one step. We're going to show Kira that her little nipples are ours to use and abuse, Hanna."

"S--sure..." Hanna said, looking down to evaluate the chain in her hand. "Also, um, your wife, she can...I don't want her, like...left out..." she shrugged.

I was honestly impressed and pleased at the sentiment. "I understand, Hanna...how do you suggest we rectify this situation?"

Hanna seemed a bit surprised, "You don't want to... put clamps on her too, do you?"

I stifled a laugh and looked over at Wendy, who had probably been subconsciously begging me to pull her off the bench for twenty minutes at this point and was ready to rip off her clothes and subject herself to whatever I would give. "I think Wendy would agree to such things... right, my dear?"

"Of course..." Wendy said, trying her best to seem calm and collected.

"Perhaps, Hanna, I can show you on Wendy what I want you to do on Kira. It might be the one learning experience where the teachers enjoy the curriculum just as much as the students..."

NINE

I STOOD NEXT TO HANNA, both of our subs sitting on their chairs, a matched pair, a mirror image of subjugation. I had affixed more threatening nipple clamps to Wendy, little alligator clips tightened by a screw, without the training wheels of the rubber tips, but the rest of the scene was virtually the same.

"Now, Hanna, the thing to remember when binding a sensitive area like this is that subtle contrasts can make a world of difference. You see, if I pull the chain back just an inch, increase the pressure just a bit..." I did just that, watching the clips pull at Wendy's nipples, drawing them toward me, the weight of her large breasts feeling wonderful, allowing me to move so subtly but still see pleasing results "...it can drive a little slut crazy, can't it?" I said.

"Fuck...fuck yes it can...thank you Mistress Morrigan." Wendy gasped.

We had disposed of the ball gags on both subjects because I worried that Kira would need to reassure

Hanna that the pain was acceptable. "Do the same for your subject, Hanna. Pull the chain tight, just a little, lift Kira's little tits toward you..."

"Um, ok." Hanna reached out for the chain, but looked toward Kira. She gave her a look of 'I'm not sure I should be doing this,' which Kira nodded, and then Hanna took the chain in her fingers and gave it the slightest pull, tugging at Kira's nipples. Kira bit her lip and grabbed the underside of her chair at the pressure. "Fuck...Kira, is it OK?"

"Oh...no...the pain...it's too much, Mistress, I can't take it..."

"Oh...uhh...sorry..."

I saw Hanna give the chain some slack and decided to step in. "Mistress Hanna, do remember that whiny, bratty subs like these will lie to you and tell you they don't want more pain, that it's too much, but look into their eyes...in their depraved minds, they're enjoying all of this, somehow."

Kira whimpered. I could tell she was loving the admonition, and Hanna got my point, because she tugged again, harder. This time Kira groaned against her gag. "She really did like it..."

"She may have loved it, Hanna, which is why it's our job to correct them. This is not normal behavior..." I pulled the clamps on Wendy, tugging her rather roughly, harder than Hanna would with Kira. "Is it, Wendy? Aren't you ashamed of the fact that you enjoy this?"

"Mmm...oh...Mistress, yes...I'm so ashamed..."

"This isn't how normal girls should act...they should be obedient and proper. But look at you two...tits on display, begging to be hurt." I twisted the chain in my hand, pulling Wendy's nipples to their limit just for a moment before easing up. "Wendy, crawl to me. I want to see just how a good girl can end up as tarnished as you."

Wendy complied because, well, she had to, I was in charge. She crawled toward me, her large breasts dangling, the chain making soft clinking noises as she approached. She was only wearing a pair of striped blue and white panties because we genuinely did not think that Hanna and Kira would have agreed to bring Wendy into the mix, but my wife wasn't going to let something like boring underwear keep her from having fun. With knowing movements, as Wendy had gone through this routine with me many times before, she completed the short distance of her crawl and sat up on her knees, her heels against her ass. Her face shimmering and beautiful, ready for punishment. Perfectly obedient.

"They are fun, though, Hanna...don't think something this broken and far gone can't be worth at least a little joy before they're so used up you just discard them..." I ran my hand through Wendy's hair, messing it up, trying to chip away at her beauty, as tough as that was. "They'll do what you want...anything..." I put my hand on the back of Wendy's head and pushed her face against me, lifting up my skirt to let her head slip underneath. Wendy needed no further instruction. "They're usually not that good..." I said, outright lying as my mind exploded with pleasure when Wendy started eating me out. "But...they'll do, and they usually are half decent with their tongues..."

I tried not to show it too much, but it was extremely difficult to hide how well Wendy was working me over. I tried to look like I was still in complete control, even with my dress pulled up around my hips, Wendy's head between my thighs.

"If you need some relief, Hanna, you should bring your pet over..." I said through tremors of pleasure running through my body.

"Oh, fuck, I mean, if that's ok..." Hanna looked to Kira and bit her lip, trying her best to be Mistress Hanna and failing a bit. "Sorry, Mistress Morrigan, it's just so hot and..."

"Hanna, have that sorry little slut eat your pussy right now, you're getting too distracted..."

It was, yes, a risk to go over the top and out-domme Hanna, but my intuition told me that I was just expressing what she wanted. That's another thing I loved about all of this unusual hobby...sometimes in the heat of passion, in letting your impulses run free, in just fucking *saying it* because you could, you found deeper truths. You dared yourself to cross thresholds you never thought you could. And yes, it was scary, but sometimes you found yourself on the other side, wondering how you'd lived so much of your life being afraid of trying that thing, of making that demand, of expressing your deepest desires and having them fulfilled.

"On your knees." Hanna said, staring at Kira with a newfound intensity. Another tally mark for intuition.

"Wendy, don't think that gives you any fucking right to stop." I said, slapping my wife's face lightly to direct her back to me.

Kira dropped to her knees and approached her wife. I was too distracted with Wendy's mouth, which was truly working me into a frenzy. "Slower." Hanna said, her hands trembling slightly.

Now this was a moment I didn't want my dear wife to miss, so I pushed Wendy's head back to silently tell her she needed to pause. She stopped and looked up at me, awaiting another command, when I jerked my head to the side slightly for her to point her attention toward the scene unfolding between Hanna and Kira.

"Earn the right to come to me." Hanna said, the tone of her voice becoming more firm and decisive. Kira padded along the ground, trying to take as much time as she could to cross the ten or so feet between the two of them.

Hanna watched her, like a cat about to pounce on an injured bird. I was thrilled. When Kira reached her wife, Hanna looked down at her, expression motionless and stoic, despite the certain storm that was rollicking Hanna's desires.

"Do you know how to remove a woman's clothing, pet?" Hanna said. I could tell that this was the moment when the character really started to set in, when the domme was able to detach from reality and let her base instincts play. It was truly freeing. And, sometimes, it was dangerously freeing, so myself and Wendy watching this wasn't entirely for our prurient interests, but also for safety ones, so we could intervene if it looked like Hanna was going too far.

"Y-yes, Mistress Hanna...I can, um, help you get out of your clothes..."

"Good, pet, good. I hope your hands don't fail you, I don't like my things to disappoint me..."

Kira was truly shaking now. As if all of this lead-up hadn't been enough overload for her, the prospect of her wife really, really getting into it must have sent her into another dimension. She reached up and unbuttoned Hanna's jeans, then drew the zipper down. Kira then reached up and gently tugged the jeans down from Hanna's hips, letting them fall to their knees. Hanna was wearing an understated red thong, but one didn't really need fancy underwear when they had tattoos that made them already look like art.

With whimpers and sounds of effort, Kira got the pants down to Hanna's ankles, and Hanna stepped out of them.

"Fold them." Hanna commanded.

Now I knew it was probably a breach of ethics or the psychosexual contract a domme and sub agreed upon to demand they do something as debased and profane as household chores, but I did make a mental note that Hanna had just given me a new way to make laundry day go smoother next time.

Kira, looking properly chastised, picked up Hanna's jeans and folded them carefully. As she did this, Hanna watched every move with rapt attention.

"Do you think you've earned the right to taste me, pet?" Hanna said.

Kira whimpered, and her face looked crestfallen.

"Answer the question. Do you think you've earned it?" Hanna repeated, more force in her voice this time.

Kira whimpered. "No...I've barely done anything for you, Mistress."

"You're right...you have to earn the right to my pussy...

but I want you to taste it, just so you know what you're going to miss out on." Hanna said.

Kira's face brightened a little bit. "Th--thank you, Mistress" she said.

Hanna nodded and slipped her thumbs into the elastic waist of her underwear. "Come and taste it." She let her thong fall to her feet and Kira approached her wife, hands grasping Hanna's firm thighs.

Kira moved her head forward, her tongue tentatively moving outward toward Hanna's slit. As soon as the tongue made contact, Hanna took hold of her wife's hair.

"You think you've earned more than that?"

"Please...please...Mistress..." Kira begged.

"Fine." Hanna sighed and pressed Kira's head into her hips. Kira moaned following the sudden movement and got to work on Hanna.

My crush on Hanna was already pretty intense at the start of this, but seeing her standing there, body chiseled like a Greek statue, her muscles tensing and flexing as she opened herself up to her submissive wife, I had no defenses to falling deeply for the woman right then and there.

But I knew that right now, despite all I had said before about ceding control and letting base instincts take over, I knew it would be wrong to even think about joining Hanna and Kira. As a matter of fact, I halfway wondered if they even realized we were still in the room.

"Good girl...do you like how I taste, baby?" Hanna groaned.

Kira answered Hanna's question by intensifying her efforts, lapping at Hanna, taking her clit into her mouth, using every ounce of knowledge she had on the woman. It seemed like this was the moment they had both been waiting for.

"I want an answer, Kira, I want you to tell me..." Hanna grew in intensity, and I was overwhelmed to see the emergence of a side of her that she probably thought she wasn't capable of.

Kira pulled away, her mouth shining from her wife's juices. "I love how you taste, Mistress." Kira said.

"Then get back to eating me, slut."

Kira dove back in, more energetic than ever, and it seemed like Hanna was balancing all of her weight against her wife's face...maybe to a slightly dangerous degree.

"Very very slightly yellow light, but, that angle can be a little...risky once it comes time to...well, I don't think it's much of an assumption to say that Hanna is going to come pretty soon..."

"God...fucking yes I am..." Hanna looked up at me, her eyes glittering, recognizing my and Wendy's presence once again.

"It might be safer if I just...held you from behind to stabilize you?"

This wasn't just me trying to get close to Hanna, I swear. The chance of strained muscles or compressions on either party when things got this intense was a genuine concern...but, OK, I also did just want to be close to Hanna.

"S--sure..." Hanna said, barely able to focus even though Kira wasn't actively eating her out.

I got behind her, wrapping my hands around her

torso, holding her tight. This also gave me a much better view of the proceedings.

"Green light?" I said.

"Fucking...green, yes." Hanna said and Kira echoed.

Kira resumed, and now that she knew Hanna was close to the finish line, she wasn't letting up. Hanna's skin was warm against mine, her shoulders pressing back into my chest. I was close enough to hear every breath, every adjustment, every lap of Kira's tongue that was driving Hanna wild.

Hanna moaned, and her muscles clenched under my hands, "God...god I'm about to..." Hanna moaned, then I heard her breath catch. "Kira...god yes..." I felt Hanna's body shaking, but my own grip held her tight so she wouldn't fall. "Grab my tits, Mistress, please..." Hanna winced as she boiled over.

I didn't have to be told twice. I slid my hands up Hanna's front and took her breasts into my hands, grabbing them and straining the fabric of her bra. So hard that I probably stretched it out and I would need to gift Hanna a new one, but that was a problem for later, for after her earth-shattering orgasm.

"Grab me harder!" Hanna yelled, a fury and intensity firing off in her, unlocking new realms of power to lay with. It was enough to scare an inexperienced domme, but I could tell passion from aggression, and Hanna was entirely occupied with passion. I complied, digging my hands into her breasts as much as I could. "Yes! I'm coming! Fuck...Kira...I love you..."

My grip was all that was keeping her upright as Hanna lost all of her senses to the power of her orgasm.

When things were this intense, standing up sometimes became a very dangerous proposition. "Yes, Hanna...give yourself to her...feel how good Kira is making you come... she feels so good against you..."

Hanna shook, my grip helping her stay upright. Kira pulled away, breathing just as heavily as her wife was. She stood up and watched Hanna recover for a moment, then placed a hand on her cheek and kissed her softly, gently, giving her all of the care and affection she could in the moment. I loosened my embrace as Hanna regained her own wherewithal so that the two of them could once again share the moment to themselves.

"Kira, that...baby...I'm so sorry I was skeptical..." Hanna laughed, her breathing calming from gasping heaves to something more controlled.

"It's...it's OK, I'm just glad you were willing to try it."

"Oh, we're definitely going to keep trying it, don't worry."

Kira smiled at Hanna and then looked up at me with a silent 'thank you' for orchestrating all of this. But I had only done so much...this would have been exceedingly normal if Hanna hadn't decided to step in.

Hanna went back in for another kiss and Kira pushed back slightly. "Baby, respectfully, I would love to make out with you all night but if I don't get off really soon I'm going to literally pass out..." Kira laughed a bit at the admission.

Hanna smirked at her wife. "You know, I was so fucking turned on, I kinda forgot the whole reason we were here in the first place...did I leave you hanging, baby?" Hanna took her wife into her arms.

"A little, but...it's OK..." Kira grinned.

"Well, I mean, I get you every night, but Mistress Morrigan's only here tonight, so..." Hanna looked back at me.

"Is that...OK? If she...does it?" Kira said.

"Of course," Hanna said, releasing her embrace and stepping to the side, so I was in front of Kira again. "She's all yours, Mistress..."

"Oh, little lamb, you're going to regret that decision..." I said with a smirk, reminding Kira we weren't here for sweet kisses and warm embraces, at least not entirely.

TEN

HANNA HAD JUST HAD what was probably one of the best orgasms of her life, so her collapsing on the couch she'd begun the night on, still reeling from everything, wasn't much of a surprise.

"What makes you think you even deserve to come, Kira?" I said, reaching for the nipple chain and pulling it. "Because you licked your wife's pussy? Do you think that makes you special?"

Kira let out a scream and whimpered at the sudden pain, her breasts pulled forward from my tight hold.

"N...no...it's...I just..."

"I didn't give you permission to speak. I'm going to ask your Mistress if you deserve it, and you're going to stay quiet until I say so."

Kira was clearly getting back into the groove, hard, and was almost too excited to return to the pain and pleasure I had planned. I could tell she was about to reply with a 'Yes, Mistress', but caught herself and bit her tongue in a way that was so utterly adorable.

"Mistress Hanna, do you believe sweet little Kira deserves the right to come after all she's done?"

"Hmm...she does look pretty pitiful." Hanna adjusted herself on the couch, her long legs folding, "But I wonder if she needs to earn that orgasm by showing Mistress Morrigan how well she can eat pussy." Hanna leveled a seductive smile at me.

"Do you think so, Hanna?" I said. I was so close to crossing that boundary. Tonight was supposed to be about giving, not receiving, and I genuinely didn't have plans on having Kira get me off during the scene, but, if given the offer. "Kira, do you think that's an appropriate way to show your worth?"

Kira nodded, keeping her vow of silence intact.

"Mmm, yes, I think she'd look quite lovely in between your legs, Mistress Morrigan." Hanna said. Wendy joined Hanna on the couch, but was maintaining a respectful distance.

"God, you're a depraved little slut, aren't you, Kira?" I said, lightly tapping her face with my fingers, feeling the sticky sweetness of Hanna still on her. "You're salivating at the idea of eating another woman's pussy while you dear wife watches...what do you have to say for yourself?"

"I--I...I want to make you come, Mistress, more than anything...I know I'm worthless but..."

I pushed Kira back slightly, "You don't get to determine your worth, Kira, I do. Now give me some room and await my instructions."

Kira stepped back, the nipple chains slinking and reflecting in the light. I walked over to the chair Kira had been using that was still in the middle of the room. I made sure to swing my hips as I walked away from Kira to give her the extra tease, because this whole thing was making me feel better than I had in weeks.

I stopped in front of the chair and reached under my dress. There wasn't any particularly elegant or even sexy way to remove one's underwear from beneath a dress, but I tried. And judging by the enamored gaze Kira was giving me when I turned around to sit in the chair, I don't think I lost much favor with my awkward moves.

"Kneel before me."

Kira approached, her steps delicate and unsure, but also so aroused, her body shaking. "Mistress..."

"Don't talk, Katie. Do not say one more word before you make me come on your pretty little face." I said, sneering. I spread my legs and hiked my skirt up, since I knew Kira was already exhausted and the extra challenge of navigating things with the skirt still down would have been too much, surely.

I knew that Wendy and Hanna were watching, and that Kira was already well aware, but I decided that they should be a bigger part of this moment than just mere witnesses.

"Mistress Hanna, it should go without saying that you're free to use my wife for any purposes you'd like while I judge poor Kira's worth." I turned to the two of them with a grin. I knew Wendy was as pent-up as I was, and I hoped Hanna would be happy to take care of that.

"You...you don't mind?" Hanna said, almost unable to process the permission.

"It is our duty, isn't it?" Wendy said with a grin. "I

mean, pitiful little subs aren't being useful if we aren't working to make our Mistresses feel divine."

I let them do what they desired and turned my attention back to Kira, who was waiting patiently on her knees, begging me with her eyes for the signal to taste me.

"I could make you sit here the rest of the night, Kira. I could tell you to keep waiting, until your thighs burned, and your body gave out. I could keep you from having the privilege of tasting me for the rest of eternity. I want you to realize that. Do you understand that, Kira?"

"Yes...Mistress...I understand. I will serve you, however long you want, however you want...I want to be what you desire..."

"You're so sweet, Kira. But what ever should I do about disobedient little subs who speak after their Mistress has expressly forbidden it?" I said, the intensity growing in me.

"You punish them, Mistress. You make them your toy." Kira returned the exact same intensity. Oh, it was such a rush to get a sub who fought back.

"Give me your fucking chain, Kira. You have no idea how much trouble you're in." I snapped.

"Yes, Mistress..." Kira whimpered, her shoulders tensing as she gathered the fine silver chain into her hand and presented it to me.

"Thank you." I took it in my hands. "It looks like your clamps have loosened since I put them on, Kira. Please correct that."

"Thank you, Mistress. You're too kind to me..." she reached for her right breast and made a face as she applied pressure, slowly and surely. The chain hung taut. "Should I..."

"Push it until it hurts and then push further? Yes, Kira, you're learning." I gritted my teeth.

Kira looked at me with animalistic lust as she pulled the clamp nearly to the top so that it was the tightest it could go. Her nipple was strawberry red pinched between the two tongs. For extended use it would have been inadvisable, but it was safe enough for the finale.

Kira did the same with the other clamp and presented herself to me, her nipples bound tightly.

"It's good to know you can occasionally follow instructions, lamb." I wrapped the chain around my hand and tugged, drawing Kira in. "Now, get to licking, and pray to your gods you don't disappoint me, Kira."

"Thank you, Mistress...I don't deserve..."

"Now. Or you'll spend the rest of the night in handcuffs while Wendy, Hanna and myself go off and have a wonderful evening out without the disobedient sub that didn't lick her Mistress when she asked..."

Kira put her hands on my thighs, gripping my skin as she started licking, tasting, making me hers. She was damn good, eager and enthusiastic.

"Fuck..." I tugged on the chain to give Kira extra stimulus and tried not to fall entirely into the bliss of having her go down on me.

I heard moans and shuffling to my left, and looked up to see Wendy's mouth on Hanna's chest as she pulled and squeezed and played with Hanna's breasts. Hanna had her eyes shut, lost to the feelings my wife was giving her.

I was glad they were enjoying themselves as much as Kira and I.

"A good girl couldn't eat pussy like this, Kira. Shame on you for thinking you were ever a good girl..." I ran my hand through Kira's hair, preening, admiring her cute face as it worked me over.

She groaned against me. I tugged the chain for my pleasure and to remind her of her place. Kira responded with even more energy, working my clit, flicking it with her tongue.

"That's my fucking girl. You only exist to eat my pussy. Do not hold back, Kira, or I'll know..."

I was beyond close. Usually when a client was getting me off, I did everything I could to extend things as far as I could, but that wasn't a choice now.

"I'm going to come all over your face, little lamb, I want you to make me come, do you understand? This is why you exist. You have a purpose in this world. You are my pet, I am your Mistress, and you get to have a purpose. Slide your tongue inside me, lamb, taste me..." I couldn't resist rolling my eyes back in my head as Kira moaned loudly against my thigh before sinking her tongue into me. When I glanced over to see Hanna's hand down the front of Wendy's panties, her fingers taking my wife over the edge as well, I lost it.

I don't even know how I managed to stay conscious with how hard I came. Kira was merciless with me, she kept licking, she knew that it wasn't enough, that my pleasure was the only thing that mattered right now, and she didn't want to risk her very fragile standing with me, even if in reality I would protect this girl to the ends of the earth.

"Kira...fucking hell..." I continued to feel the orgasm releasing from my body, Kira keeping pace. "Good...girl..." I said, looking up to the ceiling.

After a long while, when it seemed like I had emptied everything I had, Kira pulled her mouth from between my legs, "Please, Mistress...please..."

"Lay on your back and take off your panties. I'm only going to give you one chance to have me do this to you." I said firmly. I had no idea how I was able to summon any more Mistress Morrigan energy after being so utterly drained by Kira.

"Th...thank you...thank you...Mistress..." Kira whimpered, and fell to her back and wriggled her hips so her panties came off. "Thank you, Mistress..."

"Keep thanking me, slut..." I dropped to my knees and grabbed Kira's thighs to get her more near to me. She smelled divine, the perfect little sub. I didn't waste any time. I let my tongue trace over her, getting to know every little spot of Kira that was most sensitive, licking her, drawing her in.

"Thank you...thank you Mistress, thank you..." Kira begged me, and I was more than happy to keep eating her out. "Oh please, Mistress, don't stop..." Kira begged, "Please..."

"You're such a dirty, dirty fucking girl, Kira..." I said in the moment when I was catching my breath before devouring her more.

"Fuck..." Hanna moaned and Wendy echoed a similar

noise, both of them giving their own final thrusts against each other, sharing their own climax.

I redoubled my efforts with Kira, and the little lamb didn't last much longer.

"Oh...Mistress Morrigan...thank you...thank you... thank you....fuck....fuck my slut pussy..." Kira babbled as her pleasure poured over. She grabbed the chain at the last second to increase the pain, the pressure, to feel everything. "Oh, fuck me!" she cried out as I brought her over the edge, and the rest of her body fell limp, the chain the only taut thing on her body.

I gave her one last long, deep, slow lick to get her to the very end of her orgasm and to remind her I could give her more if I wanted, and she writhed at the sensation.

"Fuck..." Kira gasped.

"I thought you might like that, little lamb..." I said as I moved my mouth away from Kira's body.

ELEVEN

"HOW...HOW can something feel that good?" Kira said, sitting on the bed next to Hanna, an ice pack pressed to her thoroughly overworked nipples.

"Good practice, arousal, and creativity can do a hell of a lot." I smiled, wiping my neck with a warm towel while Wendy stretched her legs across my lap, brandishing the same ice pack Kira was soothing herself with.

"But, like, wow, that was really really...wow. It felt like something in my brain clicked, or snapped, or, like, got flipped in some way and I just...wanted it more."

"It can be addictive, Kira...but, remember you can't do it every time, for your sake and Hanna's sake." Wendy smiled.

"But we can...do it sometimes, right, babe?" Kira rolled to the side and bumped her shoulder against Hanna.

"Yes...yes, sometimes, we can." Hanna sighed, the euphoria of the scene and orgasm still pulsing in her body. "A...lot of times, we can..." Hanna smiled, a new edge to her voice.

DEMONOLOGY

ONE

THERE'S no firm rule saying that a dominatrix has to wear leather or latex. Sometimes, everyday clothes can be much more exciting than the shiny bustiers or forceful platform boots.

If you were so inclined, you can, at great effort, make your BDSM play room look very much like a mundane, boring office, where you could imagine a mundane, boring interview taking place...well, the interview is boring until the woman across the desk begins asking increasingly explicit and demeaning questions. Or maybe you'd like to imagine a booth at a restaurant where you can find out just how much that cute waitress despises you. Then again, perhaps you'd prefer a dressing room at a high-end lingerie boutique where the clerk will tell you with complete certainty that you're wearing the piece wrong, and she will show you how it properly fits your body...or else.

Since getting into the role of being a professional domme, my wife at my side as my chaotic and eager assistant, I started thinking about why almost all of BDSM seemed to take place within a very specific aesthetic. Nothing against the ropes, the chains, the rib-cracking corsets and the shimmery silver handcuffs, but I found that people's fantasies were far more diverse, and a little mise-en-scén could give a client that extra bit of immersion, that extra permission to engage their deepest fantasies in a place that closely resembled the initial spark of that fantasy, or the idealized location for it to take place.

It was unconventional...it required far more subtle roleplaying and research, and it cost way more than buying a bunch of costumes and toys in red, black, or purple, and I knew it wasn't everyone's cup of tea. But, for some of the women who came to Club Crescent, the ones willing to pay the premium cost of Wendy and I delivering a fully immersive fantasy...I'm pretty sure I could ask any amount, and they would still be beating down my door for the opportunity to experience it.

Today, Wendy and I were sitting in that boring interview room I mentioned earlier, awaiting our prey. My costume was easy, since I just pulled a suit that had seen enough days in the courtroom that I wouldn't mind if it got a little messy. Wendy wasn't much for suits or business wear at all, but the charming little charcoal grey dress with a matching jacket that we got at a discount store fit her like a glove, even if it was threatening to burst at the seams...which is exactly what we wanted.

"She's three minutes late." Wendy said, looking at her watch and then at me.

"Well, that certainly is going to hurt her chances at this job, isn't it, Aosoth?"

"Indeed..." Wendy smiled, her eyes locked on the door. Since we had decided to take things in this direction, both of us had really gotten into the idea of selling these fantasies to our clients. We wanted things to be at least reasonably accurate, and so today we had even gone to the effort of printing out fake business reports and writing random corporate jargon on a whiteboard behind us. In a very, very clever idea, Wendy had formatted our unlucky client's kink list as her resume. I don't know if listing biting and orgasm denial on your list of skills would do much for a person for any other job, but right now, it was very necessary information.

"I suppose she might as well give up now. If she's late for the interview, then I can't even begin to imagine how tardy she'd be once hired." I said, looking at my wife and trying to hide my amusement at her complete dedication to the act.

Before Wendy had a chance to reply, there was a knock at the door. I looked at my watch, which read 8:04. Four minutes late to a job interview...god, she must really yearn to be punished.

"Come in!" I said to the door as Wendy got up and went over to it to open it for the client.

When she opened the door, I was greeted by a short woman with wide hips, chubby cheeks, and a curvy figure that wasn't all that different than my dear wife's. Oh, this poor woman had no idea what she had signed up for.

"Penelope?" Wendy said, looking at the woman.

"Y--yes...that's me..." she said, chipper and gleeful. She probably forgot that she'd picked the code name, so the stammering in reaction to 'Penelope' was most likely genuine.

"I'm Aosoth, and this is..." Wendy turned to me and directed Penelope's attention to the desk.

"Morrigan...and, Penelope, as you sit down in the chair across from me, I think you should begin by explaining why you think it's appropriate to show up four minutes and thirty-six seconds late to an interview." I said, keeping my face neutral, verging on disdain.

I watched as she looked back to my wife for a brief second.

"Oh, uhm..."

"If you can't even think of an explanation, Penelope..."

"No...I do! There was...uh...traffic. And...my bus was late." Penelope said as she walked across the office and scanned the room. I saw a bit of Tiffany, the actual name of the woman who had signed up for us tonight, marvel in glee at how accurate everything was.

"A bus...dear...god...Penelope. Peach Corp is a high-end, demanding business. Our employees simply don't ride the bus, ever." I said.

"I'm...I'm sorry! I've had trouble getting a car!"

"We know." Wendy said, her voice sounding like she had already resigned the woman to failure, "In fact, it was the first thing I checked when I reviewed your application, and your resume..." I flipped through the papers and acted like I was reading them deeply, "I'm going to be completely honest with you, Penelope, I am not really sure why Aosoth here even thought you were worth the time to interview."

"Oh..." Penelope's voice became slightly somber.

"Yeah...you really don't have any sort of skills or qualifications that would be appropriate for a position at Peach Corp. No experience whatsoever...your red lace bra is showing through the gap of your shirt, and I can see the milky white cleavage of your big tits just begging for my attention. Were you aware that anyone looking at you in that shirt can basically see your breasts, Penelope?" I said.

"Y--yeah..."

"Do you mean yes, Miss Morrigan? You are not addressing your potential boss properly."

"Yes...yes, Miss Morrigan, I am sorry that my attire is...revealing." Penelope said.

"Sorry? Why be sorry? Those things are the only reason you're still sitting in this room and this interview is continuing. Those big tits are probably the only reason a lot of people give you any kind of attention, aren't they?" I said, putting the papers down and leaning forward at the desk.

"Yeah...probably, Miss Morrigan. My ass is really fat too...it gets a lot of attention. Men love grabbing it, pulling my skirt up to touch it, to slap it. It gets so sore when that happens."

"Do not fucking mention men in my presence..." I looked to the side and gathered myself, as if the mere reminder of the existence of men filled me with venom. I mean, not quite, but the reality was pretty close.

"Oh, shit. I'm sorry, Miss Morrigan..." she said.

"Language...Penelope...I'm just going to update you

here, things are not looking good." I took a pen and made some random, but realistic-looking scribbles on one of the pieces of paper. "Aosoth, begin the questions, I want to get out of here, I have dinner reservations."

Wendy shuffled the papers in her hands, then looked up at Penelope with a grin.

"Penelope...what skills and attributes do you bring to this company that could possibly make you stand out from our other applicants?"

"Other than your floppy tits and spankable ass, of course." I offered with a smirk.

"Uh..." She looked down and then to Wendy. "Well, I have good customer service skills...and I know how to bend over when a woman in authority demands it...I have lots of experience at that."

"What do you mean by that, Penelope? Do you think myself or Aosoth would even consider doing that to you? Do you think that's acceptable office behavior?" I said.

"Well, no, but I just...I was hoping maybe there'd be an exception." she said, looking to us, her face painted in desperation.

"Hmm...you know, there is one thing, Penelope...you do seem to be rather cool under pressure." I lied, but I had to move the story along. "But I want to test that."

"How...how would you test that?" Penelope looked around the room.

"My dear assistant Aosoth here is going to unzip her dress and she will expose her breasts to you. She will then ask you some further questions. Under no circumstances should you even glance for a moment at Aosoth's large, delicious, luscious breasts...breasts with dark nipples that will be as hard as rocks, presented to you, mere inches from your face. You will answer the questions, and you will not be distracted. Am I clear?" I said.

Penelope gulped and nodded. "Yes...I guess...I mean, I really want this job..."

"If you do, then you can ignore Aosoth's delicious, perfectly round tits." I said as Wendy undid the buttons on her shirt, and her bra was revealed, just as I promised. She pushed her breasts up out of the bra so they were mostly showing, the nipples I had described to Penelope looking particularly delicious tonight.

"You get one look, Penelope. One single glance. And from then on, I will watch your eyes. If they drift down to Aosoth's perfect, massive tits, you will be punished. You won't get the easy exit of being dismissed from the interview, oh no...the stakes are far more dire now, you miserable girl." I said.

Penelope took her allotted glance at Wendy's chest and smiled a bit. I couldn't blame her, everything I had said about my wife's breasts was completely true.

"Now, Aosoth, do your thing. Ask the questions Penelope will fail to answer sufficiently." I said, folding my hands in my lap, preparing to watch the show.

"Penelope...I am going to ask you a few simple questions. Just everyday, honestly boring things." Wendy reached out and grabbed her stack of papers, then positioned her arms in a way that pushed her tits together, making them look even bigger.

I saw Penelope gulp, and I knew this was going to be an exercise in the woman's ability to resist her every instinct.

"What are the top four selling flavors of ice cream at Peach Corp?"

"Uhm...ahh..." Penelope frittered. This was amazing, because Wendy had the genius foresight to actually provide Tiffany with a fact sheet about Peach Corp that she was instructed to memorize before our session. All of those facts were about a company that made furniture, not ice cream. No matter how diligently Penelope had prepared, there was no way for her to be correct in this. "Cookies and cream...chocolate...peppermint...and... peach." Penelope nodded confidently, and I have to applaud the girl, her gaze didn't waver from Wendy's eyes.

Wendy laughed a bit. "So...so confident. Miss Morrigan...how could someone be so confident and answer that peach is our best-selling flavor when Peach Corp has never had a peach-flavored ice cream on its menu in its entire 135-year existence?"

"I don't know...seems pretty bad, getting something that easy that incorrect." I smirked.

Penelope looked down at the desk for a second, "I'm so sorry Miss Morrigan, Miss Aosoth...I don't know why I got it wrong..."

"That's just one question...there are more. And you will answer them."

"Yes, of course..." Penelope closed her eyes and focused.

"Eyes open, Penelope. It's rude to take naps during interviews." I kicked the leg of the desk, moving it forward a couple of inches, just to scare Penelope.

She opened her eyes and nodded.

"Where is the headquarters of Peach Corp?"

"Uhm..."

"Is it Chicago?" I asked.

Penelope nodded and then immediately shook her head. "No...umm..."

"Penelope, I work here. Do you think I don't know where our headquarters are? I'm trying to fucking help you, you ignorant woman." I said.

"Oh, gosh, I'm so sorry, I...uh, it's Seattle! I know it's Seattle!" Penelope said.

"That's correct..." I smiled. The note on the fake fact sheet did indeed say Seattle, so I decided to give Penelope that one. "Aosoth, another question, dear."

Wendy adjusted the way she held her chest and the fabric shifted, revealing the bottoms of her nipples now.

"Why aren't you looking at my tits, Penelope?" Wendy said in the same neutral, dispirited tone of her previous questions.

"Wh--what?" Penelope's face fell into fear.

"I have my tits out, Penelope. It's so rude to not look at them. Do you think they're ugly?" Wendy said.

"N--no..." Penelope was looking to my face, but I stared back at her coldly. I wasn't going to intervene and give her permission to look down.

"Then look at them. I'm getting very aggravated that you're not staring at my big tits right now. What the fuck is wrong with you?" Wendy amped up the heat and the threat with an expert skill.

"I...I just...I have a really hard time concentrating and...oh god...I...I just need to..." Penelope's eyes moved down.

"Penelope." I stood up from my chair. In this position, I had incredible dominion over the short woman, and I knew I looked statuesque. "What was the one rule that I laid out before these questions began?"

"That...I..."

"What was it?"

Penelope's shoulders slumped, "That...that I was not supposed to look down at Aosoth's perfect breasts, her delicious nipples..."

"That's right, Penelope. You weren't, but you did. Do you have complete disregard for all rules, or just ones that keep you from being such a depraved fucking slut?" I walked around the desk and ambled behind Penelope's chair.

"No! It was just hard!" she whined.

"Excuses." I said, shaking my head. "You broke my one rule, you have to pay a price for that."

TWO

"SHE'S STILL LOOKING at them, Miss Morrigan." Wendy looked up to me with a devilish grin.

"Penelope...Penelope..." I put my hands on the woman's shoulders, grabbing them forcefully, shoving her harder against the chair she was sitting in. "Do you have any concept of how much you have just fucked up?"

Penelope began to cry. "No! No, I don't!"

"I think you deserve to get punished...to feel pain. You clearly have no sense of order, or structure...and...no morals." I slid my hand between the buttons on her shirt and pulled the left half forcefully, ripping off the top two buttons, the sound of the plastic clattering on the ground was the only thing audible in the room.

This was, of course, part of the plan. Tiffany had said she had a clothes ripping fetish, so everything the three of us were wearing tonight was designed to be ripped, torn, and savaged in any number of ways. Wendy had even cut small incisions into my jacket and pants and her own clothes so that they could be pawed away without any awkward (and potentially dangerous) tugging. I had to keep myself from getting too excited at the prospect of tearing Penelope's tights apart after a few well-placed bites...but, that would have to wait.

Oh, the biting didn't have to wait, though. Not at all. With Penelope's pale, shimmering shoulder exposed now that I had pulled her shirt back, I leaned down and sunk my teeth into the top of it, into her trapezius. You had to be careful when biting to not get close to any major artery or a place where the skin was particularly thin, because even though all parties tonight were properly and rigorously tested, I didn't have much of a stomach for accidental bloodletting...if people liked that, they could find other dommes that would be happy to.

But, anyway, I returned my mind to sinking my teeth into Penelope, literally. There was plenty of muscle to bite into in the bicep and shoulder, and so I allowed myself extra pressure, knowing it would be exactly what Tiffany wanted.

I pulled my head back and held Penelope's cheek from the opposite side of her face. "You taste pretty sweet for someone so utterly rotten, Penelope."

"Thank you...thank you so much..."

"Aosoth...touch those big, gorgeous tits for me, dear. Make them jiggle for her, while she stares at them...she's clearly not going to stop staring."

Wendy smiled and did just that, rolling her breasts in her hands, pinching the nipples, giving Penelope and me a hell of a show.

"Do you like them, Penelope? You can be honest with

me. Tell me what you think about Aosoth's tits." I whispered.

Penelope gulped, "I love them...I would suck her nipples so much...if I could...if that were appropriate..."

"Is that an appropriate thing to ask, Penelope? At a job interview of all things? To ask if you can suck the interviewer's delicious nipples?" I said.

Penelope gulped.

"Answer, slut. Answer. You better be fucking honest with me or there is going to be more biting."

"N--no, it isn't appropriate!"

"Wrong!" I bellowed, taking the other half of her shirt and pulling at it, the rest of the buttons skittering across the ground, leaving Penelope exposed in her strawberry-red bra. "If the interviewer is offering it, you can ask to suck their tits. I can't believe you could miss such an obvious question."

Penelope pouted a bit. "Aosoth...can I...am I able to suck your...your nipples?"

"No..." Wendy said with a smirk, the line so deadpan and cruel I could have passed out at how perfect it was.

"It was worth a try." I said, smiling as I wrapped my arms around the woman, grabbing at her bra, pulling the cups down and allowing her tits the freedom of the cool air. They jiggled splendidly with the motion, now free from their confines. "Can you suck these yourself, Penelope? Give yourself a bit of a thrill if you're so fucking obsessed with sucking tits?" I gently flicked upward against Penelope's right breast, the nipple hardening.

"Yes, I...I can..."

"Well then...what are you fucking waiting for?" I said

as I moved to the front of the woman. She was, indeed, already beginning to suck on the nipple, her other hand finding the other breast and playing with it. "Do not touch that left tit, Penelope. God, just learn to follow directions and this interview will end with far less trauma."

Penelope was tearing up a little, and she looked up to me as she pulled her lips away from my tit, the nipple coated with her spit.

"This is all so mean, Miss Morrigan, but I don't want it to stop..."

"Then..." I took my foot and stomped it on the front of her chair, between her legs. I made sure there was plenty of room to bring my toe down with such force so close to her, but the dramatic thud had the exact effect I desired. "Don't. Fucking. Stop. Suck your tit, Penelope. Show me how you do it when you're alone in your bed, when nobody else is watching."

Penelope began again, the noise she made with each suck sounding more and more erotic, the motion of her lips more and more depraved and animalistic.

"That's right...she really loves it. She probably has to suck them herself because nobody else will..." Wendy said, eager to be the agent of chaos and the one with the meanest lines of the night. If I was the bad cop in our dynamic, Wendy was the utterly insane one.

"Can...can you step on me again...please..." Penelope begged between sucks.

"Hmmm..." I brought my foot down again, this time harder, since I knew that the landing zone was clear. "Like that?"

Penelope nodded, sucking her nipple with such fervor I was almost concerned, but she seemed to be enjoying it.

"It's pretty fucked up..." I stomped again in the same place, eliciting another yelp, "to want to have a woman come so close to crushing your little cunt while you suck your big, floppy tits..." I said.

"Fuck...yeah...I don't care how fucked up it is...I fucking need it..." Penelope was crying in joy at this point.

"Aosoth...I think little Penelope here was hiding a thing or two from us in her resume, and in this disaster of an interview." I ran my hand through Penelope's hair and guided her head back, denying her the pleasure of being able to suck her tits more. "I think Miss Penelope here is a depraved little slut that likes to be roughed up...likes to be told how fucking awful she is...I bet she even gets off on a beautiful woman tearing her tight clothes from her body and ravaging her...doesn't she?" I stared at Penelope, the glee in my eyes quite clear.

"Fuck..." Penelope muttered as Wendy walked to her side, "I...yeah...I want all of that. I need all of that."

"Oh, sweetheart...you don't need anything. You may want some things, but you don't deserve one single bit of my attention or labor." I straddled Penelope in the chair and put my hands on the center panel of her bra, between the cups, where she told us she had perforated the lace and removed the underwire so it could be torn off of her. And I'm sure she thought I was going to do that right now. "I may choose to bestow your little slut body with just a bit of attention to keep you from being so annoyingly fucking horny, but you don't get to demand a goddamn thing from me or Aosoth." I tightened my grip on the spot that would tear, but held off on putting enough pressure there, delaying the release that Penelope was screaming for inside.

"You may have given us that permission, but we don't want you, Penelope. You're too fucking weak. You're not worth our time." I leaned down and kissed the woman. Penelope returned my affection and opened her mouth. I loved this little inversion of things, following disgust and demeaning with sloppy, passionate lovemaking. It made the sub's body feel the emotional whiplash that they desired, and also gave me a little bit of pressure relief to get some kind of physical release after purposely denying myself from my subject.

"You are our plaything. You are a toy we might break. That's it." Wendy said, kneeling next to the two of us.

Penelope pulled her lips off of mine, "Can I be broken?"

"Oh, Penelope...I think you'd like that far too much for us to even consider it." I trailed my hand down the woman's thigh, felt the heat through her leggings. I felt a small irregularity in the smooth fabric, a tiny hole. I dug my finger into the hole, not having much help from my nails because, well, I had many reasons to keep my nails short. But, I found enough purchase to get my nail underneath the fabric and pulled, the ripping sound utterly satisfying. "Penelope...I guess you really are on the road to being broken if you come to a job interview in ripped leggings, aren't you?" I pulled a little harder, opening the rip more. The shimmering white of the inside of her thigh stood out so deliciously against the black fabric of the leggings.

Penelope whimpered, her voice dripping in desperate pleasure, "Yes, I'm such a fucking slut...I'm such a piece of trash...I'll let you break me...just break me."

THREE

I TURNED toward Wendy with a grin, "Aosoth, dear... what was it you said when Penelope here was begging to suck your tits? What was the word? I can't seem to remember it, but you delivered it with such venom..."

"I'm...I'm not sure, Mistress Morrigan." Wendy said, shrugging, playing up the melodrama of it.

"Oh...that's right...I remember..." I stood up and slammed my foot down in between Penelope's legs, hammering it harder than I had before. I leaned forward, craning my body toward her and taking my centre of gravity to a perilously dangerous spot, but it was worth the effort and I believed in my yoga skills. With my foot still planted firmly between Penelope's legs, the toe pressing ever so slightly against her vulva, I leaned forward and put my face next to Penelope's beet-red ear. "The word was...no." To make this moment even more euphorically overwhelming for poor Penelope, I used the position of my face next to her ear and closed my teeth gently on her earlobe, pulling it just so, enough that it hurt, enough that she loved it.

Penelope came, just from that, I knew. Her legs were trembling and her whole body tensed and released, and her voice became a guttural cry. It was perfect. I leaned back and took the center of her bra between my hands once again. "Oh, really, Penelope? You're so far gone, that made you come? How fucking pitiful..." I ripped the bra apart from the middle, Penelope's breasts spilling out as her body heaved and shuddered with orgasm.

"God, I've never seen someone orgasm for that long in my life." Wendy said, almost impressed. "She's playing it up. Mistress Morrigan, little Penelope is faking..."

I stepped back from my position. My yoga was good, but it wasn't good enough to hold that pose forever. "Is that so? Did you fake that orgasm, Penelope?"

"N--no! It...I can't fake an orgasm that long..."

I slapped Penelope across the face, utilizing the sly stage combat trick of bringing my left hand against my right after grazing Penelope's face with my fingertips, but still being able to end it with a painful sounding snap. "Don't lie. Fuck. Penelope. Don't fucking lie. I could fake an orgasm for an hour if I needed to...you're telling me you couldn't fake one for a couple of minutes?"

Penelope shook her head and winced. I think my slap was more powerful than I had planned. "I couldn't. I...I came...I really did..."

I leaned down to the ground and took one of the buttons off her shirt, then flicked it with my finger so it careened off of the back wall and danced along the ground. The echo of the button on the slate tiles was an acoustic orgasm in its own right. "I hope you don't expect us to reimburse you for the clothing we're ruining on your awful body tonight, Penelope..." I smiled.

Penelope's head drooped a little, and she began to tear up. "Please don't do this, Mistress Morrigan..."

"Oh...you're learning some manners now, huh? You didn't call me Miss Morrigan...you called me by my proper name. Aosoth...this little slut is learning! Isn't that cute?" I said, circling Penelope like a bird gliding around, looking for the next bit of prey to snatch.

"She's got such a big mouth now..." Wendy said.

"I know..." I swiped my thumb over Penelope's lips, dragging a crimson streak of lipstick across her cheek, "Imagine all the trouble she gets up to with this mouth, Aosoth..." I took my index finger and slipped it between Penelope's lips, drawing her jaw open and pressing the pad of it against her tongue. "Suck it, Penelope. Now."

Penelope obeyed, taking my finger deeper into her mouth. "That's good, Penelope..." I smiled as I looked at her with the finger between her lips. "Good girl...you're a fucking natural at sucking, aren't you?"

"I am..." Penelope said.

"Good girl...what do you want to do with that mouth next? How do you want to prove your worth?" I asked as I looked toward Wendy and raised my eyebrows. "Are you imagining one of Aosoth's big, hard nipples in your mouth? Do you have any idea how good she tastes, Penelope?"

Penelope looked up at me and nodded as I pulled my finger from her lips with a slight popping noise.

"Maybe...you want to put that mouth on my pussy..." I

trailed off as I looked at Wendy. "Do you think that's a good way to get a job from this interview? Putting your future boss on the desk and eating her pussy to show her how good of a girl you can be?"

Penelope's eyes lit up, "Please, please let me, Mistress Morrigan! I've wanted to taste you so much."

"Really..." I walked toward the desk. "Have you wanted to taste Aosoth's pussy as well?"

"Yes...god...yes, but...I think you deserve it more, you're the Mistress."

"Hmm..." I raised my eyebrows and looked at my nails, then back at Wendy. "Do you find that insulting, Aosoth? That Penelope thinks I taste better than you?"

"No, Mistress Morrigan, I know you have the most delicious pussy in the world." Wendy said with utter glee. She really did think that, and I had a lot of proof of it.

"You're a good girl too, Aosoth...just in a different way." I grinned. I walked toward the desk and turned around, sitting on it. Keeping my eyes fixed on Penelope, I reached under my skirt and pulled my panties down my thighs and then off of my legs entirely. I held them between my fingertips and dropped them on the desk, subtly telling Penelope we were not done with them tonight. "OK, Penelope, if you're such a pussy craving slut, come over here and prove it, eat my pussy."

"Fuck..." Penelope said, "Thank you...thank you so much for this...thank you for letting me be so lucky as to eat you..."

"It's a privilege...not a right. And don't disappoint me, Penelope."

I opened my legs just a little, enough that the space I

created would be frustrating for Penelope to work with. She had put orgasm denial on her card, and we had sort of blown it with her own orgasm, but I wondered how she would react to me denying my own orgasm.

Penelope put her face in between my legs and the feeling was pure bliss. Wendy walked toward us and then stood to my side.

"Let her eat it for a bit..." Wendy said as she stroked Penelope's hair, then grabbed a handful of it, pulling Penelope's mouth tighter to me.

"Oh...she's down there? I barely felt it." I said, sounding utterly bored. Because Penelope obviously couldn't see my face, I did flash a massive gleeful smile at Wendy to show her that Penelope was doing an amazing job, but I think my wife understood the game I was playing.

"She's working so hard, Mistress Morrigan. It's a shame it's doing nothing." Wendy said.

I looked down to Penelope. "Do you need some help? Do you even know how to eat pussy?"

Penelope looked up from her position and nodded. "I know, I know...I...I do. It's just that your skirt is keeping your legs together, I can't do it as well as I should."

I hiked up my skirt with a smile and presented my entire vulva to her, making it easier. "Here, take this as a favor...I doubt it will change the situation, though."

Penelope got back to her task and began eating me out with even greater intensity, her tongue darting, flicking, teasing...and I was enjoying it a great deal. I don't know how I did it, but I managed to keep myself calm and unmoved during this, not letting my body lead on one bit that Penelope's licking felt beyond stunning.

"Penelope..." Wendy said, "It's been two minutes now and not a single moan, or whine, or grunt from our Mistress..." Wendy crouched down and got her face level with Penelope's, "I really, really don't think you know how to eat pussy, because anyone else would have already made Mistress Morrigan come...listen," Wendy patted Penelope on the back, mocking her as she reassured her, "some women just can't eat pussy...it's fine... you can give up on it, you shouldn't keep doing something you're so fucking awful at."

"I'm...not...fucking...awful at this!" Penelope said between laps of my vulva. "I am great at this!"

"No..." I said. "She's not, Aosoth, you're right...it's like she's doing literally nothing." I sat back, containing the feelings inside myself. Suppressing my pleasure for this long wasn't sustainable, but I didn't want to make the mask slip. "Penelope, you're done, get your face away from my pussy right now."

"What? No...please!"

"Don't beg!" I bellowed, and then took my finger and wiped it down, spreading the mess from my pussy across her cheek, making it look like she was so terrible she didn't even manage to get the job done and get me wet. "God, I don't even know where that wetness came from, because it wasn't from me." I roughly pushed Penelope's head back, resisting the urge to spit in her face...she'd marked it as a no on her kink card, so I was good, but...it took every bit of my overloaded self to not. "Penelope, that was the worst pussy eating I've ever experienced. How completely pitiful."

"It...I did my best, Miss Morrigan! I tried my hardest to make you feel good!" Penelope's eyes were filled with tears. She was overwhelmed too, playing this up, and I could tell feeling this used was exactly what she wanted.

"Aosoth, please eat my pussy properly, now." I said.

Wendy moved to take her position where Penelope had just been, and I felt her warm breath on my wet folds. She wasted no time and began, taking me as she usually did when she had permission, like a woman possessed by her one true mission. I decided coming right away fit with the story well, telling Penelope she was so utterly bad and Aosoth she was an expert...but, beyond that, my body did not give me any contemplation in the matter.

"Fuck...yes...Aosoth...you're already making me come..." I stared at Penelope, trying to look as cruel and degrading as possible as the orgasm unwound my spine. "Oh...fuck yes..." I looked up toward the ceiling and let out an exaggerated, pornstar-worthy groan of pleasure. My eyes rolled back, and I slumped a bit, still sitting, still making sure Penelope knew I had a full, hard, and complete orgasm from her amazing work, even if Mistress Morrigan was going to give all of the credit to Aosoth.

"There..." I stroked Wendy's hair as I came down, "Penelope, do you see how easy that was for her to do that? Do you realize that shows how utterly awful you are at pleasuring a woman?"

"I'm so sorry, Miss Morrigan." Penelope said.

"You really should be...this is pathetic. Now..." I

pulled my panties up from the desk and put them into Penelope's mouth, being sure to not stuff them in and choke her, but Tiffany had put so many clothing play kinks on her card that I was sure my panties in her mouth would be a thrill. "Keep those in your filthy mouth while I recompose myself. Do not make a sound, Penelope, I need to meditate."

I went back to my chair behind the desk and sat down, then closed my eyes. I put a cloth mask over my eyes that looked completely opaque, but allowed for some visibility, because no way in hell I was going to miss seeing this next part. The room was silent other than Penelope's gasps for air around the fabric of the panties.

"How dare you even breathe?" Wendy said with such vitriol and disdain, I could feel Penelope shiver. "Shut your mouth and taste those fucking panties."

This next planned bit was something Wendy and I loved to play out. That emotional whiplash I talked about earlier? This was the most powerful, most dastardly implementation of it. I sat there, looking as calm as I could, meditating as if I needed to rid myself of some serious bad vibes. I heard Wendy pad her way across the floor on her bare feet, and when she stopped, I knew she was in front of Penelope.

"Hey, Penelope...I need your help..." Wendy whispered in a conspiratorial tone. "Morrigan has me do these depraved things, but...I don't want to. I hate doing this stuff. It's so painful to me to be so mean. I'm a nice person..."

FOUR

I WATCHED THROUGH THE MASK, trying not to have any emotional tells, as Wendy was saying every word with the same calm intensity and clarity she always used.

"Do you understand why Morrigan is like this? Is she...evil? She has to be...I don't know how to escape her...I've been here so long, I don't even know if I can escape, and I don't want you to end up like me. I'm going to take the panties out of your mouth, OK? Morrigan is in one of her states, she can't hear us right now..."

Penelope nodded, and Wendy pulled the panties out of her mouth, allowing her breathing return to normal.

"Thank you for trusting me..." Wendy said with such sincerity and care that it sounded so convincing. I had heard her do this so many times and still had no idea how she did it. "You're very pretty, you know. Morrigan says you're such an ugly, broken slut, but I don't really believe it."

Wendy sat on Penelope's lap, arm around her shoulder, looking so soft and calm and kind. I had to not let myself get excited about the fact that Penelope was about to learn a major lesson.

"Can I kiss you? I want you to know I care about you, that it's OK, that I'm going to help you...help you get out of here before the darkness takes over" Wendy said. "Please, I really like you."

"Y...yes..." Penelope said, her voice shaky, seeming to buy into the act completely.

The two women kissed, and the moment their lips touched I was done for, I wanted to burst out of my seat and run toward the two of them, but I knew I had to control myself for another few moments, at least.

Wendy pulled back and nuzzled her nose against Penelope, really selling it. "Penelope, you know...in demonology...there are the ones that you know to be afraid of just by nature..." Wendy kissed Penelope's cheek, extra sweet, and I could tell the air of trepidation was finally revealing itself on Penelope's face. "The ones with the claws, with the fangs, the ones that look threatening at first blush. They're scary, aren't they?" Wendy clasped her hands behind Penelope's shoulder, conveniently where I had bitten her earlier, leaning back, putting subtle additions of her body weight into leaning back, straining Penelope. "Penelope, those are the scary ones, right? Tell me you've learned to be afraid of them."

"Yes, that makes sense..." Penelope said, nodding.

"Well...do you know a rather funny thing about those demons, Penelope?" Wendy asked, a sly smirk spreading on her face. "They look that way because secretly, they're scared of you. They can be bested by humans. The minions of Azazel have to bare their fangs and rend clothing and flesh, they have to use clumsy methods to deal with their prey, because they're just so fucking dumb and craven, Penelope." Wendy kissed Penelope again, but was met with a far less enthusiastic return.

"Those are the amateurs, Penelope. The ones that use clumsy tools of flesh and bone to do their work. Do you know there's others? That there are ones you should be more scared of?"

Penelope shook her head. "No, Aosoth..."

"The ones you really need to look out for...they're called the succubi. You see...they draw you in, befriend you even. They are so sweet to you, Penelope, it might even make your teeth hurt." Wendy was now almost fully hanging off of Penelope, but had her foot a few inches above the ground, just in case she needed to brace herself if Penelope gave way...but I didn't think our sub for the night was going to give way any time soon, she was enjoying this way too much.

"The succubi, Penelope...they have no claws, they have no teeth...but they can make you beg for what they do to you..."

Wendy brought her fingers into Penelope's mouth. "They can demand pleasure, Penelope, and you will find yourself happy to comply, no matter how depraved that pleasure is." Wendy moved her middle and index fingers on either side of Penelope's mouth, crowding the space, forcing her to lick her fingers like a rude gesture. "The most fucked up thing, Penelope...it's that, when a succubus has you in their thrall, you might even be convinced that you're enjoying it. That you like giving pleasure to something as fucked-up and evil as me--"

Wendy giggled. This was a line she had practiced a lot at home, so I was able to keep myself from laughing at it, "--I mean...as fucked-up and evil as a succubus..."

Wendy now put all her body weight against Penelope's body, and I saw her struggle with keeping herself upright.

"Penelope...can you tell me..." Wendy ran her lips down the side of Penelope's face, planting kisses like flowers, "What kind of demon Mistress Morrigan is? Can you show me that you've been paying attention?" Wendy kissed Penelope on the neck. "Please? It might save your life."

Penelope stuttered for a moment. "She...she...Aosoth, she...is she a servant of Azazel?"

"Yes...good girl...I'm so glad we've become such fast friends...you're so smart." Wendy kissed Penelope on the cheek and began bouncing her leg over the side of the chair. She had been subtly tangling herself more and more with Penelope, but I don't think the poor girl even noticed. "Now, Penelope, do you want to have a guess at what that makes me?" Wendy said. She pulled herself up and licked Penelope's face from the chin to her temple, her movements getting more wild and loose as this all came to a head.

"Ahh...I...you..." Penelope was sobbing now. The line between being scared, being aroused, and being overwhelmed by emotion was a very thin one to tread on tonight. I was almost jealous at how much of her pleasure we were pulling from Penelope.

Wendy licked Penelope's face again and dragged her canine teeth along the woman's neck. Then, in the cheeriest tone a human could possibly muster, my lovely wife said, "Tell me what you think I am, Penelope, or I'll rip your heart right out of your chest just to see how much you love me..."

I had never been more aroused.

"I--you..."

"Yes?" Wendy asked as she ran her hand over Penelope's body. The two of them were still entwined, and Wendy kept the cloying tone. "Have you forgotten how to speak, you little slut?"

Penelope let out a cry, the tension and confusion finally cracking through to her soul, the moment so beautiful in its ugliness. "Please stop! You...you're a succubus!"

"Good girl...turns out you do have a brain, don't you?" Wendy said, rolling away from the grapple she had around Penelope and standing up. "You know, Penelope... you should have appreciated the safety you had when Morrigan was still here, because right now...while she's still off in la-la-land? You're mine to ruin, you dumb girl."

Wendy dropped to her knees in front of Penelope, and although the theatrical blindfold kept me from seeing too much detail, the ripping sound that accompanied Wendy's head movements in Penelope's lap gave me a wonderful idea of what was going on.

"Did you think these leggings were going to keep me from getting my tongue inside of your pussy, Penelope? Did you think it would impair me?" Wendy said.

"God..." Penelope said, "this is so fucked up..."

Wendy grabbed Penelope's thighs hard, pointing her face up toward her target, and Penelope loved every bit of it. "You shut the fuck up while I eat you." She laid her head to the side and started tearing away at more and more of the leggings with her teeth, leaving larger holes that showed more and more of Penelope's milky skin.

Penelope gasped, "That's so fucking good..."

I decided that it was time for me to emerge. "Oh...are you still alive?" I asked with an evil glee in my voice. I pulled the mask off of my eyes and looked around as if I were seeing this new scene for the first time. I stood up and walked the few steps toward Penelope and Wendy, standing over the two of them, my wife's face ripping the redhead's leggings to tatters. "Poor girl...you trusted a succubus, didn't you? I hope you don't expect me to get you out of this..."

Penelope was too far gone for words. She shook her head, knowing her only path now was down.

Wendy moved her face to the side and grabbed a section of fabric. With a great big tear, the hole in the leggings opened enough for Wendy's hand to move under the fabric enough to tear it wide and expose Penelope's pussy. It was magnificent...even though Penelope had already been through so much pleasure tonight, there was no question that she was more than ready for plenty more.

"Penelope, dear..." I stood behind her and put my hands on her shoulder, digging my thumb in hard in the growing red bruise from the bite, "I will warn you to not enjoy this much...depraved little demons like Aosoth, when they slide their hot pink tongue inside of your pussy, you might think it feels good, you might think it's the best thing you've ever felt, but remember, they are draining your very being. With every lick, they own you a little more. And if you get too far, well, I just hope you've made peace with the world..." I peered down at Wendy, who was ready to utterly devour Penelope and had been practically begging to do it since this morning.

Penelope, still in that same breathy, exhausted voice, said, "I'm OK...if this is what it takes...I...I am more than willing..."

"Poor girl, you have no idea what you're agreeing to..." I reached down and swept my hands over Penelope's breasts, teasing her nipples. "Don't say I didn't warn you... if you can say anything at all soon, that is."

Wendy started eating Penelope out, lapping her tongue across Penelope's clit and pussy, not giving the poor woman any time to adjust or ready herself. Wendy proceeded to devour the woman, her mouth working in a fury of sucking, biting, and licking that I was so lucky to bear witness to so often, but Penelope hadn't seen such a thing in her whole life, I was sure.

"Fuck...yes, Mistress...oh god...thank you...Aosoth!"

My hands trailed down from Penelope's tits and I rubbed my thumbs against her nipples in rhythm with Wendy's eating of her pussy, "Thanking her gives her more power, Penelope. You're giving more lifeforce to a monster..."

"Oh..." Penelope gasped out in the pleasure, "Thank you...thank you so much, Mistress Morrigan! Fuck, oh my god...thank you for making Aosoth...fuck..."

"I have no control over that horrid little thing, Penelope. I'm just trying to soothe you to make your final moments more palatable. Give yourself to Aosoth, Penelope. Your life is forfeit to that disgusting little succubus tonguing your cunt...she's consuming all you have left..."

I couldn't help myself, and leaned down and put my tongue on Penelope's ear, tasting her sweat, kissing the side of her face, licking it, loving it. I brought my teeth to the side of her neck and nibbled it, tasting her flesh in a way that was both erotic and primal. I bit down on her ear, enough that she'd probably have a couple nice little red dashes on the helix of her pretty little ear, something I knew she'd love hiding from coworkers and friends. With the cartilage still between my teeth, I gritted, "come, Penelope...it's over...she won...give it to her."

I released the flesh from my teeth, and Penelope's body gave itself up completely, shuddering, twitching, moaning, crying out for more pleasure and for this horrible curse to be over. "Fuck...oh my fucking god...oh fuck..." Penelope panted. Her chest was dripping with sweat, her exertion soaking the torn white shirt and the scraps of leggings that remained on her.

Penelope's back straightened, and her eyes closed like steel shutters. Everything in her body tightened. It was like she was having a demon exorcised from her body, which was maybe a little ironic considering the context.

After another minute or so, Wendy pulled back. “Ohhhh....my god, Penelope...what a treat. I've never had a woman squirt that much..." Wendy raised her head up, her chin slick with the milky liquid, a small pool of it on her tongue.

"Lovely...Aosoth, would you mind giving me a taste of that instead of lapping it all up with your greed?"

"Yes, Mistress Morrigan." Wendy stood up and met

me in front of Penelope, who was still a wrecked mess, and kissed me, letting me taste Penelope's nectar on my tongue. We were both exhausted beyond all measure, but we'd had a hell of a lot of fun.

"Oh...she's still alive..." I looked down at Penelope with a small smile, "Well...this is an unusual development to say the least..." I bent over Penelope, stroking her hair, and she smiled as her eyes opened. She had an utter look of ecstasy and pleasure on her face, one of pure satisfaction that we had done everything she'd hoped. "Welcome back, my dear."

"Oh...my...fucking god...you two might actually be demons..." Tiffany said, laughing, finally sitting up from her wasted state.

"Hate to burst your bubble, but we're unfortunately just lesbians with really great imaginations..." I walked over to the towel warmer that we had hidden behind some printer paper boxes and grabbed a couple warm towels, handing one to Tiffany and one to Wendy.

"Fucking...god...I am...I can't even speak..." Tiffany said, her eyes glittering.

"You should speak to say 'I need some water because you two just drained me'" Wendy said with a smirk. My wife walked over to the small refrigerator and grabbed three bottles, distributing them between us.

"You deserve an Oscar, Wendy...or...whatever awards they give to that...you...how are you that good?" Tiffany took a long drink of the water and laid the cool bottle against her chest.

I put the bottle of water down and laid a kiss on Wendy's lips, then broke it with a small laugh, "That's one of my favorite things about Wendy...she has the sweetest, nicest face, but...I actually am still a little concerned I married a literal demon." I said.

"Thank you...thank you both...god, I needed that. And you didn't let up." Tiffany smiled.

"You didn't say 'Calcium', so, we knew we could push you..." I said, invoking Tiffany's unused safe word.

"You two pushed me plenty. I've never come that hard. Or...squirted that much..." Tiffany's eyes went wide with realization, and she looked around the room. "God, all other sex is just going to pale in comparison now..."

"Well, we have bookings open in August, and we'll even give you a ten percent total depravity discount." I leaned down and kissed Penelope, sweetly this time, enjoying the moment.

HOME

ONE

"DO YOU BELIEVE YOU REALLY, truly deserve it, Wendy?" I said, looking at my wife who was standing in the hallway of our apartment, trying to lead me to the bedroom. Of course I'd go there, eventually, but she had to work for it. I was enjoying relaxing on the couch, so she was going to really work for it.

"Baby...this week has been so stressful, I just need...I need Mistress Morrigan to ruin me." Wendy twisted on her heel, genuinely anxious about all of this, and maybe she even thought there was a chance I wouldn't end up fucking her tonight. But how on earth could I resist that face, those hips, that...everything?

"Over here." I pointed to the space in front of me. "On your knees, in front of me. Now, Wendy, before I lose interest." Suddenly, I wasn't Brenda flipping through Netflix trying to find something to watch before eventually just giving up, I was Mistress Morrigan holding court.

My wife practically skipped over to the couch and

dropped to her knees in front of me. This was a far more casual encounter than we usually had, as neither of us were in any kind of costume tonight...well, except for the black leather choker with the silver ring that Wendy wore almost all the time...but otherwise things were a rather boring affair, with Wendy in a t-shirt and sweatpants and myself in a pair of rather ragged jean shorts and a tank top. That didn't mean we couldn't have fun, though.

"You poor, poor thing..." I took my thumb and rubbed it on Wendy's lips, and she instinctively took it into her mouth, licking and sucking it, showing me her eagerness. "Look at you, you're practically feral..."

I pulled my thumb out of Wendy's mouth and licked it. "You taste wonderful, my love..."

"Baby..." Wendy started, before I gave her a sharp smack across the cheek.

"You don't get to set our timelines, slut. We will do this when I'm damn well ready to do this." I hooked my finger into the silver ring on the front of Wendy's collar and tugged gently. "Understand?"

Wendy nodded, and then added "Yes, Mistress" a few seconds after she remembered her proper place.

I released my grip on Wendy's choker and let my finger wander down her body. "Did you not think to get dressed up for your mistress tonight, Wendy?"

"No, I'm sorry Mistress Morrigan, I should have been dressed up for you, I-" Wendy looked up at me with overly affected sorrow, selling that she was so genuinely sorry for her mistakes...and she looked so sexy doing it. Her sub acting was really something else.

"Are you at least hiding a cute bra under that t-shirt,

my dear? Can you salvage my very low opinion of you and show me something that can truly amaze me?" I grinned.

"Mistress, please, I promise, I'll show you right now if you let me!" Wendy pulled her t-shirt off and threw it to the ground, and I saw that she'd indeed picked a beautiful, lacy green bra for tonight.

"That's quite decent, Wendy. Your dark nipples look particularly delicious under the lace. Good girl." I said.

"Thank you, Mistress!" Wendy looked delighted to get even that bit of praise.

"I'm going to challenge you now. This will determine if we take this night further or if you end up begging and wasted in our bed, your pussy aching for attention that I will not give it." I pulled the ring again, feeling the heat of Wendy's skin, the rapid pulse in her neck. "Are you ready for your challenge, slut?"

Wendy swallowed, a bit of nerves getting to her, and then she answered, "Yes, Mistress. I can take your challenge. Please."

"Eat my pussy...through my jean shorts. And you need to make sure I feel it." I said, opening my legs a little to give her more room to work.

Wendy took on the challenge without pausing or protest, pressing her face between my legs, licking and nuzzling the denim that was all that separated her mouth from my wetness. She looked up to me as she did it, seeking approval and trying to read my reactions, but I was giving her nothing.

I smiled at her but didn't provide any further feedback. In truth, it didn't really feel that good because there's no way I could feel much through the thick fabric. But the pressure and eagerness of Wendy was nice, at the very least.

"I'm going to fall asleep if you don't pick up the intensity of this, Wendy." I slapped her face lightly and dragged my nails along her jaw.

That got a reaction from her. She shoved her mouth more forcefully onto me, her tongue seeking the sweet spot it couldn't reach through the thick jean shorts, her teeth pulling at the legs. I have to admit, even through the difficulties, she was doing enough to get me going.

"Are you that desperate, you poor girl? Gnawing at a woman's lap just to see if you can get a rise out of her?" I gripped a handful of Wendy's hair, pulling it a little, just enough to hurt her a bit.

She yelped in response. I could see the desperation in her face, the way it seemed like her soul was starting to seep out through her eyes as she searched for a way to push me.

"Enough, this is embarrassing, Wendy." I jerked her hair back, away from me, to get her to stop.

Wendy didn't have the heart to stop though, and kept mouthing at me even while I pulled her away, until she finally said something that broke me out of character, "No, no, no, I want it so badly, I need this tonight, please don't..."

"Yellow light..." I whispered. "Baby, we'll do it, don't worry. I'm going to fuck you so goddamn hard tonight. But, patience is a virtue, my dear."

Wendy sighed and grinned. "I'm just...god, you

already have me so fucking gone, Bren, how are you this good at this?"

"Some people are just naturals...green light?"

"So fucking green." Wendy smirked.

"Stand up." I snapped, tapping Wendy on the bottom of the chin with some force. "If you're that desperate to feel something against your pussy, get those sweatpants off right now."

Wendy's grin became more maddened, her eyes wide. "Oh my god..." She stood up and pulled her sweatpants down, letting them fall to her ankles. Wendy was an eager woman in all regards, and especially an eager one when it came to sex, but this desperation and energy was notable even for her.

"No panties, Wendy, really?" I said, leaning back on the couch, taking in my gorgeous wife's wide hips and the stark black triangle of pubic hair at the tops of her legs. The restraint and withholding of BDSM was quite fun, for sure, but times like this made me want to abandon the whole act and just devour her because she looked so fucking good.

"I..." Wendy said, "I'm yours tonight. Every bit of me. No need to get dressed up, no need to keep my clothes on. I am your subject, Mistress."

"Yes, yes you are..." I flourished my hand, waving away the effusive praise. "Words don't mean much to me, slut. I want to hear how wet you are for me already. Let me listen to the sound of your fingers dipping into that desperate cunt, Wendy. I want you to be dripping for me before I even consider starting us off properly."

Wendy pushed her fingers into her pussy and

moaned out loudly. She'd already been quite aroused, her pussy a deep, dark shade of pink. "You like my fingers going into my cunt, Mistress?"

I didn't react, wanting to make this harder for her. "Stop with the theatrics, Wendy. Don't moan, don't sell this with your facial expressions. My one source of truth is how sopping wet you are, so, that is the only thing I am paying attention to...and I haven't heard anything convincing yet." I crossed my arms, looking more defensive. This would burn Wendy up on the inside so much, but I knew it would make it all that much more worth it in the long run.

"Okay..." Wendy said, her voice a bit shaky, the intensity of it all making her falter. She pushed her fingers in again, letting them press all the way against her palm, and I watched as her knuckles disappeared into herself. In the silence of the apartment, the sound was delicious, my wife pleasuring herself, preparing her body for me, showing off just how turned on she was.

"More..." I said, a little heat and want in my voice. I felt myself getting more tense, the spectacle of Wendy doing this making me feel warmth all over. She was so fucking wet, already.

Wendy did more, drawing her fingers along her labia, the wet sound filling my ears like a symphony. She had this funny little thing she did when she masturbated standing up, she would almost go on her tiptoes, seeming to want to lift herself up. I watched her try to keep her balance, the sight of her almond-tan hand disappearing into the thicket of her pubic hair.

"Let me see your fingers." I commanded, my voice not

hiding the fact that I was turned on at all. My nipples strained against the thin fabric of the bra I was wearing, every movement causing a gentle prickle of pleasure.

Wendy walked to the couch and presented her fingers to me. They were covered in her juices, sticky and smelling strongly of her arousal.

I pulled one of her fingers into my mouth, letting the flavor of her flood my tongue and wash over me. It was almost unbearably delicious, my wife's body sending so many signals that it was ready for me. "Do you like it when your Mistress sucks your fingers, Wendy?" I said, biting down ever so slightly on the pad of her middle finger as I continued to clean it off.

"Oh my god, I'm just..." Wendy shivered, her other hand starting to reach down between her legs to try to quell some of this intensity. I grabbed that wrist, though, pulling her away.

"You don't fucking touch yourself unless I give you permission. You need to appreciate the attention I'm giving you, slut. Licking these filthy fingers, tonguing all of your juices off of you." I bit her finger again, this time with enough force to feel the tendons shift under my teeth.

Wendy winced and bit her lip, holding back the instinct to pull away from the pain I was inflicting. It wasn't much pain, but enough to get a reaction. "Fuck..."

"I can't believe someone as depraved as you would have such a sweet little pussy, Wendy." I pushed her hand back toward her. "Get me more, I want more of your nectar. I want to drink from you, slut..." Something about sucking and licking liquids off of each other was the fast track to get me or Wendy going utterly full-throttle in record time, and I admit that I was already being selfishly greedy to taste Wendy's bounty.

Wendy returned her fingers to her pussy and rubbed her clit. Her head rolled back and she exhaled sharply. I could see her hand start to shake as the tension and pleasure built inside her. I know it was maybe too much to ask to see if a woman could literally drip from arousal, but Wendy was certainly testing if it was possible.

"Take it out, Wendy, take your fingers out of your slick pussy..." I said. The lustful edge to my voice was evident, I could feel it in my throat as my voice dipped down into its lowest register. "Clean your fucking hand off. Every last bit of your juices, Wendy, clean yourself for your Mistress." I sat back against the couch again, my legs spread open, the short hem of my jean shorts letting a little air in to relieve the red-hot arousal at my core.

Wendy diligently licked her fingers, her pink tongue looking gorgeous and enticing as always. Her mouth was opened slightly, and the light hit her tongue in such a way that I could see a pool of liquid pooling at the very tip.

"How do you taste, slut?" I said. It took every last bit of my energy to not masturbate, but I knew I couldn't do it yet.

"I'm delicious...I'm fucking ambrosia." Wendy said, and then licked up another drip of her arousal from the base of her ring finger. "I'm so wet, I'm literally dripping for you, Mistress."

"Don't lie to me, Wendy...don't tell me it's dripping if it's not truly dripping..." I smirked.

"It...it is, Mistress...may I approach and prove it?"

"You may." I leaned back further, sinking myself into the couch.

Wendy approached and put her leg against the back of the couch, spreading herself open, her dark pink vulva exposed, making me swoon like always. "Mistress...see... on my thigh..." Wendy turned her thigh and put her thumb next to a sticky trail sneaking down her leg.

"Mmm...and you didn't put that there, did you, slut? Did that really drip from your tasty little snatch onto your soft little thigh?" I said.

"I swear to you, I swear to you, Mistress, it dripped, I swear it..." Wendy said, the intensity building again.

I reached down and pressed my palm to Wendy's knee, feeling the heat of her body, the sticky, humid feeling of her juices emanating from her. I licked along the trail, tasting the sweetness from her.

"Well...all that work is gone now, isn't it?" I looked up at her with an evil smirk.

Wendy swallowed hard, feeling the challenge in my words. "I can drip for you again, Mistress. Please, please, just tell me what I have to do."

"You'll go to the bedroom, get naked, and lay on your back while I figure out how I'm going to punish you for being so eager and dripping for an evil woman like your Mistress." I dragged my fingers along Wendy's labia, my fingers sliding along the complete wetness.

"Oh my fucking god..." Wendy exhaled, feeling me tease her so lightly, barely brushing against her. "Thank you..."

"Thanking me is the last thing you'll want to do after tonight, you poor thing..." I grabbed Wendy's ass before she could lower herself down, digging my short nails into the soft skin, pressing as hard as I could. I kissed her pussy, sucking the lips into my mouth, sliding my tongue between them. I was giving her an unbearably pleasurable experience in preparation for me denying her even further, edging her just the way she liked.

Once I could tell Wendy was getting a little too into me eating her out, I pushed her thigh back, dismissing her.

"Go. Fucking go, before I change my mind." I snarled.

TWO

I WALKED into the bedroom and saw my wife naked on her back, legs spread open, one finger inside herself. Her pussy was pink and glistening, ready and primed for me, set for the edging I was about to put her through.

I had thought about putting on a whole outfit, really going all out for this, but I was probably just as exhausted from the week as Wendy was, so casual domme it would have to be. The bra I was wearing already was black, so that was what I stuck with, and I swapped my jean shorts and their utterly soaked panties for a pair of latex boyshorts that were so tight they practically shrinkwrapped to my ass.

"Wendy, Wendy..." I said, hanging my head. "Please explain to me why you thought you would be allowed to finger yourself while your Mistress was not in the room? I have no idea why a submissive like you would even fathom that being anything near appropriate."

I walked over and slapped her hand away from

herself. I saw a little tremor in her leg, a little hiccup of pleasure at the slap.

"I'm sorry, Mistress."

"Sorry is never enough, Wendy, and you know that. Explain yourself." I knelt on the bed, towering over her, my height even more apparent from our positions.

Wendy had an impish little look in her eye that betrayed just how excited she was, "Mistress Morrigan, I was just too turned on to resist. You made me feel so good, I couldn't wait to keep it going while you were out of the room."

"Goddddd..." I groaned in desperation. I took Wendy's right nipple between my thumb and index finger and twisted, hard. "How many times can I explain to you that you only feel pleasure with my permission?" I twisted a little harder, causing Wendy to yelp and shudder.

"Mistress..." Wendy whimpered.

"Does this hurt you, Wendy?" I said, kneading the nipple between my fingers, pulling at it, taking it to its limit.

"Yes...fuck...yes....it's excruciating, Mistress."

"And do you know that the only reason I do this is because you didn't follow my rules?" I twisted harder and pulled the nipple upward slightly. My wife's nipples were some of my favorite things on the planet, and so I relished every time I got to do anything with them.

Wendy let out a whine, her breathing getting more sharp. I knew she was loving every moment of this. "I'm so sorry Mistress, please punish me. Make me yours."

"What the fuck do you think this is if it's not punishment, slut?" I pinched at the nipple harder, exerting as much force on it as I knew I could.

Wendy's face scrunched up and she whimpered in pain. I released my grip, her nipple dark red and swollen, almost concerningly so.

"You pitiful fucking thing.." I said.

"Yellow...just...really quick." Wendy gave me a sheepish grin.

I came down from my dominant high and softened my posture, leaning down to Wendy. "What's wrong, baby?"

"That just..." Wendy rubbed her overworked nipple with a wince. "That was good but a little too far...I might need a little time with an icepack before we go further."

I felt horrible. I loved testing my wife's limits, but sometimes I had a tendency to go too far, be too eager, and this was one of those times. "Shit, Wen, I'm so sorry..." I felt a wave of shame flash over my body.

"Hey, it's alright...come here, kiss me." Wendy reached for me, placing her hand at my side, drawing me in. I leaned down and kissed her, a sweet kiss, a loving moment. "It's alright, just, you got a little overexcited, I'm not mad...but, I will need to literally cool my tits before we do more."

"God, you're too nice to me...I don't deserve you, I really don't." I kissed Wendy again. I felt terrible for making my wife feel any pain or discomfort that she didn't desire, and it's true that even dommes could get maudlin from time to time.

"Oh, Bren, you deserve every last thing you get from me..." Wendy returned a wicked smirk.

I walked to the kitchen and pulled out a soft, fabric-lined ice pack that we used frequently after scenes. It was well-insulated and just cool enough, because putting a freezing block of ice on an already overstimulated body part was quite the shock...but, I supposed some people based entire fetishes around that, too. For our purposes, though, the puffy cool pad was exactly what the moment called for.

I handed the pack to Wendy, and she put it on her still-red nipple, wincing ever so slightly from the sensation.

I sat down on the bed next to her, looking over my shoulder as she nursed her wounds.

"Damn...you really worked it..." Wendy laughed, pulling the pack up to inspect her nipple before putting it back against her skin.

"Yeah...I went a bit too far..."

"A bit, yeah..." Wendy smiled.

"You sure you still wanna do this? I can just go down on you, and we can watch something on TV?"

"Oh, Brenda..." Wendy looked at me, the blue puffy ice pack laying against her large breast. "There is no way you're getting out of this that easily, my dear..." She bit her tongue playfully. "Perhaps I should be the one who breaks you tonight, you naughty girl..."

Wendy was almost always a sub, or if she was dominant it was in addition to me, but she rarely felt the desire to domme me when it was just the two of us. I'll admit I didn't mind the feeling, being able to relax, take a more directed role in this game, every once in a while. Plus, after the nipple incident, I sort of owed her.

I laid down on the bed, my shoulders resting on Wendy's thighs, "You wouldn't have the first clue about how to ruin someone like me, Wen..."

Wendy pulled her legs back, causing me to flop down onto the bed now that her thigh wasn't propping me up. She quickly got to her knees and towered over me...well, towered over me as much as a five-foot nothing woman could. "I think I'll be able to pick up on it..." She looked down at me, hands on her hips, her beautiful soft body ready to dish out punishment that was so rare for her to give.

"Green light?" I smiled, wanting to disappear into the role of the wayward sub, to let Wendy truly have her way with me.

"Green...so...so fucking green."

Wendy didn't hesitate for a moment, she swung her leg over my head and a moment later her sopping wet pussy was pressed against my face.

"Fucking. Lick. Me." she commanded.

I followed the command because I knew she wasn't going to give me any choice in the matter. I lapped at Wendy, my tongue pressing up and parting her folds, diving inside her as my lips wrapped around her outer lips and I gently sucked them. They were so fucking delicious. She was so, so, so fucking wet, I felt like I could almost drown in her. I have no idea what I did to find such an unbelievable woman to be in my life, to marry me, to join me on this journey that a lot of people would think was too fucked-up.

"Yes, yes, you goddamn animal..." Wendy pressed down against me, her thick thighs wrapped around my face. I snaked my hands up around her ass, bracing them against her hips, holding her tight. She wrenched my left hand away and gripped me at the wrist. "No hands. I'll tell you when you can use your hands, Brenda."

I pulled back, gasping, "Yes, ma'am..."

"Ma'am? Not Mistress Aosoth??" Wendy laughed.

I smiled, though my expression was more felt than seen. "Fuck..."

"Yeah, you better learn my name and how to use it, or I'm never going to lift myself up off your little pink mouth." Wendy pressed harder, the wetness now coating my face and chin. God, what a fucking way to go if this would be the end of me.

I opened my mouth again, pushing my tongue into Wendy, trying to feel and taste every bit of her. Wendy ground down against me, moaning, getting closer and closer. I knew she wouldn't want to come right now, but I could still get her close to the edge.

"You talk so much with that tongue, but I know its real use, Brenda. You're a natural pussy eater, you disgusting little woman..." Wendy said with venom that was beyond rare and turned me on that much more.

I ate Wendy out with vigor, her dirty talk sending my body into a heated state, my pussy throbbing, my skin on fire. Wendy moaned again and pressed her hips down harder, her clit practically resting on my tongue, aching for stimulus.

"Stop licking. Now." Wendy said, and I reluctantly complied. "You're having too much fun...you need to just live in the reality of feeling such a hot little pussy spread over your face. Don't lick it at all. If your tongue moves, I'll break your nose..."

I went completely still. Wendy sat down harder, and the weight of her body pressing me into the mattress felt amazing, I was so utterly covered by her.

"Do you like the taste of your Mistress' pussy, Brenda? Do you like the feeling of it dripping down your used-up little face?"

With every quickened breath Wendy took, her body pressed against my face just a little bit, the pressure increasing in such a subtle way that it couldn't be experienced if we were doing something more vigorous, but the feeling of the small rises and valleys of her labia and thighs touching and pulling away from my skin was lighting up my brain.

I was so aroused. Every moment of this felt like I was getting more and more worked up. The anticipation, the pleasure, the inability to get off, all of it was adding to my own arousal, my body screaming at me to come.

"You need to answer me, slut. I will not hesitate to suffocate you with my cunt...do not test me."

Wendy's threats were always a little darker, a little more powerful...and if I'm being honest, a little scarier. But her domination was more rare, so I wasn't too worried about her going mad with power or leaving me with truly hurt feelings or panic.

I answered with an affirmative whimper into Wendy. The pressure on my face increased further, my ability to breathe slightly compromised.

"Your Mistress is so very wet right now...but she's not done punishing her little sub." Wendy swung her leg back over my head, allowing me to see the ceiling and breathe fresh air again...although, being completely honest, I preferred the previous climate much more.

"I'm going to deprive myself of getting off because your punishment must continue. Do you have any idea how charitable I'm being to you right now? Any scrap of recognition?" Wendy gripped my chin, digging her nails into my jaw. I'd always had hard, model-like features in contrast to Wendy's softness, and my wife loved calling attention to them.

"Thank you...I..."

Wendy gripped my face tighter, "Shut the fuck up, you silly little girl." She slapped me, and I overreacted, tossing my head to the side, really selling it.

I looked back up at her, a grin on my face. Wendy knew exactly what I wanted and slapped me again, even harder this time. I really was enjoying all this.

"Are you going to fuck me, Mistress?"

"No, no no...we're definitely not doing that tonight." Wendy tapped my chin again, and I exaggerated the movement in reaction. "I thought you'd be able to understand you being punished does not equate to you getting off, but, I guess I can't expect you to be that smart..."

Wendy leaned down and kissed my forehead, a strangely tender and sweet action after the slapping, the degradation...and I loved it, I loved when my wife was gentle with me, more even than I loved the harder stuff.

"Fucking moron..." Wendy said derisively.

And, maybe I loved being hated by her even more...

THREE

WENDY ROLLED off the bed and went to the floor, standing over me. "Get up. Sit at the top of the bed."

I did as I was told, my back resting against the pillows that Wendy had lined up behind me.

“Why aren’t you naked?” Wendy deadpanned me.

I smiled, I loved this kind of direction. I reached behind myself and pulled the clasp of my bra free, pulling it off, letting my small breasts free. I envied Wendy’s big tits, but I enjoyed mine just as much, mostly.

I unzipped my shorts and pulled them off, tossing them to the floor. Now naked, I got back into position.

“You need to learn pain, dear...” Wendy held a candle in her hand and flicked a lighter, the flame glowing gently.

God, I fucking loved wax play.

"Do you really think you deserve to feel pleasure?" Wendy tilted the candle a little, letting the flame dance across the wick.

"No...Mistress..."

Wendy chuckled, a low, dirty, wicked laugh. "Right answer, for once. No...my sweet, dear Brenda, you seem to understand you don't deserve even the slightest bit of it." She stood at the edge of the bed, the dark purple candle in her hand, a spout on one side for easier pouring. Wendy held the candle about two feet above me and tilted it, a stream of wax splattering right above my navel.

Fuck, it was hot against my skin. Not scalding, but certainly enough heat to cause notice. I tensed but kept my body flat, allowing Wendy to pour a more generous stream up my stomach toward my ribs, the heat radiating through me.

Wendy smiled down at me and dribbled more wax onto my left thigh. "God, it feels so fucking good defacing something so beautiful..."

I had to hold back the moan that was building up in my throat, the feeling of Wendy doing this, the sensual feeling of her dominating me, her words...

Another stream of wax dribbled down, the hot liquid pooling in the hollow of my hip, hardening quickly.

Without words, Wendy placed the candle on our dresser and blew it out, snuffing the wick with her fingertips. "I hope you're used to the pain now because I'm not going to let up on hurting you, you know that, right?"

"Yes, Mistress, I know I deserve the pain." I stayed still on the bed, the wax now cracking and flaking from my skin, exposing the bright pink marks underneath.

Wendy pulled a harness out of the top drawer and began tightening the straps around the thighs. "I never fucking strap you, do I? We're going to change that..."

"Mistress...please...no. I'm too tight for it, you can't..." I gasped in theatric shock. Yes, I was usually the one using the strap, but I found myself wanting a round with it here and there, and tonight it especially sounded fun with how fucking worked up I already was.

Wendy laughed at my pathetic attempts to get her to stop. "Shut your mouth, or I'll give you a real reason to be sore, slut."

"Mistress...it won't fit..."

"Guess we'll find out, huh?" Wendy turned around from the dresser and showed the dildo she had chosen to put into the harness. It was one of the bigger ones, and it was going to be a hell of a challenge, but right now I could have taken her whole hand inside me. After our fun with Cassidy, I still couldn't convince Wendy to do it, but maybe one day...

"Hands and knees. There's no fucking way I want to see how ugly your face will look when I'm doing this." Wendy approached the bed. The dildo was a pale green and white, the silicone swirled to make it look almost nauseating in how unnatural it looked. But, god, it sure did feel natural shoved inside of me.

Wendy climbed onto the bed and slapped the back of my thigh hard with an open palm. My flesh jiggled with the impact and I let out an embarrassing yelp.

I heard Wendy laugh and saw her turn back toward me, a bottle of lube in her hand.

"You don't deserve lube, but I don't want you yelping during this shit, you're already so fucking annoying, so I guess you'll get it." She squirted a generous amount of lube on her hand and rubbed it into my vulva. I was already fucking soaked, but with this dildo, I probably did need a little extra.

"Do not make a single noise when I put this in you. Do you understand? I want you to be completely silent while this thing splits you apart."

I was so ready for it, the pain and pleasure mixing together to be almost too much to handle already, and I hadn't even started. "Yes, Mistress. I understand."

Wendy pressed the head of the strap into my vagina and I moaned immediately.

"My fucking god. Already moaning." Wendy slapped my ass hard. "Do I need to gag you or can you promise you'll shut the fuck up until I tell you that you can speak again?"

"No gags..." I whispered. "I can be silent." I took a deep breath. I needed this, I needed this so badly. I wanted Wendy to fucking wreck me, to feel so full, so sore, to just have the sensation of it all.

My wife pushed in more, the feeling overwhelming as the toy stretched me. God, it was so much pressure on me, the width causing me to open my hips more to accommodate it.

Wendy pressed deeper and I moaned out. It was such a loud, needy noise, the pleasure of being stretched like that causing the moan to spill out of my lips.

Wendy gripped the back of my neck, her nails digging into my skin. "Fucking. Silent."

I held myself back and tried not to let out another noise as Wendy pushed the last bit of the dildo into me. It was so fucking big, I marveled that my body was elastic enough to envelop it.

"Why the fuck are you even a lesbian?" Wendy slapped my ass, making me tense around the dildo, causing a spike in pleasure. "You look like you were made to be railed from behind."

The pleasure of that last little movement made it feel like my eyes would roll back into my head and my brain would go totally blank. I bit the sheets in a vain attempt to keep from moaning again, but the tension made the moan arrive in the form of a hiss.

"Now you're the one dripping...just so fucking messy..." Wendy drew her hand against the inside of my thigh and wiped the dripping wetness across the small of my back, making me feel slightly sticky and cold in the spot as the wetness settled in.

Wendy pulled out slightly, my body protesting at the movement, causing me to gasp. My pussy clenched at the lack of something filling me, and as she pulled out, I knew she would notice my body begging her to push back in. I was begging for it, needing this punishment, this overwhelming attention.

Wendy pulled the strap out, tapping my ass. She laughed. "You really need it, don't you?"

I nodded, but still kept silent. Wendy's words, her hand on my body, it was so much to deal with, the need to have her inside me again, to just be wanted and used so much.

"I'm going to fuck you with it a little because you've been a good little sub, but you cannot fucking come while I do it. Don't even think about coming." Wendy said, lining the dildo up with my now more relaxed and stretched entrance.

I wanted to say I was a good little sub, but the dildo sliding into me again made my jaw go slack, the moan escaping me before I could even begin to protest.

Wendy chuckled. "You're so fucking far gone...I own you with this big cock, don't I?"

I nodded again, my face still pushed against the mattress.

Wendy put her hand on the small of my back and gripped it as she slowly pumped into me, the thickness of the strap on still making my pussy stretch around it as she pushed in and out. The wet, squishing sound of the rod sliding into me was fucking addictive to hear, my body providing wetness and the ability to provide room for such a monster.

Wendy picked up the speed a little, pulling out more before pushing back in. Each push into me felt like she was pushing the air out of me, the stretch making my breath shallow and ragged.

I was so, so, so, so fucking close to coming I had no idea how I could hold it back.

"Please...I..." I could barely breathe.

"Oh, no you don't." Wendy stopped, pulling the dildo out. "I said no, Brenda..."

I panted and tried to get control over myself. "Yes... yes Mistress...yes." I tried opening myself more, relaxing, to reduce the overstuffed pleasure that was causing me to lose it, but it was a losing battle for sure.

Still, Wendy said not to come, so, I wouldn't.

I heard her take a deep breath, "God, you're a mess." Wendy slapped my ass again and pushed the dildo in, my body letting her in as if she owned me, because my fucking god she did. "I'm training your pussy to not be so impulsive...you need to learn how to restrain yourself, don't you understand that?" She grabbed at the hollow of my hip, digging her fingers into the softest bit.

I was a bit astonished how much my pain tolerance increased as Wendy and I got into BDSM. Wendy did her time as a line cook, so she was already used to a wide array of almost daily scrapes, cuts, burns, and bruises, but, I mean, I was a lawyer, and court cases haven't been decided with gladiatorial combat in at least a thousand years, so enduring pain wasn't much of a priority to me.

But, god, now I lived for it. That shock of pain coming alongside the pleasure, it fucking sent me.

I whimpered as I tried to contain my impending orgasm. It felt like a tightening rope around my midsection, my whole body straining to keep my composure. "Fuck...fuck...." I panted, every single impulse in my body telling me to let it out, to come, to just give in because I needed to. This was beyond edging, this was a test of endurance.

"Please, Wendy..."

"No..." She pulled back again, the strap sliding out of me.

Wendy held the dildo against my ass and ran the shaft through my wetness a couple of times, teasing me more, before moving off of the bed, the sound of her feet hitting the floor feeling like a hammer to my ears, the knowledge that I wouldn't get to feel myself swallow the massive dildo any more today.

"Look at you, you're so obscene, presenting your little gaping pussy to me...as if I'm going to give it any more attention today." Wendy said. I heard her unsnap one of the straps on her harness and knew definitively I wasn't in for a surprise encore.

"I'm...I'm sorry, Mistress Aosoth."

I started to shift back into a more neutral position when Wendy's hand slapped the back of my thigh, hard.

"What the fuck do you think you're doing?" Wendy growled.

I was confused. "Mistress...you...I...what do you want?"

"I said it was obscene to see you presenting yourself like that, I didn't say to stop doing it...in fact, I want you to spread yourself open as far as you can..." Wendy gripped my thigh, her nails scraping the sensitive skin. "Spread yourself as wide as you fucking can, and stay in that position until I tell you to stop."

This woman was going to cause me to pass out. Thank god.

"Yes, Mistress, yes..." I pressed my palms against the insides of my thighs and pushed myself open, my pussy stretching a little again, a slight twinge of pain from the feeling of opening myself up. I had no idea what was coming next, and was even enticed by the idea that absolutely nothing was coming next, she would just leave me here like this so that I would suffer.

"Stay there..." Wendy commanded, walking out of the bedroom. I didn't know if I could, but I was definitely going to try. I listened for Wendy's footsteps as they disappeared into the living room.

Oh my fucking god, she was really just abandoning me. I shuddered at the feeling that I would have to keep waiting, that I would be allowed no release, that I would have my orgasm when Mistress Aosoth damn well pleased.

FOUR

AT LEAST I could breathe now and allow my body to cool down from the intensity of the strap-on. I knew I had to keep myself in my current position, but I was able to relax to some degree.

My knees were getting tired, I wasn't very used to staying on all fours. My right thigh cramped ever so slightly and I was tempted to try and move the leg.

No...stay. I had to. Of course, Wendy couldn't memorize the *exact* position I was in when she left the room, but I'd know I had shifted myself and betrayed her order. That's what being a good sub was about, behaving whether or not your domme had her eyes on you.

"Oh, Brenda...you poor, poor thing." Wendy said, re-entering the bedroom. "Look at you, still so fucking spread open, begging. How does it feel to beg to come, darling?" Wendy stayed behind me so I couldn't see her, and I yearned deep inside myself that she had a surprise prepared.

"Mistress..." I whimpered, feeling the cool air from the hallway brushing against my swollen labia. "Please..."

Wendy moved up closer behind me, her hand trailing from the back of my thigh to my pussy, sliding into it without resistance, the pressure of her finger feeling like it caused sparks to dance across my skin.

"Here, let me cool you off..." Wendy said, and then my body felt utter shock as an ice-cold washcloth caressed the back of my thigh. Fuck, it was so cold, and it felt even colder against my red-hot skin.

I jolted at the sudden coldness, feeling the muscles in my thigh twitch as a shiver of surprise went up my back, goosebumps spreading across my skin. "Mistress..."

"I'm cooling you off, dear, you're so flush..." I could hear the edge to her voice, she knew how much this was pushing me. "You should be thanking me, and, in fact, you need to be thanking me while I do this, slut..." Wendy pressed the cloth against my hip, the water still freezing cold. I didn't have to look back to know that she had a glass of ice water with her, dipping the towel back in, refreshing the freezing cold.

"Thank you..." I managed. "Thank you, Mistress..."

"Don't move your legs." Wendy pressed the towel into the hollow of my hip and let the water dribble along my stomach and hips, my muscles reacting against my will.

She swept the towel over my ass, which already felt raw from the spanking. It was heaven to feel the cool water, but hell to feel that cool water slip down the contours of my body, the icy liquid ticking every sensitive part on the way down.

"I have one more test for you, Brenda, my lovely little

whore." Wendy took an icy cold finger and toyed with my labia, making my eyes roll back. "Are you smart enough to know what that test could be?"

I tried to speak, but couldn't even get the words out as Wendy pushed her finger inside of me, my muscles tensing in the frigid sensation. "Fuck...I..."

"Do you know what you need to do? Make a guess. I won't do it until you guess. If you're right, I'll do it twice as hard as I was planning." Wendy dipped her finger into the glass again and returned it to between my lips.

"I..." I couldn't think. Her words, the sensation of the water...it was too fucking much. I was already at my limit before and she knew I had no brainpower left. "I'll need to...make you come before I do...fuck...I don't fucking know, Mistress."

"Oh, Brenda...no, I wouldn't be cruel like that. What do you take me for?" Wendy trailed her fingertip around my soaked pussy, teasing me to high heaven. "My challenge, my dear wife, is quite simple, really. All you need to do is..."

I heard a shuffling behind me and felt a sudden, exceptionally cold presence inside of me, sliding into me. Fuck, fuck, the chill and size of the ice cube as Wendy pushed it into me felt like being fucked by an angel.

"You just need to chill out a little, my darling..." Wendy pushed the last bit of the cube into me and giggled.

God, the freezing ice, the extreme temperature shift of it, the size of it as it reached deeper inside me, fuck...I didn't even have any words.

"Mistress..." I stuttered, the water inside me dripping down onto my thighs.

"If you want it to end quicker, Brenda, just make your pussy warmer. The moment it's fully melted, your Mistress will allow you to come." I felt her fingers press against me again. "Oh, and, don't let it slip out. If it does, I'm just going to put it back in...and if it happens twice, it's going to have a friend put in there with it, so stay tight, my love..." Wendy smacked my ass playfully, my reaction threatening to push the ice out already.

"Thank...thank you Mistress."

Wendy pressed against my entrance again with an ice cube in her hand. "You're welcome...oh, and, because I love you so, so much, I figured I'd give you a friend anyway..."

My body was overworked and taken to the limit. My wife had bested me in every possible way. I was happy she wasn't a regular domme because she'd have a harem of hundreds of women on their knees begging for her, with no time for me. Knowing that Wendy's domming was just for me for the most part made it that much more delicious.

Wendy pushed the second ice cube inside of me and my body reacted, clenching, keeping them where they needed to be to melt as quickly as possible.

"There's a good girl." Wendy said, her words dripping with poisoned honey.

I focused on the feeling between my legs, the cubes getting smaller and shifting slightly. I was angled to where there wasn't much of a chance of one being forced out unless I had a sudden cough, but they were secure otherwise.

The water ran out of me and down my thighs, leaving little trails of coolness on my skin. The ice had the effect of slightly numbing my vagina, which was a blessing in a way, because I knew with one move at the wrong angle, I'd find myself a blubbering, orgasming mess, and the ice reduced those chances, a little.

Wendy sat back on the bed and I heard a faint, slick noise. She was touching herself. I didn't look back because I didn't want to ruin what she had set up, but I was pretty sure my wife was playing with herself right now, my desperation was turning her on.

"You're so fucking hot...fuck..." Wendy said from behind me. I knew her lack of experience in being a domme would mean she couldn't help herself but to give herself a release during a scene.

I felt a trickle of water drip out of me and heard the sheets rustle. "Good girl...good..." Wendy breathed, "Fuck, Brenda...your Mistress is so turned on right now."

"Wonderful..." I said, my voice low and resigned, my body taken beyond exhaustion long ago.

I heard her shift again, and the sound of her fingers diving into herself seemed to grow more and more insistent. "Oh, I'm fucking close, Brenda. You're making me feel so good. Your dripping pussy is so fucking hot, baby..."

"Yes...of course...yes..." my brain was on autopilot, and I knew orgasm was the only path back to sanity that I had, but I couldn't do it until instructed. I felt that the ice cubes were probably almost entirely melted, but I didn't want to tell Wendy too early to risk being wrong.

I could hear Wendy begin to tense, her breathing deepening, and knew that she was so, so, so, so, close.

I waited another ten seconds before relaxing my shoulders. "Mistress, Aosoth, the ice cubes are melted..."

Wendy seemed to lunge forward and grab me around my midsection, her hips colliding into mine. I felt her hand working between her own legs as she pressed me into the bed. One of the last bits of ice cube slid out of me and lingered on my inner thigh.

"Then come for me, baby...come with me..." Wendy masturbated on top of me, not even touching me, but the feeling of it all was enough.

It took a lot for me to have an orgasm without direct stimulation, but after all this edging and sensation contrast, my body wanted to release me in any way possible.

"Wendy!" I called out, feeling her weight press down onto my lower back, the heat between our two bodies almost overwhelming. She moaned, the noise primal, and pressed herself even closer to me, her breath against my skin. "Oh baby, yes...yes...fuck!"

"I love you Bren, I fucking love you..." Wendy grinded against me, the soaked feeling across my entire lower half was powerful and overwhelming, and the heat and sweat from my wife's body pressing against mine as her orgasm tore through her made mine that much more toe-curling.

My brain short-circuited, and my whole body clenched and tensed. The heat in my body boiled over and exploded out of me in a violent shock of pleasure that left me utterly senseless. I kept enough of a hold on reality that I was able to ride the orgasm out without dissociating, something that was always a risk after prolonged edging.

"You're fucking mine." Wendy whispered in my ear as I rode my orgasm out. "All mine, baby. You're so beautiful, and you're all mine, all of you. My girl, my girl..."

Our bodies rocked against each other, skin seeming to meld, our individual essences subsumed into each other. The energy from Wendy's body pulsated through me, and I returned it just the same. I didn't know if other people had felt pleasure like this before, but I was at least beyond happy that I got to feel it with my wonderful wife.

"Fuck...." I sighed as my body finally calmed down. The limits of my physical form made themselves known, with my knees and back aching and my core feeling stunningly cold and rippled with strain.

Wendy rolled off of me, collapsing onto the bed, the biggest smile possible on her face. The makeup she'd been wearing today was a jumbled mess across her face, eyeliner streaks halfway down her cheeks from the exertion. "Baby...oh my god...that was...that was top ten at least."

"Top five..." I giggled.

Wendy shook her head, "Top five..." she seemed to have to think for a second, "Okay, yes. Top five. Holy shit. That was crazy." She pushed a sweaty lock of hair out of my eyes, her nails feeling cool on my warm, damp skin. "You're so beautiful, baby..."

I would have reached out and embraced Wendy, but

my body had finally decided to give up for a while, prohibiting movement in an act I could only assume was self-preservation. "Thank you...you are...so gorgeous, Wen...I love you so much." I dragged the last molecules of energy I had in me to generate a smile that was mostly lost since half of my face was pressed into a pillow.

"I'm going to draw us a bath...and, well, I'll get the candles ready because I know you're a hopeless romantic like that..."

I closed my eyes and let the comfort of the bed wash over me for a moment. "No candles...please...enough candles for one day." I laughed.

"Oh, right..." Wendy laughed a bit, seeming to forget the wax play, and I didn't blame her. A LOT had happened.

"I could go for an...unused...glass of ice water, though." I said, finally gaining back enough energy to roll myself over onto my back.

Wendy leaned down and kissed me, our bodies still covered in sweat. "Of course, my love."

Mistress Morrigan had been bested, turned into an absolute fool for the utterly wonderful woman I shared a bed with...shared a life with. I wouldn't want it any other way.

ABOUT THE AUTHOR

Chloe Slate is an author of steamy sapphic romance stories and novels. She is deeply committed to write stories that are fun, edgy, over the top, and inclusive of people of the LGBTQ+ spectrum in all forms. A former music journalist and academic, Chloe lives in Indianapolis with her wife.

ALSO BY CHLOE SLATE

THE EROTES CIRCLE

Novels

The Mansion

The Startup

Short Stories

The Wait

Shopping

Re: Stacks

OTHER WORK

Speed Dates: Book One

Ashwood Resort

Made in the USA
Middletown, DE
10 November 2024